**Robert Geddes and
Cameron Geddes
Children's Book Fund**

of The Library Foundation

Library
THE
FOUNDATION

Enhancing the work of our library
libraryfoundation.org

CITY *of* ISLANDS

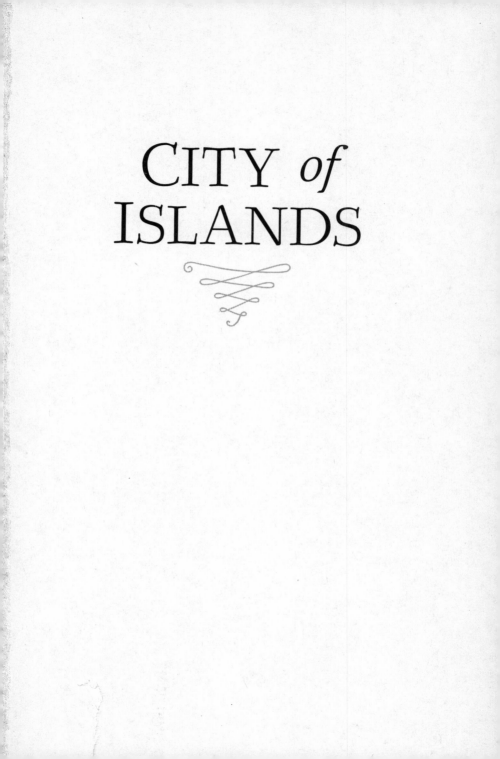

CITY of ISLANDS

Kali Wallace

KATHERINE TEGEN BOOKS

An Imprint of HarperCollins Publishers

Library of Congress Control Number: 2018933267
ISBN 978-0-06-249981-3

Typography by Carla Weise
18 19 20 21 22   CG/LSCH   10 9 8 7 6 5 4 3 2 1
❖
First Edition

For my classmates from Clarion 2010,
who have offered encouragement and
support at every step of this journey

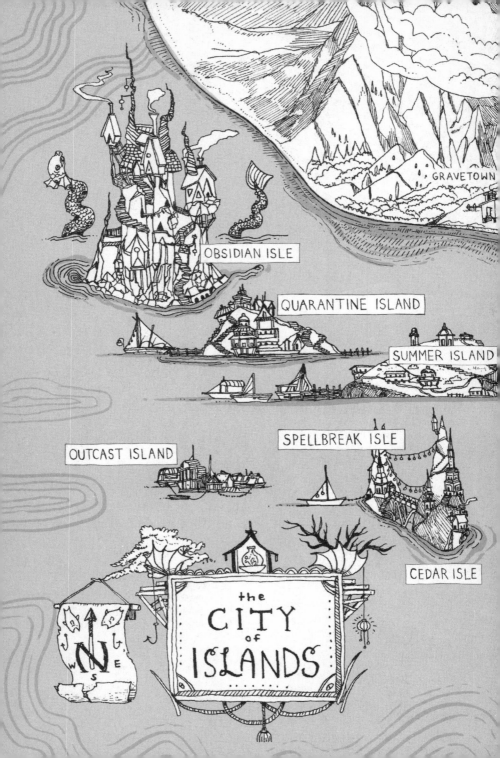

1

Mara the Fish Girl

Mara found the bones on a cold, gray morning.

Fog shrouded the City of Islands. The air stank of fish and salt and smoke, and underneath it all was the rich green scent of low tide. Somewhere across the water a woman was singing a cheerful spell-song for good weather, and fishermen shouted greetings between boats. Throughout the city, buoy bells rang, marking the places where ships had to navigate carefully to avoid running aground on the abandoned spires beneath the water. The sea was calm.

Mara sat in the prow of Driftwood's boat. Her legs were drawn up to her chest, her arms wrapped around her knees. She wore only a thin linen shift over the shorts and sleeveless top of her swimming clothes, but she didn't mind the cold. Beside her, Izzy was dressed much the same. Like most people born in the city, they both had brown skin, brown eyes, and curly black hair; sometimes people mistook them for sisters, which always made Izzy smile. On mornings like this, they both liked to get used to the chill before it was time to dive. Summer was nearly over, and the sea was barely warmer than the air.

"I think this is where the *Fool's Girl* sank," said Izzy, peering into the water.

"I don't remember that one," Mara said. Hundreds of ships sailed into the city every season, carrying people and goods from all over the world. Not all of them sailed away again. In some places forests of wooden masts jutted from the water; in others bubbles rose in sporadic gulps, as though the ghosts of trapped sailors were gasping and gurgling still.

"There was a fire," Izzy said. "It was terrible. You could see it glowing all across the city."

Izzy was eighteen, six years older than Mara. Like Mara she worked for the Lady of the Tides as a diver. The Lady was the head of one of the city's wealthy ruling families. She was also an eccentric mage who collected ancient artifacts left behind by the founders, the magical people who had built the city a thousand years ago.

The founders had lived under the sea, with scales rather than skin, long tails instead of legs, fingers that ended in long fins, huge round eyes, and pointed spines forming a fan across their shoulders. Of course nobody alive had ever seen a founder, but their images were everywhere in the city, in fountains and statues and mosaics. The founders, when they lived, had been in command of magic so powerful they had lifted entire islands from the sea, carved fortresses and towers from solid stone, called storms to rage on clear days, and raced through the water in sea chariots pulled by swift black sea serpents.

The founders were gone now, vanished forever into legends and myths, but the city's mages still studied the founders' artifacts, always hoping to find a bit of magic nobody else had found before. The founders had never written anything down, so their discarded belongings were all that remained. It was Izzy and Mara's job to retrieve objects from beneath the sea for the Lady's collection.

But Izzy was planning to leave the Lady's employ soon. She had been saving her wages to marry a pretty candlemaker's apprentice on Summer Island.

Mara told herself she wished Izzy well. She liked the way Izzy's eyes lit up with happiness when she spoke about her fiancée, Nila, or when she joked about taking Mara with her so they could work together in the candlemaker's shop. Mara laughed along with Izzy's jokes to hide her true feelings, which were part jealousy, part fear. Izzy was the closest thing Mara had to a friend in the Lady's household. When she was gone Mara would be alone.

"There's not much as bad as a ship on fire," said Driftwood. "You never forget that."

Driftwood sat in the stern of the boat, pulling the oars with smooth, strong strokes. He was broad shouldered and dark skinned, and his voice was as low and deep as a foghorn, with the smooth, rolling accent of faraway Sumant. Mara didn't know his real name. He was called Driftwood because he had been swept from a Sumanti galleon during a storm, washed ashore at Greenwood Island, and decided to stay in the City of Islands.

"You better not be bringing us to a boring old shipwreck," Izzy said.

"I'm not," Mara promised.

It was all she could do not to bounce with excitement, but Izzy's words put a pinch of worry in her gut. Mara was hoping the same thing, more fervently than Izzy could imagine. The Lady of the Tides normally told them where to dive, but this morning Mara had wheedled and pleaded until Izzy and Driftwood agreed to ignore the Lady's instructions and go to a spot of Mara's choosing.

It had been weeks since they'd recovered anything; their last find had been a brilliant blue glass window from a founders' palace, nearly intact, with only a single crack, and still humming faintly with ancient magic. If they didn't find something else soon, the Lady would spend the winter looking for divers to replace them.

That wouldn't be a problem for Izzy, who was leaving

anyway. But for Mara it would mean having to go back to the fish market on Summer Island, where she had worked for a year before coming to work for the Lady. Mara would still be there if Izzy hadn't come to Summer Island last year, offering a job at Tidewater Isle to a strong swimmer and fast diver. Mara had jumped at the chance to prove herself and leave the fish market; she never wanted to return. Work in the market meant endless days of dull knives and freezing water and stinking rotten fish, earning only a drafty attic room and a thin crust of bread for her wages. Even worse, if the cruel fishmonger with his snapping leather strap wouldn't take Mara back, she would be on the streets again, alone and hungry and scared, as she had been for months after her old guardian, Bindy the bone-mage, had died.

Mara closed her hands into fists. She wasn't going to think about Bindy this morning. She wasn't going to think about the cold winter she had spent begging on the streets of Quarantine Island. A fine, calm morning on the water was no place for sadness.

She unfolded her legs and stood. Driftwood slowed his strokes. The boat bobbed gently.

"What exactly are we looking for?" Izzy asked. "There aren't any sea caves out here. It's all sandy shallows and seaweed."

Mara didn't want to explain. If she was wrong, she didn't want to be scolded for chasing wild stories.

A few days ago, when she had a rare afternoon free, Mara had gone to visit her best friend, Fish Hook, a boy who worked in the fish market. They had been sitting on the Summer Island docks, enjoying the late season sunshine. Mara had been talking about how little she had found diving this summer, how worried she was that the city's mages had already uncovered all the founders' treasures. She hadn't realized somebody was eavesdropping until a boy had interrupted them. He was a foreigner, with pale skin and freckles and a shock of orange hair. In a nervous Roughwater accent he told them he had seen something strange underwater, something she might be interested in. He had fallen from his master's fishing boat, and beneath the water he found big, strange bones, the likes of which he had never seen before. He hadn't told his master, as he was new to the city and afraid the fishermen would laugh at him.

Fish Hook had rolled his eyes and said, "Next you're going to tell us you found a lost tower of the founders too," but Mara had shushed him. Strange bones were exactly the sort of thing the Lady of the Tides coveted for her collection. Her most prized possession was a sea serpent skull so massive it took six men to move it into the ballroom when she wanted to show it off at parties. Mara had demanded the Roughwater boy tell her *exactly* where he had fallen from his master's boat.

Now, out on the water, Mara turned in a slow circle to search for the right landmarks.

To the south stood the elegant twin spires of Lady of the Gales Isle, the last island separating the city from the remote southern seas. Directly to the north Glassmaker Isle and the Hanging Garden looked like a single jut of rock melded together. From this distance, in this thick fog, Mara could see only the faintest suggestion of the towering glass statue that loomed over the southern flank of Glassmaker Isle; the writhing serpents, the gleaming sea chariot in the shape of a half shell, and the grim-faced founder driving them to battle all vanished completely as the mist drifted.

To the east of Glassmaker Isle, a bit farther away, smaller but steeper on all sides, was Mara's current home: Tidewater Isle. The island had been carved into a single glorious palace centuries ago by the founders' stone-mages, using magic no human mage could ever wield. They had crafted the great island fortresses as a gift for the humans in the city above the waves. That had all happened very long ago, when founders and humans had lived side by side, before they had fallen to fighting and the founders had gone away.

Reluctance tugged at Mara as she turned again. To the northeast was the Winter Blade. It was a sliver of black, delicate as a needle, just barely visible through the heavy fog. Looking at that fortress of stone so dark and terrible brought back the churning, sour feeling of grief Mara had tried so hard to stamp down.

For centuries the Winter Blade had been home to the city's most infamous mages. Rather than staying in a single family or passing from parent to child, the island changed masters every time somebody more powerful ousted the previous inhabitant. The island's current master was a man called the Lord of the Muck. He had held the Winter Blade for two years, since he had taken it from a Greenwooder mage named Gerrant. Mara remembered the night he had claimed it well, as it had been the second-worst night of her life. It was the night Bindy had died.

Mara *knew* the Lord of the Muck was the reason Bindy was gone. Mara didn't know why or how. She had no proof. All she knew was that Bindy and the Muck had known each other, and one stormy night Bindy had shoved a bunch of her magic journals into a satchel before going to meet the Muck on the docks. She had never come back. In the morning, when the storm calmed, a fisherman had found Bindy's rowboat overturned east of Quarantine Island.

In one terrible night, Bindy had drowned, Gerrant of Greenwood had disappeared, and the Winter Blade had passed into the hands of a new mage.

And Mara, who had lived with Bindy since her parents had died when she was five, had been left with nowhere to go. She missed Bindy with an ache that had never faded, sometimes even more than she missed her parents. She hated the Lord of the Muck with a wild, helpless sort of anger. She still seethed to think of all the people who had refused to listen or care when Bindy died.

But right now that wretched black tower and its mage were only a landmark. Mara turned deliberately away from the Winter Blade. Fog drifted to reveal tiny Starfish Isle to the east. A fragile bridge harnessed the uninhabited island to the Broken Tower, an abandoned lighthouse said to be haunted by the ghost of Old Greengill, a mage who had died centuries ago. According to legend, Greengill had hidden a vast treasure in secret caves all over the islands, then retreated with his treasure map to the very top of the lighthouse and smashed the steps so no one could follow. Adventurers and braggarts were always daring each other to climb the tower and retrieve the map, but the tower was too tall, its ruin too treacherous. Without wings nobody was ever going to make it to the top.

"We're almost there," Mara said. The sea was brighter here, green and mottled thanks to the shallow, sandy bottom no more than four or five fathoms below. Izzy was right: it wasn't the sort of undersea landscape that normally hid ancient treasures.

"Here?" Izzy asked. "How can you tell?"

"I just know," said Mara, trying to sound nonchalant. She liked it when she knew things Izzy didn't. It made her feel like less of a little kid trying to prove her worth and more like an equal diving partner. "This is the spot."

Driftwood stopped rowing. It was time to dive.

"Where are the lights?" Mara asked.

There was a scrape and a hiss as Izzy lit a match to ignite the murk-lights, a pair of magical lanterns enclosed in glass globes. She passed one to Mara and smiled crookedly. "I suppose you want to go first, just in case you find something special."

Mara's face warmed and she ducked her head. "Maybe it's nothing. I'll come right back."

But in truth she was glad for Izzy's offer. If there was a magnificent ancient creature in those shallows, Mara wanted to be the one to find it.

"As long as you let me help bring up anything important," Izzy said.

Mara pretended not to hear. She didn't make promises she had no intention of keeping.

She dropped the murk-light overboard. It sank slowly, a golden glow descending into the dark. She stripped off her shift and smoothed down the front of her swimming clothes. She took a deep breath, let it out, then another, and another, until she felt a calm come over her. Mara couldn't remember a time when she didn't know how to swim. Her earliest memories were of splashing happily with her parents on the black-sand beaches of Greenwood Island. Swimming was as natural to her as walking. Even on gray mornings like this, the sea was welcoming and familiar.

She was ready. She dove into the water.

She kicked toward the murk-light, grabbed it with one hand, and aimed herself downward. She exhaled as she dove, but carefully. She needed to save her strength and swim with a clear mind.

The bottom was only three fathoms down. The murk-light's glow didn't waver as Mara descended, but she felt it draw in on itself, as though it knew that fire, even magic-stoked fire, had no place in this underwater world. The water was clear, the current weak, the conditions perfect. Small green fish darted about, startled by her passage. Beyond them she saw a great shadow. Her heart leapt, but it was only a bulge-eyed bayfish. They were huge and ugly but gentle. Mara silently wished it a good day as she swam past.

The seafloor was lumpy and overgrown with seaweed. Mara spotted ribs of rotten wood and broken barrels, the trunk of a charred mast, and the sloping remains of a deck. The ship's figurehead, a carved image of a founder with its spiny fins splayed around its head like a crown, was jutting from the silt.

She had found the *Fool's Girl*, but she wasn't looking for a sunken ship. She returned to the surface for air before diving again.

And again, and again, growing more and more frustrated.

Her third time up for air, Izzy called out, "All right, Mara?"

Mara waved to indicate she was fine, but she didn't head back to the boat. She wasn't giving up yet.

She treaded water slowly, conserving her energy. The Roughwater boy had been very clear: the bones were right on the seafloor, there for anybody to see. She had to be looking in the wrong place.

Mara wished she knew some of Bindy's spell-songs. Bindy had been a bone-mage, which meant she could use her magical songs on any kind of bone. Most of the mages in the city thought Bindy's kind of magic was a joke, no better than soothsaying or fortune-telling, more fraud and trickery than real magic. Mara knew they were wrong. She had seen Bindy sing to the bones of dead mages in the Ossuary, chanting in mysterious languages to coax the bones into revealing long-lost secrets. Every time Mara had asked to learn those songs, Bindy had said, later, later, there would be time later.

There had been no later for Bindy, and Mara remembered only a little of her magic.

It was worth a try. Driftwood's boat was far enough away that he and Izzy wouldn't hear Mara if she sang a spell, just a little one. She racked her mind for one of Bindy's songs, and all she could come up with were a few random spell-notes. She felt silly singing them, a babbling melody of *la-la-la* and *oh-ah-oh*. She didn't even know what she was singing. While some spells were based on ordinary songs anybody could learn, others were sung in the language of the founders, with words whose meaning had been lost centuries ago. When Mara was very little, before her parents died, she used to make up songs and pretend they were spells, because so often that's what spells sounded like to an observer: mere gibberish.

For all she knew she could be casting a shark-summoning spell, and wouldn't *that* be an unfortunate way to start her day?

Mara hummed softly to herself as she considered her next move. Not a spell this time, just a song her mother used to sing as she sharpened her chisels. Mara's mother had been a stonemason in Gravetown. Every morning she had filled their little house with warm cheerful songs as rain lashed the windows and the gray sea roiled outside. Mum had had no talent for magic—stone magic had been impossible since the time of the founders—but she had loved to sing.

Mara often sang her mother's favorite song to herself when she was scared or lonely, as a way of remembering those peaceful mornings. She knew every word: *Over the sea and under the sky, my island home it waits for me.* It was an old sailors' song about missing Greenwood Island from far away, which had always made Dad laugh when Mum sung it, because Mum had never left the city, didn't even like to visit the other islands. She always said she had everything she needed right there in Gravetown. *Over the waves and under the storms, my heart is bound but my dreams are free.* A cool breeze slid over the sea surface, a gentle warning of the changing seasons. Mara ducked her head underwater to dispel the chill. *Older I grow and farther I roam, and my green island I yearn to see.*

She liked the way the song changed underwater, dropping into lower tones, vibrating in her bones rather than dancing in her ears. She shifted the words from her mother's song into the melody of one of Bindy's spell-songs, just to see how it sounded. She was expecting it to feel weird, burbling out a song underwater, and it was.

She was not expecting the sea to answer—but it did.

2

The Singing Bones

A rolling low song filled the sea around Mara. It was as deep and sonorous as a gong on a foggy night. She felt it in her teeth, in her bones, over every inch of her skin.

She was so surprised she gasped, gulping a mouthful of seawater. Coughing and spitting, she bobbed to the surface.

As soon as she hit the air, the sound vanished.

Mara could hear the lap of water, the distant buoy bells, Izzy and Driftwood chatting on the boat. The air felt colder than it had before. Goose bumps rose all over Mara's skin.

Cautiously, frowning in thought, she tilted her head to submerge one ear.

The song was still there. Lower now, eerie and wavering, but still there.

All magic in the City of Islands came from songs. Anybody could sing a bit of magic, if they knew the right combination of words and melody. Fishermen had songs for luring fish into their nets, crafters for gently shaping wood and metal and glass, sailors for asking the clouds and waves about the weather. That didn't make them mages. Becoming a mage meant apprenticing when you were young, or studying at the Citadel on Obsidian Isle under the High Mage, both of which required money. True mages spent a lifetime learning spell-songs in any number of living or dead languages, including the founders' language, which nobody knew how to speak anymore. It had never been meant for using above water anyway.

Mara wasn't a mage. She didn't know why the sea reverberated in response to her song. Sound traveled fast and far underwater—a diver in the city might hear whale song from miles and miles away—and spell-songs carried even when they weren't very loud at the source. All she knew was this magic.

Like calls to like, Bindy had always said, explaining why you couldn't sing a woodworking spell to a stormy sky any more than you could sing a weather-wishing song to a pile of kindling.

Mara had been singing the words of her mother's song, but Mara's parents hadn't been mages. They had been stonemasons, and there was no stone magic anymore. The founders had once been able to lift towers from the seafloor, carve maze-like fortresses into solid rock, and hurl great boulders at their enemies from afar. The massive valley that nearly rent Greenwood Island in two was said to have come from two cruel founder sorceresses battling each other for the same suitor, hundreds and hundreds of years before any people came to the islands. Of all the great elemental forms of magic, stone magic was the one that had died utterly with the founders. Most people agreed it was probably for the better.

No sailing song from a Gravetown stonemason could be magical. That didn't make any sense. She had to be mistaken. It had to have been Bindy's song.

"Mara?" Izzy called out. "We're coming over to you."

There was the slice of oars through water. Mara took a deep breath. She ducked her head underwater, and she began to sing Bindy's song.

Nothing happened.

She tried again, enunciating as much as she could.

It was no use. The only words she managed sounded like nonsense to her own ears, and she didn't even know if the *la* and *ooh* and *ah* she remembered corresponded to words in the founders' language. She returned to the surface and treaded water again, thinking of all the times Bindy had taught her that you had to be *bossy* to do magic, you had to *know* what you were singing, even if you didn't know what the words meant. Mara had never really understood that—how could you know a song without knowing what the words were saying?—but she figured it was unlikely a random collection of sounds would get her anywhere.

Well, she thought. It can't hurt to try.

Mara sang her mother's song again: *"Over the sea and under the sky, my island home it waits for me."*

The answer was immediate and overwhelming. The water trembled with a deep, slow melody, a sound so strong she felt it in every bone. It was just about impossible to pinpoint the source of a sound underwater, but spell-song was different from ordinary sound. It had a feel to it: teasing, feather-light brushes on the skin, prickles of hot or cold, even phantom pressure if the spell was powerful.

Mara swam in a careful, ever-widening circle, coming up for air before ducking down again to sing a few lines from the second stanza: *"The rich green slopes that haunt my dreams, they are beloved as treasure to me."*

When she felt the first shiver of tiny hot-cold bubbles on her skin, she knew she was right. There was something here, something more magical than a shipwreck, something emanating its own spell-song.

With her murk-light in her hand, Mara dove straight down.

There, among the mounds of green seaweed and brown sand of the seafloor, a bright spot caught her eye.

Mara's lungs began to burn, but she kicked down, down. The eerie music was fading, but she didn't have breath to spare for another bit of song.

Jutting from the sand was a clean white object both curved and angular. There was an empty eye socket; and there was the slope of a brow; and there, reaching up from the side like a spire, was a twisted horn. It was a skull.

Mara dropped her murk-light to mark the spot and surged upward. She surfaced a few feet from Driftwood's boat.

"I found something!"

Izzy was already perched on the side of the boat in her swimming clothes. Her murk-light bobbed on the surface on the end of its chain. "What is it?"

Mara gulped salty water, spat it out again. "A skull," she said, grinning.

"There's a shipwreck. It could be a sailor."

"Do you know any sailors with horns?"

Izzy's doubt turned to excitement. She dropped into the water and came up a second later with her rows of braids slicked back, her eyes shining. "Where is it?"

They dove together. The song had faded completely. Izzy followed Mara to the seafloor and dropped her own murk-light beside the skull. They began to dig in the suck-ing, sticky mud. Every motion stirred up gritty clouds of silt. When it got too bad, Mara closed her eyes to work by feel, prying her fingers around the skull's eye sockets and the smooth twin arches of the brow. She felt the sharp ridges of teeth, a twisted length of its horns, a long snout.

It took them two lung-burning dives to tug the skull free from the silt, along with the length of rope and woven sack of lumpy, angular rocks that had been used to weight it down. Mara left Izzy to retrieve the jaw and kicked to the surface. When she burst into the open air, she grabbed the side of the boat to set the skull inside, dragging the rope and sack in after it. She broke away clumps of mud and strands of clinging seaweed.

She looked up at Driftwood. "What do you think it is?"

Driftwood leaned over the crossed oars and frowned thoughtfully. "Hold it up," he said.

Mara obliged. Out of the water, the skull was heavier than she expected, the bone denser. "It's not a sea creature, is it?"

Izzy surfaced a moment later and passed the jawbone to Mara. "Well?"

All three of them studied the skull in silence.

It was about the size of a horse's head, but it had horns like a Greenwood Island mountain goat, long and twisted, protruding from behind the eye sockets. Its teeth were neither a horse's nor a goat's; they were too sharp for munching grass. The lower jaw, when Mara fitted it to the rest, jutted from beneath the upper with long, curved fangs. Mara wanted to hold it up to her ear like a conch shell to listen for the spell-song, but if she did, Izzy and Driftwood would ask what she was doing.

The Lady of the Tides had all manner of strange creatures in her collection. The massive sea serpent skull was the prize, but there were also animals of every size and shape gathered from all across the world, birds from the far east and snakes from the far west, horned deer from the north and leviathan ribs from the southern seas. She even had a handful of fine, frail bones she claimed had come from the founders themselves, locked in a glass case in her library.

But in the whole of the Lady's collection there was nothing like this.

Izzy clung to the side of the boat. "What *is* that?"

Mara opened her mouth to say she had no idea, but something stopped her. A memory flashed into her mind like a darting fish.

She *had* seen something like this creature before. But where? Not in the Lady's collection. Not in a cage in the dockside markets. Not among the jumbled bones in Bindy's shop. She had been hurrying somewhere—running, even—racing back to the fish market because she had been listening to the storm-mages atop Summer Island and the fishmonger would be angry she was late—she could already feel the stinging slap on her cheek—she had to find a shortcut, and there at the corner of her eye—

Mara's heart began to beat faster. Her throat was dry.

It wasn't a living animal she had seen, nor was it a skeleton.

What she remembered was a stone carving.

The crooked streets and rambling stairways of all the city's islands were filled with ancient mosaics and statues, fountains and friezes. Many depicted the strange animals that had not lived in the city since the time of the founders: fish with wings to fly above the water, great cats with webbed feet and fins for tails, birds with talons as long as swords. In addition to calling up fierce storms and carving islands into fortresses, the founders had also been able to create wondrous creatures with their magic, filling the sea and land and sky with strange, magical hybrids. Some were created for battle, some for beauty, some for no reason anybody could fathom. The animals, like their creators, had been gone from the city for centuries.

On a weather-worn carving in an alley not far from the great fountain in Seafarers' Square, Mara had seen an animal with a horse's head, a goat's horns, and the curving fangs of a predator. She couldn't remember what its body had looked like. Horse-like, she thought, but perhaps it had wings? Or catlike claws rather than hooves?

She didn't even want to say it out loud, for fear of making the skull vanish in a puff of smoke.

The Lady's sea serpent skull was impressive for its size and great age, but sea serpents were natural creatures. They had been tamed by the founders, not created by them. This skull was different. Mara was holding in her own trembling hands a creature made by forgotten, ancient magic.

And magic, Bindy had always said, was a duet. If a mage sang the right song to an ancient spelled object—or skull—that object might be persuaded to echo the spell that had shaped it right back to her. Dedicated collectors like the Lady, with piles of ancient artifacts to study, spent their lives coaxing small bits of melodies out of the oldest treasures.

The skull had responded to Mara's song. It had answered her with a spell, and that spell might not have been heard by anybody for hundreds of years.

She took a steadying breath.

"Doesn't it look a bit like one of the old creatures?" she asked. She tried to keep her voice light, as though she wasn't asking the most important question she had ever asked. She had never believed she would find anything so special. Nobody had ever found anything like this. "Like in the stories?"

Izzy tilted her head to one side. "A little. But you don't think—" She looked at Mara sharply. "Is that even possible? Could this really be an animal from the time of the founders? An animal they *made*?"

"I think it could." Mara's voice fell into a ragged whisper on the last word.

Izzy looked at Driftwood. "What do you think?"

Driftwood was quiet for a long, long moment. Finally

he said, "I think you should find the rest of the body."

With a scramble and a splash, Mara and Izzy were diving again.

They didn't find the rest of the body, but they found more than enough to make up for it.

There was the skeleton of a lizard as long as Mara's arm with spindly, bat-like wing bones. Another looked at first like half of an ordinary bayfish, only instead of a tall caudal fin, it had a long tail, like a sea snake but twice as big around. In a sticky hollow of mud, Izzy found a bird skull and a scattering of hollow bones, but the skull alone was bigger than the largest birds that migrated through the islands. Tangled in a mat of kelp, Mara found the bones of a creature that she would have guessed was a seal if only it didn't have long talons on the ends of its flippers. They both spent several long dives bringing up what could have been a shark, but its head was too long, its teeth too blunt, and strangest of all it had a tail split into two sinuous ends.

It was difficult work, far more tiring than their usual searches for small objects in rocky caves. The bones weren't buried very deep, but many were covered with silt and seaweed. All had been weighted down by knotted ropes tied to sacks full of stones.

The more bones they pulled from the water, the more puzzled Mara grew. The ropes and woven bags weren't old; they hadn't been sitting on the seafloor for hundreds of years. Somebody had dumped these animals not very long ago. But because the skeletons were so strange, it was hard to know when they'd dug up the whole skeleton. She couldn't even be certain she and Izzy were putting the right skulls with the right bodies and limbs. What were they doing half buried in the seafloor mud? Why would somebody have discarded them at all? How long had they rested there, humming with magic, before the Roughwater boy spotted them? Had whoever dumped them here known what they had?

And most of all: Had her mother's old Greenwood sailing song really called to them? Mara had so many questions and not a single answer.

Mara and Izzy dove all morning. Driftwood helped them lift the larger remains into the boat, along with the bags of stones and knotted ropes. He said little about what they found except that he had never seen such animals in his travels. His reticence gave Mara a nervous feeling, but she ignored it. She didn't have time for doubt, not when there was so much more to find.

Near noon she and Izzy came up from a dive empty-handed. The sun had burned away the fog, and the day was bright and warm.

"We should probably stop for today," Izzy said reluctantly. "We've got plenty already."

Mara wanted to keep diving, but the burn in her lungs and hunger in her stomach told her Izzy was right. They couldn't afford to grow careless; they might miss something.

The rest of the bones would have to wait for another day.

She dove one more time to retrieve the murk-lights. Just for a test, just to see what would happen, she sang a few words of her mother's song: "*Over the waves and under the sky, my island home . . .*"

She stopped as the sea hummed in response. A little bit quieter, maybe, but no less eerie. Mara returned to the surface, giddy to have that lovely old song echoing on her ears.

"I wonder what the Lady will think," Izzy said as she helped her into the boat. They had to shift some of the larger bones around to find a spot to sit. "She's got nothing like this in her collection."

"I bet nobody does," Mara said. "Not even at the Citadel."

"You know the High Mage would be bragging to everybody if he had anything like this." Izzy smiled at Mara, who grinned right back at her.

"They're even better than a sea serpent, because they were made with magic," Mara said.

"Don't get ahead of yourselves," Driftwood said. "You don't know that yet."

Mara opened her mouth to argue, then changed her mind. Part of her wanted to blurt out that she *did* know. She knew they were magical bones because she'd used magic to find them. It was the first time in her life she had actually sung magic that worked. Real magic, not silly household spells any child could do, and she had done it without help! She was almost bursting with the need to brag, to impress Izzy and Driftwood, to prove to them and everybody else that she was meant to be doing magic.

But another part of her, the bigger part, wanted to wait. Wait to see what the Lady said. Wait to see how pleased she was. If she was as delighted as Mara expected her to be, she would ask how Mara had found these bones, and *then* Mara could reveal what she had done. The Lady was a mage herself. She would understand.

She might even give Mara a special reward. Mara had never earned a reward from the Lady of the Tides before, but others in the household still spoke of a previous diver, a woman who had found a trove of ancient mariner's instruments in a sea cave beneath the Hanging Garden. The Lady had been so pleased with the find she had given the woman enough money to retire from diving altogether and buy her own spice shop on Quarantine Island.

Mara settled back against the pile of bones to enjoy the sun on her face and the warm breeze drying her skin. She had spent so long daydreaming about what she could do if she found a sea serpent skull or a long-lost underwater palace or a trove of magical artifacts, and now she was lying right on top of such a treasure.

All her life she had wanted to study magic. She had thought she would become Bindy's apprentice someday, but then Bindy had died and Mara had feared her chance was gone for good.

For the first time in two years, Mara was hopeful again. If she could recall enough of Bindy's magic, she might even be able to help the Lady study *these* bones, delving into magic that had been forgotten centuries ago. That would surely earn the Lady's gratitude and more. She could earn the Lady's patronage and go to the Citadel, or persuade a mage to take her on as an apprentice. When she was a fully trained mage she could have a shop of her own, spelling herbs to cure fevers and amulets to protect fishermen, or hire herself out to the city's rich merchants and ruling families, who paid mages to shield their ships from storms and guide their traders along dangerous routes.

She would never again have to worry about finding enough food or a dry place to sleep, or having her entire life upended by a single storm or shipwreck. She could help Izzy and her fiancée buy their own candle-making shop. She could give Fish Hook a job away from the market and the cruel fishmonger.

Someday she would be her own master. She would never again cry herself to sleep knowing the people meant to care for her were gone for good, and all they had left behind was an aching loneliness and deep, cold fear that never truly subsided. She would be the person who cared for others instead.

She could do all of that, if she became a mage.

And these strange, magical bones were her chance.

The Lady of the Tides

Renata Palisado, the Lady of the Tides and mistress of Tidewater Isle, was a tall, sturdy woman. She had been beautiful when she was young, or so everybody claimed, but she was now better described as intimidating. Her skin was smooth brown, her face broad, her chin strong, her neck long. Her eyes were the color of pale green sea glass—proof, some claimed, that there was a Pinnacle Isles pirate somewhere in her long family history. Her hair, once deep ruddy brown, bore white streaks that only made her look more severe.

Mara felt like a tiny dull fish when she stood before the Lady. She had to fight the urge to stand on her toes to make herself taller. The library was imposing enough on its own, lined as it was from ceiling to floor with hefty tomes and crackling maps, delicate astrolabes and polished mariners' compasses. Amid all these human artifacts were the stranger objects from the founders: a long harpoon with a barbed end, the broken curve of shell that had once been part of a sea chariot, a greening metal harness that had been used to subdue sea serpents, a section of pearl and gem mosaic taken from an abandoned underwater tower. The Lady's display of founders' bones in their glass case had pride of place against one wall.

Colorful silk tapestries covered the thick walls and muted the sounds of the household. They showed scenes of the founders battling each other, shaping both the city below the sea and the fortresses above from raw stone, racing their serpent-drawn chariots, and surrounding a tiny human emissary who had traveled down to their city in a fragile underwater globe.

Mara had been hoping for another look at the bones she'd found, but they were nowhere to be seen. The Lady had commanded a line of servants to carry them up to her tower laboratory.

"You made a very interesting discovery this morning," said the Lady.

"Thank you, ma'am," said Mara.

"Thank you, ma'am," said Izzy.

The Lady's lips curved, not quite a smile. She was standing beside the map table at the center of the library.

"I'm not yet sure what to make of it. I shall reserve judgment until I've had a chance to piece them all together."

Mara's heart thumped nervously, but she kept quiet, and so did Izzy. It was better not to speak until the Lady invited them to.

Renata Palisado was the last surviving member of a very old, very rich family that could trace its line all the way to the very first Sumanti explorers who had found the islands. Although the stories told about those long-ago days were more lore than history now, that still meant the Lady's family had interacted with the founders themselves, which earned her no small amount of awe and admiration even among the city's other old families. She had studied at the Citadel when she was young; she had never taken a husband or a wife and had no children of her own. She regularly threw parties for the city's rich and important people: great banquets where the High Mage and his acolytes rubbed elbows with the Lady of the Glass and the Lord of the Garden, and they all vied for the attention of foreign traders, learned scholars, and daring adventurers.

Bindy had always said the Lady of the Tides was a mediocre mage, notable more for her vast wealth than her magical skill, but Bindy had disdained all Citadel-trained mages. She had laughed when Mara had sheepishly admitted that she might want to attend the Citadel someday.

The Lady smoothed one long-fingered hand across the great map. Behind her an expanse of tall windows overlooked the sea. The afternoon's brief blue skies had not lasted. Clouds were crawling over the city as the day waned, surrounding the islands in a cool gray shroud.

"Driftwood tells me there is more to be found in the same location," the Lady said.

"Yes, ma'am. We think so," Mara said, before Izzy could answer.

"Show me where," said the Lady.

The map detailed every island in the city, from the smallest wave-battered rock to the broad mountains of Greenwood, each labeled in neat script. There were notes indicating where the founders' underwater city had been, with its crumpled, abandoned towers traced in vague outlines. The Lady had scribed small crosses and naughts to show where her divers had either found interesting artifacts or come up empty-handed.

"We are here," the Lady said, pointing to Tidewater Isle.

Mara resisted the urge to roll her eyes. The Lady, like almost everybody, assumed that an orphan fish girl couldn't read her own name, much less a complicated map.

Mara had to stand on her toes to point to the spot north of Lady of the Gales Isle. "There. It was near where the *Fool's Girl* sank."

"I see," said the Lady. She dipped a quill into an inkwell to mark a black cross on the map. "I do not recall asking you to dive in that location."

Mara's heart stuttered a warning. "No, ma'am."

"In fact I recall asking you to search the water near the sea caves north of Obsidian Isle, where we have had success before."

Mara swallowed. "Yes, ma'am."

"I did not give you permission to seek your own dive sites." The half smile was gone from the Lady's face.

"No, ma'am," Mara said, her voice small. She felt the weight of Izzy's stare on the back of her neck. They had been hoping the Lady would be so pleased with their discovery she would overlook the fact that they had disobeyed her. They should have known better.

"Would you care to explain why you ignored my instructions?"

"Ma'am," Izzy began, but Mara interrupted her.

"It was my idea to look there," she said quickly. "Izzy had nothing to do with it."

"Yes, I had supposed that to be the case," said the Lady, even as Izzy made a noise of protest. "What I want to know is why. Why, of all the places in the sea, did you choose that one?"

Mara's thoughts whirled. This wasn't going how she had expected at all. She didn't know what to say. She could tell the truth. She could lie. It was *better* to tell the truth—she hadn't done anything wrong, not really. All she had done was disobey the Lady and use a bit of magic. That wasn't so much.

But she couldn't force the words past her lips. All at once she was thinking about the days after Bindy had died—after the Lord of the Muck had killed her. Nobody had wanted to hear what Mara had to say when they found Bindy's boat. The storm had swept her away, they said, and what was the foolish woman doing on the water during weather like that anyway? Bindy had only been an eccentric bone-witch on the Street of Whispering Stones, obsessed with magic they all believed to be half fraud and half delusion. Mara had tried to get the other mages to listen, to believe that the Lord of the Muck had killed Bindy, but nobody cared. They said Mara was lying for the attention. She had been stunned and bewildered and so very alone, and every bit as frightened as she had been when she was little and her parents died, before Bindy found her. She'd had to leave Bindy's shop, taking only the clothes on her back and not even a cloak against the cold. For all that they had scorned Bindy's magic while she was alive, the other Quarantine Island mages were quick to claim her belongings for themselves.

The way the Lady of the Tides was looking at Mara now reminded her very much of those dismissive mages on Quarantine Island. It was the look of a woman who had already decided not to believe whatever answer Mara provided.

Mara felt a hot spark of anger. The magic she had used to find the bones was *her* magic. She was *not* going to let the Lady take credit for it. Mages had to protect their songs from thieves and eavesdroppers: that was as much a part of life in the City of Islands as the towers of black stone and howling winter storms.

But she had to tell the Lady something, so she decided on half of the truth. "A fisherman's boy told me. He said he fell from a boat and saw some bones."

Renata Palisado raised a single eyebrow. "And?"

"I thought I might find another sea serpent," Mara admitted. "He didn't say what kind of bones. I just thought . . . it would be okay to look?"

The Lady stared at her for so long Mara began to tremble. She was sick with fear. She was going to be dismissed. The Lady did not mistreat her servants, but she did not indulge them either. Mara had been so stupid to expect praise and a reward just because she found some bones. Tears sprang into her eyes and she felt her face grow hot. She dropped her eyes to the floor. Her bare feet looked small and grubby against the woven carpet.

Finally the Lady said, "For now, I will not punish you for your disobedience."

Mara was so relieved she felt dizzy. "Yes, ma'am."

"But if it happens again, I will not be so forgiving, no matter what curiosities you find."

"Thank you, ma'am."

"You will dive again tomorrow at the same place. If there are more bones to find, you will find them."

"Yes, ma'am."

"Yes, ma'am," Izzy said. "We promise—"

The Lady quelled her with a look. "Do not try my patience. You are dismissed. Tell the kitchen staff I've released you from your other duties for the evening. Both of you. Go."

"Thank you, ma'am," said Mara. Izzy echoed the words half a beat later.

"One more thing," said the Lady as they reached the door. "You will keep this discovery to yourselves. You will not gossip with the kitchen or boat staff. I don't want to give other collectors a chance to steal our find. Is that understood?"

Mara didn't like the way the Lady said *our* find, as though she had been the one out there on the boat, shivering in the morning cold and diving until her lungs burned. But she nodded, and Izzy did too, and they fled the library.

Izzy waited until they were descending the stairs to say, "You'd think she'd at least thank us for what we found." She slapped at the stone wall and made a face. "She didn't even care."

Mara also felt the sting of disappointment; her hopes of ending the day with rewards and admiration had withered on the library floor. But even worse than the disappointment was the knot of fear in her gut. She had been so caught up in her dreams about magic and the future she had forgotten how precarious her position was. She had forgotten how dangerous it was to be a servant who upset her master. In the fish market she had never forgotten, not with the fishmonger always looming with his switch at the ready. But here, in the warm, protected rooms of Tidewater Isle, she had grown as careless and naive as a Greenwooder newly descended from the hills, and that was unacceptable. She wasn't angry at the Lady—not entirely—but at herself. She knew better.

"We're lucky she didn't decide to punish us," Izzy said. "She wasn't happy we disobeyed her."

Mara mumbled, "You didn't have to listen to me."

"That's not what you said this morning, when you were begging and pleading."

"I was right, wasn't I? If we didn't go, we wouldn't have found anything at all."

"Oh, did *we* find something?" Izzy's voice was sharp. "Here I thought you were taking all the credit for yourself."

"That's not what I meant! I didn't want—"

"It doesn't matter anyway," Izzy said. "No matter what we find, she'll be just as angry tomorrow. What good is a night off? She could have given us something *real*."

"She might still," Mara said, but weakly. She hated the way the Lady made her feel like she ought to be grateful for a night of rest after a long day on the water. That she *was* grateful made it even worse.

By the time they arrived in the kitchen, Izzy was ignoring Mara entirely. She found her other friends, the older girls and boys on the kitchen staff, and began complaining to them at once about how she had dove all morning and gotten nothing but a scolding for it. They responded at once with sympathy and kindness. Everybody liked Izzy; they were all going to miss her when she left.

Mara didn't join them. Izzy was nice to her when they were diving together, but here at Tidewater Isle Mara was just the little fish girl, and the older servants wanted nothing to do with her. Izzy would be no better in her current mood. It didn't matter that Mara had only been trying to keep Izzy from getting in trouble, telling the Lady it was all her idea. The Lady was angry, it was Mara's fault, and Izzy had better friends to talk to anyway.

And there was a little voice in the back of Mara's mind whispering: the bones *were* Mara's discovery. She didn't think it was wrong to want credit for that.

She took a bowl of spicy fish curry and went down to the sea cave, hoping for a chance to see Fish Hook. Even if she couldn't tell him anything about the bones, Fish Hook would know just the right thing to say to cheer her up. But the fishmonger's boat had already come and gone that day.

Feeling even lonelier than usual, Mara retreated to the girls' dormitory above the kitchen. The room was warm, tucked in the embrace of the kitchen's numerous chimneys. As the newest girl in the household, having been here only half a year, Mara's pallet was crowded against a drafty window. It was the least desirable spot, but she didn't mind. The stone wall at her back reminded her of her parents' Gravetown workshop, and she could look out at the city and sea any time she wanted.

Through the rain she could just see the tall silhouettes of the Hanging Garden and Glassmaker Isle, and beyond them Spellbreak and Cedar islands, connected by a slender metal bridge lit with lanterns. The bridge was formed by long arches in the shape of tentacles, as though a kraken as large as the islands was lunging from below to swallow them whole. The bridge had been fashioned by the founders hundreds of years ago; no metal-mage knew the songs to create a structure like that anymore. Human metal-workers in the city were considered admirably skilled if they could forge harpoon heads that didn't snap and knives that didn't rust. Important things, but little things, nothing like what the founders had been capable of creating.

Beyond the bridge, lurking beneath the arch like a bruise, was the stinking brown mass of Outcast Island, which wasn't a proper island at all but a patchwork of der-elict ships, houseboats, and floating docks all strapped together.

Mara huddled on her pallet, eating spicy hot chunks of fish, watching the waves rise and swell. She had a good job, a warm bed, a hot meal to fill her belly. She even had a handful of coins knotted up in a handkerchief and hid-den in her mattress. That was more than a lot of people had in the city. It was stupid to complain just because her rich mistress hadn't given her a pile of gold for finding a few bones. The Lady hadn't even studied the bones yet. As soon as she looked at them, really looked at them, she would know how special they were.

The door to the girls' dormitory opened. Izzy hesitated on the threshold, then came in and approached Mara's pallet. She held out a knotted napkin.

"I brought you some mango cake," she said. "It's just out of the oven."

Mara recognized the offering for the apology it was. She unfolded her legs and scooted over to let Izzy sit beside her. Their shoulders pressed together, and Izzy drew the blanket over their legs. Mara unknotted the napkin. The cake was still warm. Its sweet, delicate crumbs melted on her tongue. Mangoes tasted to her like summer, like sunshine, like long-ago memories and half-remembered songs. She swallowed the first bite and did not take another.

"I'm so tired my arms could fall off," Izzy said. "I really thought she would be more impressed than that."

Mara shrugged; her shoulder moved against Izzy's. She had thought as much too, but admitting it out loud felt like defeat. There was a small part of her hoping the Lady was up in her laboratory tower even now, examining the bones through a magnifying glass and scratching notes in a leather-bound book, and by morning she would realize the mistake she had made in scolding her diving girls.

Mara leaned against Izzy. The other islands were

vanishing into the fog. "I'm sorry I got you into trouble," she said.

She didn't really know if she was sorry or not, but Izzy was her friend, and that was what you said to friends.

Izzy laughed softly. "Oh, it's okay. You were right. I didn't *have* to listen to you."

"Tomorrow we'll find something even better," Mara said. It was a promise.

4

Fish Hook

For three more days, Mara and Izzy returned to the spot to dive again and again. They piled strange skeletons of all shapes and sizes into Driftwood's boat, including a cat with wings and a monkey with grasping sharp talons. But by the end of their fourth day on the water the bones were getting harder to find. They had expanded their search to a larger area, but that only meant they kept uncovering things from the shipwreck that weren't magical or interesting at all.

"I think we might have all of them," Izzy said. They were treading water beside the boat. She playfully flicked water at Mara's face. Her murk-light was dangling from her wrist by a chain, a tiny sun beneath the greenish-gray sea. "We're digging up handfuls of mud at this point. Ready to go back?"

It was another cool gray day, with drizzle pattering over the sea. Dark clouds were gathering on the horizon, but the storm-mages on Quarantine Island had sung to the sky, teasing out a response from the restless weather. They were sure it would be only a rain shower, not a true gale.

Mara heard in Izzy's voice the same exhaustion she was feeling herself. Mara's arms were as limp as noodles. All she wanted to do was return to Tidewater Isle and wrap herself in warm, dry clothes.

One more big one, she thought. One more bone and she would be satisfied.

"I'm going to look again," Mara said.

"All right," Izzy said, "but don't take too long. If we get another night off, I'm going to visit Nila, and I want to have a bath first."

Mara said nothing at the mention of Izzy's fiancée. Even though she had spent the last four days daydreaming in every spare moment about her own future after Tidewater Isle, it still stung to be reminded how soon Izzy was planning to leave.

Along with her hurt feelings was something a little more like guilt. Mara wanted to dive alone so she could try the spell-song again.

She hadn't wanted to risk it when Izzy was diving right beside her. Mara didn't think Izzy would *mind*, exactly, but she would want to know why Mara hadn't told her about the spell from the start. Mara didn't know how to explain that she had wanted to have something that was secret and magical and most of all *hers*, if only for a few days. She had to share everything else in her life: the dormitory she slept in, the hand-me-down clothes she wore, her finds in the water. She wasn't going to share the spell-song until she had to.

She dove again, straight down, her murk-light trailing behind her. When she was about a fathom above the sea-floor, she sang a few words of her mother's song: *"Older I grow and farther I roam."*

She couldn't sing much more than that underwater, but she didn't need to. There was an answer.

It was faint and difficult to pinpoint. With a couple of kicks downward she felt a shiver of cool water over her skin. There: a coil of rope and the edge of a rock-weighted sack sticking out of the sand.

She dug through the silt and kelp, aware of the tiredness in her arms and the burn in her lungs. She felt a jolt of relief when her fingers closed over something solid; she tugged the bone free of the rope and surged upward.

Mara didn't look at her find until she reached the surface.

"Did you find something?" Izzy said. She leaned over the side of the boat to help Mara climb in. "What is it?"

Driftwood raised his eyebrows, surprised. "That's no animal."

He was right. It was a human bone. A femur, the longest bone in the leg.

Mara dropped the bone in alarm. It clattered to the floor of the boat.

A moment later, Izzy laughed uneasily. "It's got to be from the shipwreck. Right?" She looked at Driftwood, then Mara. "Right?"

"Seems likely," Driftwood said.

"I'm surprised we haven't found more from that wreck," Izzy added.

"But . . ." Mara swallowed. "But there was a rope and a sack of rocks, like the others."

Izzy frowned. "It must have gotten tangled up with them."

Mara nodded uncertainly and willed her heart to stop pounding. There was a shipwreck right there. Izzy could be right.

But as she pulled her shift over her swimming clothes and rubbed her hands dry, Mara could still hear the way the bone had hummed in response to her spell-song. So low, so quiet. There had been something almost lonely about it. A human bone from an ordinary shipwreck wouldn't be magical. But she didn't want to tell Izzy and Driftwood about the song, so she said nothing.

It was well past noon by the time they returned to Tidewater Isle. Servants were waiting at the dock to take the bones to the Lady's laboratory in the tower. The Lady had not summoned Mara or Izzy since the scolding in the library. She did, however, pass word that they had the night off again, so Izzy went to have her bath while Mara hurried to the kitchens for a late lunch.

She ate slowly, feeling tired and out of sorts. What she *wanted* was to spend her time thinking about the hybrid creatures and spell-songs, but her mind kept turning back to the human bone she had found. Was Izzy right? Had it simply been tangled up in the ropes? Or had it been purposefully weighted down like the animal bones? She couldn't be sure. She caught herself idly wiping her already-clean hands on her clothes, trying to dispel the gritty feel of the silt, still lingering hours later.

When a scullery maid announced that the fishmonger's boat had arrived with a delivery, Mara's mood lifted as though sunlight had broken through the clouds. She jammed the last of her food into her mouth and raced down to the sea cave beneath the palace, where space for the docks had been carved out by founders' magic long ago. She looked over the jostling, noisy crowd, until she spotted the familiar blue-and-yellow boat.

She jumped up and down and waved. "Fish Hook!"

Fish Hook was Mara's best friend. He was skinny and brown, about thirteen years old, with reddish-brown hair in a crown of loose, springy curls. Sometime in the last year Mara had grown taller than him, although he stood on his toes when she was close and tried to deny it. Nobody remembered Fish Hook's birth name, not even him. Like

Mara, he was an orphan, but he had never known his parents. He was called Fish Hook because of the long scar across his face, a hook-shaped line stretching from temple to jaw.

Fish Hook jumped the space between the boat and dock. He grinned when he saw Mara waving. "Shouldn't you be in the kitchen chopping the heads off eels?"

Mara punched his arm, and he pretended to wince in pain. "How can I chop eels if you haven't delivered them yet?"

"There's more than eels in this delivery. Your mistress must be feeding half the city tonight."

"Tomorrow, and only the rich half," Mara said. "They're going to dress up in founder costumes and pretend they don't recognize anybody beneath all the fins and spines. I don't have to help at all. Night off for me."

"Oh, aren't you the special one," Fish Hook said. "Did you find Old Greengill's lost treasure?"

"All of it," Mara said. "In a big cave right underneath Spellbreak Isle. I've got heaps and piles of jewels and gold, but it's all cursed so I have to hurry and sell it before boils make my face fall off. I'll trade it for a magic shop, and you can come with me so you don't have to work in the fish market anymore."

Fish Hook laughed as Mara wanted him to, but there was something indulgent in the way he said "I'd like that. We'll leave as soon as the eels are unloaded."

Not long ago Fish Hook would have playfully argued instead of agreeing. Learning to be a mage was all well and good, he would have said, but that was Mara's dream. *He* wanted to be an adventurer exploring distant lands on a ship of his own, never mind that he didn't know how to sail and barely knew how to swim. At least, that was what he used to want; Mara couldn't remember when he had last talked about it. Ever since Mara had left the fishmonger's for Tidewater Isle, she worried that Fish Hook thought she had abandoned him, even though he had encouraged her to go. She hadn't wanted to leave him behind. She had always meant to help him leave too.

She tugged on Fish Hook's arm to draw him away from the boats. "Tell me about Summer Island. How is everybody? What's going on? I don't hear *any* good gossip here."

"Well," Fish Hook began, "have you heard about the masquerading pirates?"

"Are they different from ordinary pirates?"

"Depends on who you believe," Fish Hook said. "One-Eyed Bennie swears they attacked her from a black ship. They were wearing animal masks to hide their faces."

"One-Eyed Bennie only has one eye, and that eye is half-blind," Mara pointed out.

"She says they were even wearing gloves with fake claws to be extra scary."

"But she wasn't scared, right?" Mara said. "She fought them off single-handed with only her fishing pole and chum bucket, and they sailed away crying like babies. She went straight back to the tavern to warn everybody else."

"Hey, you just ruined Bennie's story," Fish Hook said, and they both laughed. "How did you know how it was going to end?"

He told her about everything that had happened since they had last spoken, on the day the Roughwater boy told Mara about the bones: which fishermen were already ending the summer season and who was working into the winter, who was injured and who was well, whose son had eloped with a Lunderi silk merchant, never to be seen again. Magic students from the Citadel had been caught casting enchantments on turtles at the Hanging Garden. Nobody knew why the students had wanted to turn the turtle shells blue and make them glow in the dark, especially not when it got them into trouble with the High Mage, but everybody agreed it was a pretty good spell and wanted to know where they'd gotten it.

"I bet they think it was worth it," Mara said, giggling.

"You should learn that song," Fish Hook said. "That could be the first magic you learn."

It was right there on the tip of Mara's tongue: *It's too late for that. I've already found my first magic.* But the Lady had sworn her to secrecy about the bones.

Fish Hook was already going on. "If you think One-Eyed Bennie's story is great, I've got an even better one."

"Stop playing," Mara said, shoving his arm. "What is it?"

"You know Svana, from the fish market?" Fish Hook waited for Mara to nod; she remembered the woman with the long braids and braying laugh. "One of her sons brought something back the other night." Fish Hook glanced around and lowered his voice. "He said he caught it way out east, past the Winter Blade. He killed it, but it was so big he could only get part of it on their boat. He'd never seen anything like it before."

Mara had been thinking about strange sea creatures a lot for the past few days, but all the ones chasing through her thoughts were already dead. Something alive, something fishermen could catch and bring back, that was different from a muddy pile of bones.

"What was it?" she asked.

Fish Hook leaned closer to her ear. "A sea serpent."

Mara pulled back and glared at him.

A second later, Fish Hook started laughing. "You believed me for a second, didn't you?"

Mara scowled. "That's not funny."

"Svana's son doesn't think it's funny either. He keeps going around to all the dockside pubs with this sloppy rotten hunk of fish and making everybody look at it. Yesterday Big Jes had to kick him out because the smell was driving her customers away."

"Svana's son is an idiot," Mara said, even though she

wasn't sure which of the seven sons Fish Hook was talking about. She smiled and hoped Fish Hook didn't notice how forced it was. If he'd told her this story five days ago, she would have been laughing right along with him. But it was different now.

A thousand years ago, city sea serpents had been to the founders what horses or dogs were for humans. In the legends they were beloved companions, accompanying founders on quests or pulling sea chariots into battle. But the founders were gone, and the serpents too, and the city beneath the water was empty.

Mara had asked her mother once where they had gone and why they had left. Her mother's eyes had gone soft and sad as she explained that there were as many stories about the leaving of the founders as there were storytellers in the islands, but *she* believed they had left because humans had claimed the islands for their own, mages had stolen their songs, and the founders could not abide staying in a city they had built as a gift for people who repaid their kindness with greed.

Every once in a while sailors would claim they had seen a serpent way out in the open ocean, but nobody really believed them. Nobody had ever claimed to see one right here in the city.

The stories didn't feel as much like myths anymore, now that Mara had held the strange magical bones in her own hands.

"I wish it was real," Mara said.

Fish Hook's expression grew serious. "Yeah. That would be really great, wouldn't it?"

Mara hadn't meant to ruin his good mood. "Maybe One-Eyed Bennie can fight a sea serpent on her next night out and we'll know for sure."

Fish Hook snickered. "Knowing her she'll tell everyone the serpent tried to follow her home because it thought she was a founder."

Mara giggled. "Everybody knows wherever the sea serpents go, the founders are right behind them!"

"The serpents never swim alone, even if it's to a dockside tavern!"

They cracked up laughing and stopped only when a voice rang over the docks: "Mara! There she is."

Fish Hook's chin jerked up and Mara spun around. It was Izzy, striding across the dock. She was dressed for visiting Nila, with her braids wrapped in a brilliant blue scarf, her green skirt flowing around her ankles and her long earrings sparkling over a gold-threaded shawl. She looked pretty and relaxed and happy, and Mara felt renewed guilt for wishing she would change her mind about leaving Tidewater Isle.

But she wasn't leaving for good yet. She only wanted a ride on the fishmonger's boat back to Summer Island. Fish Hook shrugged and agreed, then he frowned and said, "What does he want?"

He was looking over Mara's shoulder. A houseboy was watching from several paces away, shifting nervously from foot to foot.

"Oh, him," Izzy said, distracted. Her mind was already on Summer Island. "He's looking for Mara."

"Me? Why?"

The boy jerked his thumb over his shoulder. "The Lady wants you in her tower. She's up there with the flotsam. She wants to see you right away." *Flotsam* was an unkind word for travelers from faraway lands. The Lady's only foreign guest right now was a scholar from Sumant, a woman Mara hadn't met or even seen.

"But why?" Mara asked, her heart thumping. The Lady had never summoned her to the laboratory tower. "Are you sure?"

Izzy made a face. "Does she want both of us?"

The boy was impatient. "No, just her. That's what she said. You better hurry."

"I have to go," Mara said to Fish Hook. "I'll see you around?"

"Tomorrow!" he agreed.

"Watch out for pirates!" Mara called out after them, and Fish Hook turned to flash her a grin as he hurried toward the blue-and-yellow boat.

The Laboratory
in the Tower

*R*enata *Palisado's tower laboratory was located in the old-*est part of Tidewater Isle. The only entrance was at the end of a long corridor with water dripping down the walls and moss growing in cracks between the stones. Low arrow slits provided glimpses outside, a reminder of when the island had been a battle-ready fortress rather than a comfortable palace.

Two armed women stood guard at the base of the tower stairs. They didn't say a word, didn't ask Mara her business, only unlocked the door and stepped aside.

"Thank you," Mara said as she hurried through.

The guards shut the door. Mara heard the rattle of metal on metal as they locked it again. A narrow staircase spiraled before her, and a single candle flickered in a sconce on the wall. Mara straightened her shoulders and took a steadying breath. She had always wanted to see the Lady's tower laboratory. She was excited, not scared. She had no reason to be scared. She began to climb.

The stairs had been worn slick by centuries of use, each one sloping into a polished bowl where hundreds of feet had trod before. The candles were just far enough apart that a gulp of darkness fell between each pair. Mara looked at the walls with interest. Some of the blocks were carved with intricate designs, now worn away by dropping water and creeping moss. There were patterns of shells and starfish, the silhouettes of whales and sharks and giant squid, and a scene of two founders, their long tails whipping and spines splayed, battling each other with deadly harpoons.

Mara touched one stone block, thinking.

The palace carved into Tidewater Isle had been shaped by the founders with their powerful magic centuries ago—just like the bones she had found. Maybe it would respond to spell-song in the same way?

Feeling a bit foolish, a bit hopeful, she sang out a few lines of her mother's old song: *"Over the sea and under the sky, my island home it waits for me . . ."*

She trailed off. Nothing happened.

Mara tried again, louder: *"Over the waves and under the storms, my heart is bound but my dreams are free."*

You have to be bossy, Bindy used to say, when you want a song to stop belonging to the one who sang it and start belonging to you.

Mara didn't know how to do that. She didn't even know what she wanted the spell to do. There was no answer, no echoing song, no eerie voice ringing from the stone.

Disappointed, Mara kept climbing. There was no real reason to think it *would* work. Bindy had always said that a spell that spoke to one kind of object wouldn't work on another. There was no reason for an old sailors' song from Gravetown to affect the building blocks of Tidewater Isle. But then there was no reason for that song to have worked on the bones of hybrid creatures either. Mara didn't know why it had worked before, and she didn't know why it wasn't working now. Not knowing felt like clothes that didn't fit right, a discomfort she wanted to pick at until it could be fixed.

As Mara neared the top of the tower, an acrid smoke filled the air, and she felt an odd sensation, not unlike being in the attic of a tall wooden house on a windy day. It felt as though the tower itself was swaying and groaning—but she wasn't moving at all, and the smoke was humming with spell-song. It wasn't particularly melodic, that dull droning song in a language she couldn't understand, but she was fairly sure she recognized the Lady's voice.

The smoke grew stronger and thicker the higher she climbed, scratching at her throat and stinging her eyes.

She was coughing and rubbing tears away by the time she reached the open door at the top of the stairs. She hurried inside without waiting to be invited. She was so desperate for clean air she momentarily forgot she was barging head-first into the Lady's laboratory.

"Oh," a voice said. "There you are."

Renata Palisado emerged from the billowing clouds. She wore a stained smock in place of her usual fine gown, and her white-streaked hair was tucked beneath a tattered red scarf.

"I sent for you ages ago," said the Lady.

Mara tried to say "I'm sorry, ma'am," but she only managed half before coughing again.

"Etina, this is my diving girl, the one I found in the fish market." The Lady said it as though she had plucked Mara from a market stall like a clutch of squid or a bucket of mudfish. "Her name is Mara."

Smoke swirled and another woman appeared. She was older than Renata Palisado, her face more lined, her hair a shock of white. Her skin was so dark it looked almost black in the haze.

"Don't make her stand there in the blind all night," the woman said. She had a Sumanti accent, rich and rolling like Driftwood's. "Come in, child, quickly now."

Mara gratefully took a few steps forward. The smoke cleared, revealing the Lady's laboratory.

The tower room was alight with lamps and candles, so

many Mara felt like she had stepped into a pungent, waxy oven. There were shelves crammed with books on every wall, and piles of scrolls tumbled from chairs. A metal brazier in the center of the room held a crackle of wood. Thick brown smoke rose from the fire to spread across the ceiling and slink down the walls.

On three long tables lay the bones Mara and Izzy had found. The goat-horned horse's head gleamed white in the candlelight, its sharp teeth glinting. The bayfish with a serpentine tail was spread out in a long line. The massive bird skull sat at the center of one table; an orange cat dozed beside it, uncaring of the dead creatures all around it.

Mara hadn't been in a mage's laboratory since she'd been forced to leave Bindy's shop on the Street of Whispering Stones. The Lady's was larger, finer, and altogether unfamiliar, but still it felt a little bit like coming home.

"This is Professor Etina Kosta," the Lady said, gesturing to her guest. "She is a scholar from Sumant."

Mara bowed to the professor. "Pleased to meet you, ma'am."

"Likewise. You're the one who found the remains?"

Mara glanced at the Lady before answering, "Yes, ma'am."

"I haven't got them all put together yet," said the Lady. "There are pieces of the puzzle missing. I was hoping you would find them today."

Mara shuffled her feet and said nothing.

Professor Kosta laughed. "Don't blame the girl for your failure, Renata."

The Lady's face was unreadable in the dancing candle-light. "I haven't failed. I'll have it sorted before long. The girls have kept this discovery to themselves. Haven't you?"

"Yes, ma'am," Mara said quickly, with a glance at the smoke-spewing brazier.

One of Mara's chores in Bindy's shop had been to light oily candles in every corner before Bindy sang certain spells. The candles had smelled terrible, like meat festering in the sun, but Bindy had only laughed when Mara coughed and pinched her nose. "Better this stink than those dry old bones at the Citadel stealing my songs," she would say. When Mara was very little, she had thought that meant the Citadel was populated by animated skeletons who clicked and clattered into magic shops. Only when she was older did she understand that Bindy was talking about the mages of Obsidian Isle, and the spell-smoke kept them from overhearing her songs. Citadel-trained mages, Bindy claimed, were a sneaky, secretive lot, and not to be trusted.

The thick smoke here served the same purpose as those charmed candles: to keep other mages from spying on the Lady's laboratory.

"Tell me, Mara, how did you find these curious skel-etons?" Professor Kosta asked.

"They were in the mud of the shallows," Mara said, after the Lady nodded at her to answer. "A fisherman's boy told me where to look. I didn't mean to disobey the Lady. I was only curious."

The Lady of the Tides snorted delicately. "And you were not at all thinking about what reward you might receive."

Mara's face grew warm.

"Don't tease the child," the professor said. "Curiosity should be nurtured in children, not quashed."

"Oh, I agree completely," said the Lady. "I think you'll find Mara has more than enough curiosity—especially on the subject of magic."

With that the warmth in Mara's face became a full-blown flame. Mara was only a servant. She wasn't supposed to want anything at all except to please her master. She had never suspected the Lady would notice her interest in magic. The Lady didn't even know she had spent half her life with a bone-mage; and even if she had, she would have dismissed Bindy's magic as worthless, like all the other mages did. She had only ever cared about how well Mara could swim and dive.

Professor Kosta asked, "What do you think of these creatures, Mara?"

Mara's embarrassment gave way to a faint panic. Both women were watching her, but she didn't know what the professor wanted her to say. She had come up to the tower expecting scolding or commands, not questions. She didn't know why a learned scholar would be asking her anything at all.

"They could be very old," she began hesitantly. She looked again toward the remains on the tabletops. By the bird skull, the orange cat had awoken and was cleaning its paws. "They look like they're from . . . they look like the creatures the founders made with their magic before people lived here?"

The Lady and the professor didn't say anything, only waited for Mara to go on.

"But the bones haven't been on the seafloor for hundreds of years. Somebody weighted them down with rocks to make them sink," Mara said. "Not very long ago."

The Lady picked up one of those black stones from the table and passed it idly from hand to hand. "Yes, someone certainly did. You've had a busy few days. Will you be well rested by tomorrow?"

Mara nodded uncertainly. "Yes, ma'am?" It came out like a question.

Professor Kosta's lips turned in a frown. "Renata . . ."

"She's a very strong diver."

"It's not her swimming ability that concerns me."

"We won't find out any other way."

"Have you tried to find another way?"

The Lady gestured dismissively. "She'll be happy to do it."

"She's your servant. She can hardly say no."

"Of course she can say no. We don't keep slaves in this city."

"No, but you do force children to work and earn wages."

Mara looked back and forth between the two women, her eyes wide. She had never seen anybody argue with the Lady of the Tides before.

"Mara likes her work," said the Lady airily. "And I think she would very much like an opportunity to do more. She's a skilled diver, but I don't think it's a job that fully occupies that curious mind you so want to nurture. Is it?"

Mara trembled when she realized the Lady was speaking to her. "Ma'am?"

The Lady raised a single eyebrow.

"I do like diving," Mara said carefully—and truthfully. She felt shaky and nervous all over. It didn't sound like the Lady was going to punish her. It sounded like the Lady was leading up to the exact opposite of punishment. "But I wouldn't mind other tasks? If that's what you wish," she added.

"At the very least you must explain to her what you're asking and give her a choice," said Professor Kosta.

"I suppose that is reasonable," the Lady agreed.

"And we are so very concerned with being reasonable." The professor's voice was dry as kindling.

The Lady said to Mara, "If you know about the magic of the founders, then surely you know how many mages have tried through the ages to draw those ancient songs from artifacts and once again use that magic. I've devoted much of my own life to trying to determine where the myths end and the facts begin."

"Yes, ma'am," Mara said. Bindy used to say that so many mages had tried to wake the magic of the founders that the magic, if it even existed anymore, had probably rolled over on its ancient bed and covered itself with its pillow to keep from being bothered. Like every child in the city, Mara had grown up hearing stories about mages who had claimed to wield the founders' great elemental magic: Old Greengill, Hars the Half-witch, Nevena the Mad, the Three Drowned Sisters, and so many more. None of them, in the end, had been able to calm storms or turn away waves or shape islands to their will, or achieve any of the magnificent things the sea dwellers had been able to do.

The Lady went on: "It's something of a family hobby, in fact. One of my kin first tried his hand at it some years ago. Nobody important, a cousin from a minor family line. He's been dead for decades. Every family needs an embarrassing failure or two tucked away in their history, don't they?"

Mara looked away. The orange tabby on the table was blinking at her, as though to say, with its judgmental cat eyes, that everybody in the room knew Mara had no family.

"I assume somebody has been attempting to glean the songs of the founders from these bones," the Lady said.

That was what Mara had thought as well. That was, after all, the main reason the Lady and other mages collected magical artifacts at all. Bones weren't much different than artifacts. "Of course they haven't a hope of succeeding, but that wouldn't stop some misguided pretender who claims to sing to bones."

"That's not—"

The Lady frowned, and Mara stopped.

"Sorry, ma'am," she said.

That's not fair, she had been about to say. Bindy hadn't been a pretender; she had been a skilled and clever mage. Just because none of the other mages understood her bone magic didn't make it any less powerful. Maybe not everything she tried had worked—she'd had her share of failed experiments—but Mara had seen her sing to skeletons of long-dead mages in their Ossuary crypts and hear their replies in eerie, whispered spells.

As for *these* bones, Mara wasn't a mage at all and she had been able to stir their song without even trying. The Lady shouldn't dismiss the possibility so quickly. Bindy was gone, but maybe there was somebody else in the city who knew bone magic. Somebody who had kept it secret rather than open themselves to mockery. Maybe even somebody who had known Bindy and shared spells with her.

The hair on the back of Mara's neck prickled.

The Lady was still passing the black stone from hand to hand. "I doubt whoever discarded these bones was able to glean anything useful from them, but I should very much like to know more before I draw any conclusions."

Mara swallowed nervously. "How will you do that, ma'am?"

The Lady exchanged a glance with Professor Kosta. "There are a few mages who might be responsible, but this—" She held up the black stone between her thumb and forefinger. "These stones used to weight the remains have certain magical characteristics that lead me to suspect one man in particular. But I have no proof. That is why I need your help. This seems to be a task only you can do."

"Me?" Mara's voice rose to an embarrassing squeak.

Did the Lady know Mara had used a song to find the bones? Izzy and Driftwood didn't know—and even if they did, they would have said something to Mara first. Did the Lady know Mara used to be a bone-mage's servant? It was Izzy who had brought Mara to Tidewater Isle, and all Izzy knew was that Mara had been working in the fish market. Mara had never told Izzy or the Lady about Bindy, never spoke of her at all except with Fish Hook. She was too afraid of being scorned and dismissed as a magical crack-pot before she even had a chance to prove herself.

Whatever the Lady knew about Mara's past, however she had found out, Mara wasn't about to betray Bindy's memory by sharing her spell-songs with another mage, even if she could remember them clearly. The Lady was Mara's master, but the Lady wasn't her *mage* master, and

Mara wasn't her apprentice. She could say no. She could suggest a trade. She could—

"You are a very strong swimmer," the Lady said. "For this task, that is exactly what I need."

Mara's shoulders slumped. The Lady wasn't talking about bone magic. She was only talking about diving.

"How old are you, Mara?" Professor Kosta asked.

"Twelve, ma'am," Mara said.

"Perhaps the older girl?" Professor Kosta suggested. "She's very young."

Mara bristled. She could take care of herself. She didn't need to be protected. "I'm a better diver than Izzy."

"And more humble too," said the Lady. "You haven't heard yet what I want you to do."

"Sorry, ma'am."

"We must maintain absolute secrecy," said the Lady.

"Yes, ma'am."

"If something goes wrong, I may not be able to help you. You will have to rely upon your wits."

"Ma'am?"

"And, yes, it might be dangerous."

Mara had never seen her mistress like this, plotting and scheming in her tower. It was a little bit exciting, like working for a pirate witch rather than a rich old lady with an eccentric hobby. But beneath the excitement Mara was still aware of the hair-prickle of unease. It all came back to the bone magic, and there weren't very many mages in the city who would have learned Bindy's songs. Bindy hadn't had many friends. She had been very secretive, always aware of how the other mages mocked her. She had never let Mara look at the journals where she wrote down her spells.

"Yes, ma'am."

There was a spark of satisfaction in Renata Palisado's eyes. "Are you afraid of the dark?"

"No, ma'am," Mara said. It was almost not quite a lie.

"Good." Renata Palisado ran her finger over the head of the orange cat, who bumped her hand and purred. "My cousin wasn't either. Third cousin twice removed, or thrice. Who can remember these things? The one who spent so much time seeking lost songs. He loved to explore the caves and tunnels of the founders' underwater city. He had this odd glass globe—much like the ones the emissaries were said to use to meet with the founders, only instead of enclosing the entire body, it protected only his head. I have no idea how he made it. He was a very strange man. But he was kind enough to record how he found his way into the fortress."

Mara's heart was thumping so loud she was sure the Lady could hear it. "Fortress?" she whispered.

"This is what I want you to do," the Lady said, meeting Mara's eyes. "I want you to sneak into the Winter Blade."

Mara stared, speechless.

The Lady held her gaze. "I should very much like to know if the Lord of the Muck has been collecting bones while he's shut away in that tower, and if he has been, I should also like to know what he's doing with them."

The first thought to worm its way through Mara's surprise was: that's impossible.

The Lady was mad to think that anybody could sneak into the Winter Blade. It was the most foreboding island in the city. The founders had built the tower as a gift for some long-dead mage using ancient, long-forgotten spells. Ever since then, it had been home to a succession of powerful mages, a line of women and men who stole it from one another by tricks, fights, battles, and murders. It was said to be riddled with so many curses, spells, and enchantments even the island's masters tripped its booby traps from time to time. Living there was almost as dangerous as winning it—but the rewards were great, if you survived long enough to delve into the magical secrets past masters had left behind. Nobody knew exactly what had become of Gerrant of Greenwood, the island's master before the Lord of the Muck, but all agreed he must have met a most horrible death.

It wasn't possible to sneak inside. The Lady had to know that. If there were secret tunnels carved by the founders beneath the Winter Blade, surely Gerrant or the Lord of the Muck or any of the island's past masters would have found them and blocked them up. Or, worse, turned them into deadly traps.

But if the Lady was *right* . . .

For two years the master of the Winter Blade had been the man Mara hated most in the world. The man who had killed Bindy.

Mara's chest ached as though she had dove too deep, too fast.

The Muck had known Bindy. The night Bindy died, she had claimed they were only going to the Ossuary to coax secrets from the bones of dead mages. But she had packed up all her journals before she left, which she had never done just for a trip to the Ossuary. Would she have trusted the Muck with her spell-songs? With her secret spell journals? It was hard for Mara to imagine; Bindy hadn't trusted anybody. But maybe she had thought the Muck was her friend.

Bindy's spell books had never been found. The Muck might have them; he might have stolen them from Bindy before he killed her. If Mara *could* get into the Winter Blade, she might be able to find the spell books as proof of what the Muck had done. Nobody had wanted to listen to a bone-mage's little servant girl, but they would listen to the Lady of the Tides.

"Think before you agree, child," said Professor Kosta. "It could be very dangerous."

"But it could also be very rewarding," the Lady added. "For both of us."

Mara's hands were shaking. "Ma'am?"

"Whatever you think of me, child, I do not ask my

staff to perform difficult—"

"Dangerous," said Professor Kosta.

"I do not ask my staff to perform *dangerous* tasks without offering anything in return. If you do this thing—" The Lady glanced at Professor Kosta. "If you *choose* to do this thing, a choice which is entirely up to you, upon your successful return we'll see about finding work that makes better use of that admirably curious mind of yours. I could certainly use some help with all of this."

She gestured casually to take in the laboratory room around them, but to Mara the gesture seemed as slow and graceful as a dream. Magic. The Lady was talking about magic. She was talking about Mara being allowed to help. It wasn't an offer to teach, and it certainly wasn't an apprenticeship, but it was more than she had now.

Justice for Bindy. Magic for herself. Mara's heart was racing so fast she thought it would leap from her chest like a fish from a bucket. She ignored the whisper in the back of her mind insisting it was no accident the Lady was saying everything she wanted to hear. This was Mara's chance. She was not going to let it slip away.

"I'll do it," Mara said. "I want to do it."

The Lady smiled. "Splendid," she said. "Let us make a plan."

6

Night on the Water

The next afternoon, Mara paced the dock impatiently.
The sea cave beneath Tidewater Isle was a flurry of activity. Lamplight glinted off the glass and stone mosaics on the walls, and the chamber echoed with noise. The Lady's party would be under way in a few hours. There were merchants, musicians, and players arriving all at the same time. There was even a tailor, a thin-faced woman in striped trousers and a long jacket, who had leapt from her boat and raced toward the stairs, muttering about charging double for troublesome clients.

Mara had been excused from helping with party preparations. She was supposed to be resting for the long night ahead. Tonight she was going to the Winter Blade.

She was far too anxious to sleep. She wanted to talk to Izzy before it was time to go. Izzy hadn't yet come back from Summer Island, and Mara hoped she would be returning this afternoon. She knew she couldn't tell Izzy about the plan for tonight. She only wanted to know somebody besides the Lady would be waiting for her to return.

"Mara?"

She spun around. "Fish Hook!" She had been so distracted she hadn't seen the fishmonger's boat come into the cave. "Is Izzy with you?"

"She said she'd come back with an early boat. You mean she's not here?"

"She didn't come back yet," Mara said. "But maybe she just . . . decided not to? She's moving to Summer Island soon anyway."

Fish Hook shook his head. "She wouldn't just leave you, you know."

Mara looked down, embarrassed at having her fears read so easily.

"She wouldn't," he insisted. "She wouldn't go away without saying good-bye. There must have been something she had to do."

"Maybe." Mara wanted to be convinced, but it was hard when she had so many other worries crowding her mind, and she couldn't tell Fish Hook about any of them. "Can you find her when you get back? Just to make sure she's okay? She goes to the candlemaker's shop on the Street of

Two Hundred Stairs, the one that's halfway up—"

"I know where it is," Fish Hook said. "I'll go. Of course I'll go. You can even come with me, if you want?"

"I can't," Mara said. "I've got to— The Lady needs me for something tonight."

"For her party?"

"No, it's . . ."

Mara looked at his familiar brown face with its long scar, his brown eyes filled with concern, his curly hair escaping in spirals from the tie he'd used to push it back. He didn't even know Izzy very well, but Izzy was Mara's friend, and that was enough for him to want to help.

She couldn't tell Fish Hook the truth, but she didn't want to lie, so she said, "I'm supposed to tell everybody I'm giving the Lady's foreign guest a night tour of the city so she can see it all lit up."

Fish Hook raised a single eyebrow—an expression he used to practice when he thought nobody was looking. "It's going to rain later."

Mara hoped Fish Hook understood how hard she was trying to be honest with him. "She's from Sumant. She likes the rain because it's so strange to her."

"Right," Fish Hook said slowly. He didn't believe her, but his wry smile meant he wasn't going to push. "Well, be careful. Watch out for One-Eyed Bennie's masked pirates."

"I'll be with Driftwood. We'll be fine." She couldn't tell Fish Hook anything else, but she didn't want him to worry about her, only Izzy. "Just tell Izzy everybody's asking about her."

"I will," he promised. He ran back to the blue-and-yellow boat.

Mara climbed the narrow stairs to the girls' dormitory to rest, but sleep was impossible. She watched the gray light outside the window sink into twilight while she ate dinner. The flatbread and fried fish churned in her stomach, but she made herself finish. She had to dive tonight. She needed her strength.

When it was time to leave, Mara changed into her swimming clothes, then pulled on a shirt and trousers and cloak to hide them. She had been going over the plan again and again in her mind, the same way she planned dangerous cave dives, but she could only get so far before she ran into the unknown. She packed an oilskin sack with two murk-lights, then took them out and picked two others, then switched them back before scowling at herself for being ridiculous. The murk-lights were all the same. She was only stalling.

She couldn't help but feel that no matter what happened, no matter what she found inside the Winter Blade, everything would be different tomorrow. This was bigger than diving for ancient artifacts, bigger than working as Bindy's servant. This was ancient magic and powerful mages and secret fortresses, and Mara was at the center of it.

There wasn't anything left for her to prepare. She went down to meet Driftwood and Professor Kosta on the docks.

Thin fog wrapped around the islands like a gossamer shawl. The Hanging Garden was brilliant with cascades of white and gold light, and the palaces on Glassmaker Isle glinted like jewels. The arched bridge between Cedar and Spellbreak islands was a delicate necklace of torch-light. Even floating Outcast Island was a yellow glow in the distance, soft as a sunrise. Far to the northwest, the windows of the Citadel on Obsidian Isle shone like pinpricks through a black cloth; the magic students were late at their studies. Mara stared at those lights with a nervous fluttery feeling in her chest.

"The city is beautiful at night," said Professor Kosta. She was wearing a cloak for the rain, but she had pushed the hood back to better see the city.

"Yes, ma'am," said Mara.

"I am not your master, child," the professor said, gently chiding. "I am only an old scholar far from home. Please call me 'Professor.'"

Mara couldn't see Professor Kosta's expression in the darkness, but she didn't think the woman was upset. "Yes, Professor." Because she thought the professor would not mind, she asked, "If you please, Professor, a scholar of what?"

"Ancient history and myths," said Professor Kosta, "like your city's lost sea dwellers in their underwater realm. You know, the first explorers to come to these islands were from Sumant."

"Yes, Professor," Mara said. Everybody knew that. "They landed at Gravetown and made a village there."

"Indeed they did. They were the first humans to learn spell-song as well. The songs are such a curious form of magic. It's delightful that any blacksmith can learn a song or two to make her life easier, but at the same time it seems impossible for anybody to achieve what the founders could do."

Mara glanced at the professor. She might as well be wondering why a whale couldn't climb a mountain or why a horse didn't have gills. The founders weren't human, and humans weren't the founders. Their magic would never be the same.

"They were magical," Mara said. "They didn't just know magical songs."

Professor Kosta inclined her head thoughtfully. "Indeed, but I find it fascinating how the mages of your city have adapted to a magical system they can't, by nature, ever hope to master. I can wander the wharves and hear spell-songs in twenty different languages, some nearly indistinguishable from perfectly mundane songs, and some so strange they scarcely sound like human voices at all. It's truly remarkable."

"It takes a lot of study and practice to be a mage. My—" Mara stopped herself and bit her lip. She had been about to say *my old master*. "I've heard mages say it can take years and years to find the right combinations of words and pitch and melody to cast strong spells, and even longer to invent new ones."

"It is the same with most magical traditions, I suppose," Professor Kosta said.

Mara didn't know much about how people did magic in other places. She knew about the Sumanti alchemists, a few of whom had shops on Quarantine Island, and she had heard tales of stomach-churning blood potions of the Pinnacle Isles far to the west, or the rhythmic stone clacking from Roughwater to the north. But those distant magical traditions had never captivated her like her own city's songs. She couldn't imagine how blood potions or clattering rocks could ever be as beautiful as an eerie spell sung by an accomplished mage.

She thought of the songs she used to make up when she was a child, the ones she had pretended and wished with all her heart could be spells. Her mother had always laughed and told her to keep trying; stonemasons took great pride in not using magic, cherishing their strong hands and sharp tools instead. Magic can't solve every problem, Mum used to say, even if mages sometimes forget that. But Mum had never told Mara to stop singing her made-up spellsongs, and Mara had never forgotten how it felt to yearn for them to be magic.

Professor Kosta sighed. "Oh, that is a splendid sight."

Behind them, Tidewater Isle was lit up like a flame, with golden lamplight glowing in every window. The party guests were arriving in decorated flatboats lined with lanterns, with wooden figureheads in the shape of arched sea serpents or spiny founders adorning every prow.

They wouldn't be worried about pirates; they would never believe anybody would dare attack them while they were trying to have fun. That sort of fear was for other people. The Lady of the Glass was coming, along with the High Mage, the Lord of the Summer and all seven of his daughters, the First Harbormaster and her sons, the mistress of the Glassmakers' Guild, and so many other important and powerful people. The household gossip hadn't been able to keep up. A select group of the Citadel-trained mages Bindy had so despised would be there, congratulating one another on their latest magical achievements and lucrative commissions. The palace would ring with music and laughter, and the guests would be eating and drinking and dancing until dawn. They would all be wearing elaborate, colorful costumes meant to represent the founders: gowns covered with embroidered scales, fans shaped like bejeweled fins, collars adorned with jewel-covered spines, masks with round painted eyes.

Professor Kosta drew her gaze away from Tidewater Isle and pointed to the north. "Tell me, what is that dim island there? The one with so few lights?"

"That's the Ossuary, ma'am. I mean, Professor. The graveyard island."

"A whole island for a graveyard! How fascinating. We don't inter our dead in Sumant."

"Only the rich do here. Everybody else is buried at sea," said Driftwood.

Buried at sea, or lost, with no chance of good-bye.

Mara had vague memories of playing on the steep terraces of the Ossuary when she was very little. Her parents must have taken her along when they were hired to build or repair tombs. It was during the very last of those trips that their boat had foundered in a squall and they had drowned. Only Mara had survived.

She didn't remember swimming to the Ossuary and crawling up on the black-sand beach as the waves and rain beat at her. But she did remember hiding from the storm in the catacombs. She had been terrified and shivering, surrounded by walls made from black stone and old bones, humming to herself to chase away the shadows and crying for her parents.

And she remembered when Bindy had found her. A warm welcome light appeared in the darkness, and a gentle voice coaxed her out of the tomb with kind words and a warm cloak.

It had taken Mara a long time to understand that her parents were gone for good, and even longer to admit to herself that Bindy, odd and gruff and eccentric as she was, had taken their place.

Then she had lost Bindy too.

Mara wiped a spray of rain and seawater from her face. She wanted the professor to keep talking to distract her. "What do you do in Sumant? If you don't bury people?"

"We burn the dead on pyres," Professor Kosta said. "Nothing is left but ashes. That's how we've always done it. Perhaps I will visit your graveyard island, if it is allowed. I should like to see the old graves. Do you hear that? Is that magic being sung?"

Mara tilted her head to listen. She heard music from Tidewater Isle, drifts of laughter, the ring of buoy bells, the distant moan of a foghorn. Mingling with those usual nighttime sounds was a slow, deep, sad spell-song and another that was higher and lighter, bouncing and chasing like a moth on a sea breeze.

"Yes. Those are fishing songs," Mara said.

"They sound very different," Professor Kosta said.

"They're for different things. The fast, high one is calling for slipfish—little bait fish," she explained when the professor looked at her in question. "You have to sing fast to keep their attention. The other one is for a calm night. That's why it's so slow and soft—to soothe the waves."

"Can your magical songs do that?" the professor asked. "Renata led me to believe controlling the weather was beyond a human mage's capability."

Mara liked the way the professor said "your magical songs," as though any servant could sing a spell as well as a mage. "That's true. Our mages can't really change the weather. A song like that is telling the sea it's okay to stay quiet tonight."

"Like a mother humming a child to sleep."

Mara nodded, happy Professor Kosta had understood. "Yes, like that."

"It's a lovely song, and a little sad, I think," Professor Kosta said.

"Weather songs are always sad," Mara said. "That's the only kind of song the sea understands. It's been that way since the time of the Three Sisters."

"Oh? I don't believe I've heard about them."

"I can tell you, if you like."

Mara tried not to sound too eager, but the farther they drew from Tidewater Isle, the more the darkness and the fog closed around them. If the conversation ended and silence reigned, she wouldn't have anything to do but count the oar strokes and tremble in fear until they arrived. No matter where she looked, no matter how she turned her head, her gaze kept drawing back to the east, where the dark silhouette of the Winter Blade would soon appear in the mist.

She kept thinking: it's not possible. The Lady had given her an impossible mission. There was no way Mara could succeed. She would get lost. She would be caught and the

Lady would not be able to help her. She shouldn't be here.

Professor Kosta said, "I would love to hear it."

Mara glanced at the professor to see if she was serious. In her experience adults always assumed there was somebody better to tell stories than a fish girl.

But Professor Kosta looked sincere, and Mara was relieved to have a distraction. She cleared her throat and began: "A long time ago, there were three sisters. Their parents had been lost at sea when they were very young. They had no family except one another."

Bindy used to tell Mara bedtime stories about great mages, her lively hands casting shadows on the walls as she recounted their triumphs and failures. Mara had loved most of Bindy's stories, but the Three Sisters had never been her favorite. It always made her feel a little bit jealous, a little bit lonely, although Bindy never seemed to notice. Mara would have liked to have siblings of her own, somebody who could tell her what her parents had been like, somebody who could miss them with her. That's why it stung so much when Izzy teased her about being just like a little sister. A real little sister wouldn't be left alone when a person married or moved or left one job for another.

Mara couldn't worry about Izzy now. Fish Hook would find her. She was fine. In the morning Mara would tell her all about the night, no matter how many times the Lady swore her to secrecy.

"The sisters became storm-mages when they grew up,"

Mara went on. "The founders used to stir up storms to fight each other, and those storms were worse than anything natural. The storm-mages couldn't stop them, but they could warn sailors when it was getting very bad. That's what the sisters wanted to do, because nobody had been able to warn their parents. They went to the Citadel and learned everything they could."

"I should like to see one of your city's terrible storms," said Professor Kosta. "They sound magnificent."

"They're deadly," said Driftwood. "Even without magic."

"Of course." There was a note of apology in Professor Kosta's voice. "Go on, Mara."

Mara scratched her chin with the wool blanket. With every stroke of Driftwood's oars the lights of the city pulled farther away. To the north loomed the slumbering slopes of Greenwood Island, spotted with a few lonely lights winking through the mist. She would have liked to be heading toward those lights rather than away. Her fear was only growing stronger. She was certain the professor and Driftwood would be able to see it writhing beneath her skin if they looked close enough.

"Then one winter when the sisters were grown, they learned there were two storms coming to the city. One from the east and one from the west," Mara said.

"Like two titans clashing," said Professor Kosta. "Were they magical storms?"

"Yes," Mara said. "There were two families of founders

battling each other beneath the sea. The eldest sister went west aboard a ship toward that storm, and the youngest sister went east, even though all they could do was warn sailors out of the way. The middle sister stayed home to warn the city. She was still waiting for her sisters to return when the storms joined together and blew for three days and three nights." That wasn't part of the original story, but Mara liked the sound of it. Three days of storm for three mage sisters. "She was getting desperate, and scared for her sisters. She went to the emissary to ask for help."

"The emissary?" Professor Kosta asked.

"The person who talked to the founders," Mara explained. "The founders didn't like people bothering them all the time when they had more important things to do, so they picked just one person from the city who would carry messages to them."

"I see. Go on."

"The sister wanted the emissary to ask the founders to stop fighting, because the churning whirlpools and lashing waves they were stirring up with their magical storms were hurting so many people. But the emissary said no. She was too afraid of getting caught in the middle of the battle. She refused to help, all because she wanted to save her own skin."

Ahead Mara saw a gap in the night, a slice of darkness where water and fog ought to be. The Winter Blade was completely dark. If the Lord of the Muck needed light to see, he kept it well shuttered.

"What did the sister do?" Professor Kosta asked.

Mara pulled her gaze away from the dark island. "She stole one of the emissary's great glass globes for traveling underwater, and she went down to the founders' city herself."

"Did they stop fighting?" Professor Kosta asked.

Mara had asked the same thing, the first time Bindy had told her this story. Bindy had tapped Mara's nose and said, "It's not that kind of story, little fish. Best you learn now that begging for help rarely gets you what you want." Mara hadn't really understood what she meant, not then. She'd understood a lot better after Bindy was dead and Mara had pleaded, to no avail, for anybody to believe that the Muck was responsible.

"It was too late," Mara said. "The founders were gone. The different families had set their storms brewing in hopes of driving each other away, but the storms tore up so much of their underwater city they both fled. By the time the storms ran out of magic, the founders were gone. They'd run scared from their own battle." Bindy had told that part of the story with a derisive snort, but Mara couldn't bring herself to do that. "The storm destroyed a lot of ships and a lot of the city. Whole quarters had to be rebuilt. A lot of people drowned—including the two sisters who had sailed out to try to help. Nobody saw the founders ever again."

"How long have they been gone?" Professor Kosta asked.

Mara shrugged uncertainly. That was a question for historians in the dusty Citadel libraries, not a fish girl telling an old story. "A long time. Hundreds and hundreds of years."

"How far they must have fled to vanish into mystery."

Mara's mother had said much the same thing, whenever fireside conversation turned to the fate of the founders. We should never have taken their songs, she would say, and with a sigh she would add: I wonder if they remember us as we remember them. And the other adults gathered that night for food or company would laugh, charmed by her old-fashioned Gravetown superstitions, but Mara had never laughed with them.

The bait-catching song across the water had quieted, leaving only the slow, low notes of the calming song to carry. Mara listened to it for a moment, trying to let its melody soothe her. Bindy had been one of those people who missed the founders and their magic. That was another reason the Three Sisters had never been among Mara's favorite stories; she hadn't liked the way Bindy spoke with admiration and awe about those last raging storms.

Mara's story was almost over. She wondered if it was too late to go back. To tell Professor Kosta she wasn't ready for this after all. To tell the Lady she would have to find somebody else. She couldn't do it. She couldn't go into the Winter Blade.

She felt sick to her stomach, so she made herself take a breath and finish the story. "The emissary was so angry the last sister had disobeyed her that she banished her to an island at the edge of the city. She stayed there for the rest of her life, still singing to the storms. When she was very, very old, and most people had forgotten that she hadn't always lived on that island, they began calling her the Lady of the Gales."

"Ah." Professor Kosta gave a satisfied little nod. "We passed her island as we sailed into the city."

"Nobody remembers what it was called before," Mara said. She had no idea if that was true, but neither did Professor Kosta. "Storm-mages still go there to learn their songs."

"That's a lovely story, Mara. Thank you for telling me."

Mara shrugged awkwardly. "You're welcome, Professor. I'm happy to be of service."

Even in the darkness Mara could see the professor frown. "It's a story, Mara, not a service. I am not your master."

"Yes, Professor."

They fell quiet. Across the water the calming song ended, leaving the night quiet beneath the muffling blanket of fog. Mara ducked lower into her blanket and watched the Winter Blade draw closer. She bounced her leg, and stopped. Bit the inside of her cheek, and stopped. It was too late to turn away now. They were almost there.

She had the brief, outrageous thought of diving into the water and swimming as fast as she could in the opposite direction, swimming and swimming and not stopping until the island was no more than a black smudge behind her.

The fortress was as thin as a razor and impossibly black. Not even the tiniest spark of flame escaped that darkness.

7

The Winter Blade

The face of the Winter Blade was as black as the night sea surrounding it.

When Gerrant of Greenwood had been the island's master, there had been tall windows looking down on the city, balconies above the crashing waves, and a sea cave protecting the docks.

But now all the entrances were so well hidden nobody could even remember what it had looked like before. In the first days after the Lord of the Muck seized the fortress two years ago, sailors who ventured near the island heard songs ringing from it day and night, spell after mysterious spell, until one day the sun rose and the Winter Blade had been transformed. Even merchants who had traded with

Gerrant could no longer find the cave they had entered countless times. Some people insisted the Muck must have cast those spells, but others claimed the island changed to suit its master—even if the master did not ask it to.

Nobody even knew how the Lord of the Muck went in and out of his island. Some said he had grown wings to fly like a gull or learned to swim under the sea like the founders. They always said it with a nervous chuckle.

"We'll need to get a bit closer," Professor Kosta whispered. "Let's hope Renata's cousin was telling the truth about these tunnels."

There was one part of the island that had not changed, and indeed never changed when new masters seized the fortress. All around the base of the island, just above the high-tide line, there were a hundred or more stone statues set in tall niches, all carved from the same black stone as the island. Some stories claimed they had been placed there by the founders, before the fortress's first human master, but nobody knew if that was true. The people in the statues weren't founders, after all. They were human, more or less.

Some more, some less. As Driftwood brought the boat to the base of the island, Mara stared up at the statues with a knot of fear in her throat.

Professor Kosta held up a small mage-lit candle to study each statue. They passed a woman with wings on her back, a man with two heads, a youth with the body of a horse. The black stone was wet with sea spray and gleamed faintly in the candlelight. Each statue had words in the Old Sumanti alphabet carved beneath its niche; Professor Kosta muttered under her breath as she read. This was why the professor had come along: Mara and Driftwood couldn't read a single word of Old Sumanti.

"What do they say?" Mara asked when she couldn't bear the silence any longer.

"That one," Professor Kosta said, pointing to the man with two heads, "it's a very old dialect. I can't be sure of the translation, but I believe it says *for disloyalty*. This fellow says *for betrayal*. And here is *for invasion*. Curious names for statues."

"Some people think these statues were a warning to people to stay away," Mara said. "Or punishment for people who didn't."

"That does seem like a solid hypothesis. Ah, and this one—that woman with horns—she's the one we're looking for." She spoke a jumble of syllables, rising and falling in a musical way. It sounded like she was saying "*Oooo-okee-o-ka.*" Then she translated for Mara's benefit: "*For conspiracy.* This is the spot. Are you ready?"

Mara had brought two murk-lights with her. She hid one under the blanket to light it, then blinked to chase the spots from her eyes. She stripped off her shirt and trousers and rolled them into the oilskin sack. When she was wearing nothing but her swim clothes, the fog slinking over the water felt even colder. The water was inky and black. The statue of the horned woman loomed over them, more shadow than stone. Mara breathed deeply. She was having a hard time finding her calm.

She was only nervous because she rarely dove at night. Because the Winter Blade was unfamiliar territory. Because she didn't often swim in underwater caves—they were quite dangerous, even for the best divers. Because the Lady had given her a secret, dangerous task. Because the songs of the founders were too powerful to be trusted to a man like the Muck. Because Bindy deserved to have the truth of her death revealed.

She wasn't scared. It was only that she had such an important mission before her. She wasn't *scared*.

She nodded. "I'm ready."

"Remember, it's more important for you to stay safe than it is for you to find anything," Professor Kosta said. "Don't do anything reckless. If it's dangerous, come back out."

Mara glanced at the professor. That was easy for her to say. She wasn't the one with everything she had ever wanted dependent on doing this one thing right. Professor Kosta wasn't the one who had lost Bindy because of the Lord of the Muck.

She wasn't the one going into the fortress.

"I'm ready," Mara said again.

"Luck, little one," said Professor Kosta.

Mara jumped into the water. The murk-light flashed momentarily before she pushed it beneath the surface; she hoped nobody was watching from above. She swam to the base of the tower. When she was right below the horned woman, she took a deep breath, and she dove.

Five fathoms down, and more, and she found no tunnel.

She had been expecting a rough, wave-carved face of rock beneath the surface, but instead she found a flat wall of large stone blocks. There were barnacles and mussels, small darting fish and clinging clumps of seaweed. The living things of the sea didn't care that this was the Winter Blade or that the mage within was a murderer. To them it was a stone wall like any other. Mara found that a tiny bit comforting.

But she didn't find a tunnel. She returned to the surface for air and dove again.

Three more dives and she began to worry. She treaded water for a few moments, catching her breath and thinking. Maybe the tunnels had been found and filled generations ago. Or maybe the Lady's minor cousin had made it all up. Mara did not want to have to go back to Tidewater Isle and tell the Lady her cousin had been a liar and a braggart.

She ducked her head underwater, came up for another breath.

Not just a cousin. A mage. A mage fascinated by the underwater city and the magic of the founders.

If he *had* found the tunnels, he might have used magic

to find them, or to hide them after he did. Any of the Winter Blade's masters or mistresses might have done the same. Mara had been looking with her eyes in the darkness, but that wasn't the only sense she could use.

She took a breath, not too deep, and ducked her head under. The murk-light cast a wavering light; the water was clear and free of silt. It was quiet but for the sound of the sea lapping at the tower.

She tried a few words of her mother's old song—*"Over the sea and under the sky"*—but there was no response. She took another breath and dove, and this time she waited until she was farther beneath the surface to sing. She was getting a bit better at singing underwater. It was hard to carry a melody, and even harder to make the words sound anything like they were supposed to, but she could at least do it now without gulping seawater. But still there was no response.

She resurfaced and treaded water, thinking about what else she could do. She didn't know any songs for illusions or concealing. She didn't even know what *kind* of song a mage would sing to reveal something hidden—those songs were closely guarded secrets, for good reason. Bindy had always sent Mara out of the shop when she cast a hiding or obscuring spell.

Mara looked up at the horned statue and the carved Old Sumanti words beneath it.

She turned slowly, peering across the water. She could

just see the silhouette of Driftwood's boat in the distance. Professor Kosta had extinguished the mage-candle. Mara whispered the sounds Professor Kosta had spoken beneath the horned woman's statue. *For conspiracy*, the professor had translated, that rolling sequence of syllables. Mara was good at memorizing words precisely, even ones she didn't know; stumbling over simple instructions had been enough to earn her a sharp pinch in Bindy's workshop.

It was a stupid idea. Mara could imagine Bindy snorting and saying, "What do you think you know about magic?" But at the same time she heard Professor Kosta, not an hour ago, looking over the city and admiring how they adapted and innovated to use magic that had never been meant for them. She wasn't a mage. She wasn't even an apprentice. You can't make the world by wishing, Bindy used to say. It was as true in magic as it was in anything else.

But it wouldn't hurt to *try*.

She dove again. This time when she sang underwater, it was a little melody made up of the professor's Old Sumanti words: *"Oooo-okee-o-ka, Oooo-okee-o-ka."* She turned the words into a song that rose and fell, gentle but insistent, mimicking the rhythm of waves pushing against rock, with a soft *k* sound for the slap of water on stone.

And this time there was a response: a whisper.

Mara's heart skipped in surprise and excitement. The whisper was quiet; it vanished when she returned to the surface. But she *had* heard something. She had to try again. What other choice did she have? Give up and go back to the Lady with nothing?

She dove again. Sang again. Listened again.

There it was: the answering song.

She wanted to shout with joy when she heard it, but she forced herself to listen. It sounded like many voices joined together, singing the language of the founders. Mara didn't know of any mages alive today who sang in choruses to cast spells. It had to be very old, from a time before mages became so secretive.

Once she knew what to listen for, her search was a lot easier. Through a few more short dives, Mara sang, and she listened, and she felt for the changes in the water temperature, until finally she found it.

The entrance was a round hole in the black stone, but it was hidden by a spell so perfect Mara could only locate it by feeling along with her hands until there was a space where her eyes told her no space should be. Even when she knew she was looking right at it, she saw unbroken stone.

She returned to the surface, excited by her discovery. The Lady's hidden passage was real! Part of her wanted to call Driftwood and Professor Kosta over to tell them at once, but she didn't want to waste time. Finding the tunnel was only the first step. Getting through it and into the fortress came next. She would have to swim into that magical mirage—blindly, without any way of seeing what was on the other side. She didn't know where the tunnel led.

She didn't know what was waiting behind the entrance. Her mind filled with images of a tunnel lined with sharks' teeth, or spikes, or eels. She shook those thoughts away.

Mara lifted the murk-light above the water for a brief flash. Driftwood raised an arm in acknowledgment. He would take the boat and Professor Kosta to wait at a safe distance until Mara returned.

On her final dive, Mara descended as quickly as possible, kicking hard and fast toward the mouth of the tunnel. Every instinct in her body was telling her to flinch away before she swam straight into solid rock, but she pushed her racing fear aside.

When she passed the obscuring spell she felt nothing but a feathering buzz of spell-song all over her skin, and the chorus of mages hummed briefly in her ears. The tunnel was so narrow stone scraped her knees. Small blue fish darted in the glow of the murk-light, tickling Mara's face and hands as they fled before her.

Her lungs began to ache. She needed to breathe. She couldn't see the end of the tunnel. There was no room to turn around; she would get stuck if she tried. How long could it possibly be? She really, really needed to breathe.

When the tunnel opened above her, Mara surged upward, kicking so fast the oilskin sack dragged behind her like a weight. Just when she thought she couldn't bear it for another second, she burst through the surface and sucked cold air into her lungs.

When she was breathing steadily again, she lifted the murk-light to look around.

She was in a narrow cylinder of stone bricks: a well. The water was less salty than the open sea; there had to be a freshwater spring nearby. The top of the well was only a few feet above the water's surface. Mara's light barely reached an arched ceiling high above. Water trickled somewhere, a slow steady rhythm. Otherwise it was quiet.

Mara jammed her toes into the wall and lifted herself to peer over the rim. The room was empty. There was a pile of buckets and salt-crusted rope against one wall, the remains of a crank mechanism against another. Water from the spring seeped lazily into a leaking trough. The room had been abandoned for a long time. There was only one door.

She climbed out of the well and dressed quickly, then picked up the murk-light and slung the oilskin sack over her shoulder. She shivered in the cold. It was so quiet every drop of water on stone sounded like a drumbeat.

Mara ran over to the door and pressed the latch with her thumb. It was unlocked.

She took a deep breath and pushed the door open.

8

Weeping Stone

The first thing Mara noticed was the smell.

She noticed because there wasn't any. She couldn't smell any wood or smoke or frying fish. There was no hint of damp wool or pungent cigars, no cooking fires or scraps of fish, no roasting meat and spices. There wasn't the faintest suggestion of sweet candles or incense.

Seawater in her hair, damp stone, air closed up too long—but nothing else. The Winter Blade didn't smell like a place where anybody lived.

Mara stepped into a corridor so long it vanished into darkness in both directions. Her light cast a shy yellow circle around her. When she looked back, her heart skipped a beat. There was no door, only a blank wall.

She reached out, panic tightening her throat, and found the open doorway at once. She could feel the air drifting and hear the lap of water in the well.

The doorway was still there. It was hidden by magic. She could be the first person to pass this way in centuries.

She had to search the tower, but she didn't know which way to go. She kept thinking about all the stories she had heard about the Winter Blade: the curses old masters had set upon the fortress to protect it, how many great mages had met their end in these very corridors, the sailors who claimed to hear the wails of ghosts in the tower on the darkest nights.

There were no wails now. The fortress was quiet.

It was eerily, profoundly quiet.

Creeping along the corridor, Mara heard no voices, no footsteps, no doors opening and closing. She heard nothing but her own breath. The Lady claimed the Lord of the Muck had only a few loyal servants, not an entire household, but even so, the quiet was unsettling. She tried to think of it as a good thing. If there wasn't anybody awake at this late hour, there wasn't anybody for her to run into. But she wasn't quite reassured. The silence only meant she hadn't found them yet.

Them, she thought, but she meant *him*.

The Lord of the Muck was somewhere in that tower. Every corner she turned, she risked meeting him. Every door she opened, he might be waiting behind it. She didn't know what she would do if she found him. Would he remember her from Bindy's shop? As much as she wanted to look him in the eye and tell him she knew what he'd done, she couldn't get caught.

The Lady had insisted her most important task was to find the Lord of the Muck's magical laboratory. If he had any more of the ancient animal bones, that's where he would be keeping them. In this Mara's goal coincided with the Lady's: if he had any of Bindy's journals, the written record of her spell-songs she had taken with her the night she died, those might be there as well.

Mara tried every door she passed. Most were locked, but a few were open; and every time a handle turned her heart thumped as she gathered her courage to open it. She found a kitchen that hadn't been used in years, a pantry filled with wine casks, a closet full of dusty buckets and brooms. There was no sign anybody had lived in this part of the fortress for years, or even longer.

Three locked doors past the broom closet, she finally found something useful: an unlocked door leading to the sea cave and the island's hidden docks. A short, crumbling staircase led down to the water.

Mara held her light high. It was shaped much like the sea cave under Tidewater Isle, with stone walls arching up to a buttressed ceiling over a long quay. But where Tidewater's cave was decorated with a brilliant stone-and-glass mosaic depicting the landing of the first Sumanti explorers on Greenwood Island, the Winter Blade's walls were covered with a vast frieze of roiling, toiling, embattled sea creatures: a kraken fighting a leviathan, sharks swarming a whale, serpents and octopuses dragging tall ships down from below. Most of the carvings were timeworn and faded, the details scrubbed away by storms and centuries, but here and there a creature's jeweled eye glinted in the light, as though the stone itself were watching.

There were only two boats tied to the dock. One was a flat, old-fashioned pleasure boat draped with cobwebs; it had benches enough for twelve or fifteen people and long, age-cracked oars crossed over its prow. Much of its colorful paint was long since scoured away, but what remained showed a line of flowering vines all around the saxboard. The other was a rowboat. That one, at least, was in good repair.

So much for the rumors that the Muck flew from his tower on bird wings. He bumped over the waves like everybody else.

Mara stepped to the edge of the dock for a closer look. There were two sturdy oars tucked into the rowboat, and beneath them were a coil of rope and a woven sack.

And a single broken sandal.

Mara backed away quickly. The rope and sack were a good sign: they looked exactly like what had been used to sink the bones. But that one lonely sandal with its leather strap broken put a nervous quiver into her chest.

There was nothing else in the sea cave, so she continued her search. She counted twelve more doors, all locked, and one dark hallway sloping into the heart of the island. The stones of its arched entrance looked like vertebrae, as though a long backbone was marching up one side and down the other. Mara decided very quickly not to explore *that* corridor. The laboratory would surely be above water level, not far below it.

Just beyond that hallway was a staircase, which Mara ran up with relief. She was growing frustrated, and more than a little suspicious. There had to be *something* in the fortress besides empty rooms in empty corridors. The Muck wouldn't have gone through all the trouble of taking the Winter Blade from Gerrant of Greenwood if he wasn't going to use it.

Mara was halfway up the stairs when she heard the singing.

It was so faint she thought it was the echo of a spell, but it didn't repeat itself like a magical remnant would. Magical or not, it was being sung now. A woman's voice, rasping, high, and thin. Mara didn't recognize the song. It sounded like the Roughwater language, but she couldn't be sure. All she knew was that somewhere in that great fortress, a woman was singing a song as soft and gentle as a sea breeze.

Then there was a loud shriek—metal grinding on metal—and the singing stopped.

Mara held her breath. The darkness was silent again.

Stone corridors could make sound bounce in tricky and untrustworthy ways. The song and the metallic shriek could have come from anywhere. Above or below, near or far. All it meant was that Mara had to work faster. She ran the rest of the way up the curving staircase, her hand sliding along the wooden banister until she realized it had been carved in the shape of a sea serpent, and the bumps racing under her fingertips were its scales.

At the top was another long hallway. She didn't know which way to go. There was a set of broad balcony doors flanked by windows, every pane blacked with grease to block the light. The corridor was dark and silent in both directions. Mara looked to the left, looked to the right, frustrated by her indecision. The fortress was too massive for her to explore every room and every corridor. She needed to focus her search.

She was looking for the laboratory, because the laboratory was where the bones would be. She had found the bones before by singing her mother's song. Mara took a breath.

Took a breath—and stopped. It was so quiet. The silence felt even more oppressive now. But she had to try *something*. The song was the only idea she had.

She began softly, so softly it was barely a whisper: *"Over the sea and under the sky, my island home it waits for me."*

Nothing.

A few more lines, a little bit louder: "*Over the waves and under the storms, my heart is bound but my dreams are free. Older I grow and—*"

In the darkness, something groaned.

Mara stopped singing with an undignified squeak. She couldn't tell where the sound had come from. It was nothing like the answer the bones had given to her when she was diving. It sounded more like the deep thrum of waves in a sea cave, and it faded quickly.

Gathering her courage, she finished the first stanza of her mother's old song, and this time she didn't stop when the creaking sound returned. She went into the second stanza: "*The rich green slopes that haunt my dreams, they are beloved as treasure to me.*"

Her father used to tease her mother for singing that song, in the playful way they had. It was an old-fashioned sailors' song, for Greenwooders far from home and yearning for their green island. Dad would sweep Mum around in a circle and ask, What business did a stonemason who couldn't tell a jib from a mizzen have singing a song like that? "*The trees and vines and flowers in bloom, the waterfalls spill like jewels to the sea.*"

Mum had always laughed and said she might not be a sailor but she was a Greenwooder to her bones. With a wicked twinkle in her eye she would say if he didn't like that song, she would pick another, maybe the one about the Lunderi captain and the blue-eyed boy. At which point

Dad would clap his hands over Mara's ears with mock horror and tell Mum to carry on, and Mum would, louder than before, so loud the goats in the neighbor's pen bleated in reply, and Mara and Mum and Dad all fell over laughing.

It hurt to remember them like that, so happy and safe and alive. Mara's voice trembled on the next lines: *"The black-sand beaches and hearth fires alight, oh let me return, oh let me go home, to the waves I plea."*

The noise from the corridor never grew any louder, and when she stopped singing it faded into a tired sigh. But Mara knew now which direction it had come from. She turned right and marched down the corridor, more determined than ever.

She went back to trying doors. No light shone beneath any of them; there was no light at all except the one she carried. She heard no more singing, no clangs of metal. She began to wonder if she had imagined it.

It was no use thinking like that. Just because it was unexpected didn't mean it hadn't been real. She had to trust her own senses. The noises were a mystery, but it was one she could solve if she kept looking.

Seven locked doors from the staircase Mara reached an intersection with another corridor. She paused to count back every turn and step she had taken from the well room. When she was certain she could find her way out again, she peered around the corner.

Somebody was there, barely ten feet away.

Mara pulled back so quickly she stumbled over her own feet, just barely caught herself before she fell. She gulped around the terrified hammering of her heart.

There was somebody standing just around the corridor. A tall, broad-shouldered man. She had glimpsed him for only a second, but it seemed to her he had been facing her and unmoving, standing like a sentry or a guard. Had he been armed? She couldn't remember. She hadn't noticed. Surely a guard would be armed.

She waited for a shout, for the sound of his footsteps. There was no way he hadn't seen her. She was carrying a light. It filled the hallway. He had to see it.

But he made no sound.

Maybe he was waiting for her to move first.

Or he was creeping toward her ever so quietly.

Or he was just around the corner, and he was going to step forward, and he would catch her right where she cowered. She could imagine it so vividly she knew exactly what his hand would feel like on her arm.

In a moment it would be too late to run. Her hand was shaking and the murk-light swung on its rope, its light dancing on the stone walls. She squeezed her eyes shut. Opened them again.

She stepped around the corner.

The man hadn't moved.

Mara inched closer.

He still didn't move. With the light shining directly in

his face, he didn't even blink.

Mara swallowed. "Sir?"

He wore the heavy wool clothing and leather boots of a mountain-born Greenwooder, but they were oddly smooth and dark gray in color, without a trace of the dyed reds and greens and golds favored by the mountain villagers. There were deep lines and discolored spots of age on his face; his lips were turned in a frown. His hands were calloused, his knuckles knobby. His face beneath the brim of his hat was the same gray as his coat. His skin reminded Mara of a street performer who used to work on Quarantine Island during the busy market days, a woman who would cover herself with green-tinted paint and stand perfectly still in regal poses so that travelers new to the city would mistake her for a weathered copper statue. They only realized the difference when she spoke. It was considered great fun, a way to trick sailors and children.

Only the man's eyes stood out. They were yellow, glassy, and bright.

"Sir?" Mara said again.

The man didn't move. Not even his fingers twitched.

Mara reached for his hand. It was cold, unyielding stone. The man didn't just look like a statue: he *was* a statue. His clothes had the look of wool and leather, with seams and laces carved so realistically they had fooled her, but they too were stone.

Mara looked at his face again.

His odd yellow eyes were watching her.

Mara jumped backward and knocked her elbow into the wall so hard she yelped. The sound bounded down the long corridor, and she held her breath until it faded. A shout like that could carry far in these empty stone halls.

But the tower was as silent as before.

The stone man was still watching her. It was a trick. It *had* to be a trick. The strange yellow stone had been spelled to look like real eyes. She was jumpy and nervous and he was a statue.

Only a statue.

A drop of water trickled from the corner of his eye and down the side of his face.

9

The Sorcerer's Library

Mara's sprinted away from the statue. Her feet slapped noisily on the stones, and her murk-light swung on its rope. She looked back, and she almost yelped to see somebody behind her—but it was only her own shadow, dancing wildly as she ran. Nobody was following her.

Of *course* nobody was following. Statues couldn't move.

Or stare.

Or weep.

Once, twice, three times she ducked into a doorway to hold her breath and listen. For footsteps, for shouts, for the scrape of stone on stone. There was nothing. The hallway remained empty. There was no sign of the stone man.

It was easier to think of him as *the stone man*, even though she knew who it was.

Gerrant of Greenwood had disappeared when the Lord of the Muck had taken over the Winter Blade. Everybody assumed the Muck had killed him, although nobody knew for sure, and Gerrant had no family to demand the High Mage look into it. He had been considered an outsider since he had come down from the remote interior of Greenwood Island some twenty years ago to challenge the great storm-mage Lilia the Kind for control of the fortress. Lilia had surrendered after a brief, mostly symbolic battle; she said she was too old to fight for a drafty, bad-tempered fortress anyway. She moved to live with her daughters in the crafters' quarter on Glassmaker Isle, and Gerrant of Greenwood became Lord of the Winter Blade.

Many mages in the city had never liked that a Greenwooder trained by mountain hedge witches held the fortress; they wanted a proper Citadel-trained city mage to have that honor. So everybody felt it was right that the Muck should seize the fortress. It wasn't that they *liked* the Lord of the Muck, and they certainty didn't approve of mages going about killing each other. But the Winter Blade had its own traditions, and at least the Muck wasn't an outsider. Besides, they said, it was entirely possible the Muck had chased the defeated Greenwooder back to the mountains or sent him away on a merchant ship to the

Pinnacle Isles, never to be seen again.

Now Mara knew the truth: Gerrant of Greenwood had never left the Winter Blade.

Mara leaned out from her current doorway to check the corridor one more time. Still empty. Her murk-light was fading, but she didn't want to light the spare until it was time to leave. She didn't know how long she had been in the fortress. She felt like she had crawled out of the well only moments ago, and at the same time she felt like she'd been in the dark for hours. Driftwood and Professor Kosta were still waiting outside. They had to be waiting. It hadn't been *that* long. Driftwood wouldn't leave her behind.

With renewed determination—and a strong desire to get as far from the stone man as she could—Mara ran up a second flight of stairs. As she was trying to decide which way to search, she felt a change in the air. It was so subtle she didn't even realize what it was until she had taken a few cautious steps.

She could hear the sea.

She drew in a slow breath. She could smell it too.

The murmur of the waves seemed to be louder to the left, so that's where Mara went. She passed an alcove with a dusty bench beneath a bank of windows, but every casement was bolted shut. She kept searching. Another fifty steps along she found a pair of large doors. Every other door in the fortress had been plain, grimy with dust and sticky with spiderwebs, but these were polished to a shine. The hinges were clean, the handles gleaming, and the wood carved with elaborate scenes of ships and monsters and mages.

Mara pressed her ear to one door and heard the faint sound of surf on rocks far below. Nothing else. No voices, no footsteps, nothing. She grabbed the handle with both hands and pulled the door open.

The room was as dark as the corridor, but the air was different. Clean, fresh, salty on her tongue, and the rumble of waves was louder. She stepped over the threshold.

As soon as she was inside, light flared so bright Mara winced and closed her eyes. When she opened them again, flames were dancing in candles and lamps all around the room, but there was nobody in sight. Her surprise passed quickly. For a mage as powerful as the Lord of the Muck, a hundred candles lighting when he entered a room would be child's play.

In the blazing warm light, Mara took a look around.

It wasn't a laboratory. It was a library.

Books and scrolls and sheaves of brittle parchment crowded every shelf, and the shelves stretched from floor to ceiling, from one end of the room and back again, interrupted only by narrow windows open to the night. The sky through the windows shimmered faintly; Mara recognized the distortion as a simple veiling spell. That was the reason light never shone outside the fortress.

Mara couldn't imagine how many great mages of the Winter Blade had left their libraries to be absorbed when the island was taken from them. Mara felt overwhelmed and a little breathless, trying to gape everywhere at once. She set down her murk-light. If the Muck had taken Bindy's notes the night he killed her, they might be here. She had to look.

There were shelves stuffed with books written in a dozen different languages and others overflowing with maps from lands Mara had never even heard of before. There were piles of scrolls and towers of ledgers. She found a tottering stack of books about birds and animals from Sumant far to the east, and another with books about great forest predators in the Lunderi empire to the west. She found biographies of great mages, trade reports from fish merchants, farm records from Greenwood Island, and one book as tall as she was containing nothing but sprawling family trees. She paged through the Palisado family in hopes of identifying the mage who had found the underwater tunnel, but she didn't know his name or even when he had lived.

There were dozens and dozens of books about magic, in every language Mara recognized and many more she did not, but nothing that looked like Bindy's journals.

Most of the books were dusty and old, some so brittle they looked like they would crumble at a touch. Before long Mara was sneezing and rubbing her eyes, but she didn't stop searching.

On the wall at the far end of the room hung several shelves that contained no books, but instead held a collection of mirrors. Some were small and round, some large and square; others were set in crude wooden frames like what a fisherman might use for shaving. A few were polished and gleaming, but most were made of warped glass so dirty Mara wanted to wipe them clean. The mirrors hummed with magic, all in tune with one another, the same charm echoing over and over again.

She leaned closer, trying to hear the spell-song more clearly. Her nose was just inches away from one mirror when something moved in the reflection.

Mara jumped back and spun around.

There was nobody behind her. The library was empty.

She peered at the mirror again. She hadn't imagined it. There was something moving in the glass.

A man in a brown apron stood at a high workbench. He was pouring steaming liquid from one flask to another. Wire spectacles perched on his thin nose; his hair was long and tied back at his neck. His lips were moving. She leaned closer, and she could hear, very faintly, a whisper of song.

The mirror was looking into another mage's workroom. It was charmed by a spying spell.

She watched the mage for a minute or two, fascinated. The flasks made her wonder if he might be one of the

Sumanti alchemists in the Greensmoke Quarter, or a healer on Quarantine Island mixing up potions and tinctures in preparation for the coming winter.

She turned her attention to the other mirrors. Those that were clear showed mages in their laboratories and workshops. She even recognized a few: she spotted Tulen the Storm-singer in her drafty garret, the High Mage himself visiting a bearded man in what looked like a Glassmaker Isle workshop, and the Lady of Spellbreak's eldest daughter reading a scroll by candlelight. Some of the mirrors were so cloudy Mara couldn't see anything at all, but she studied them nonetheless, watching for any glimpse of motion.

She couldn't tell if any of the clouded mirrors peered into Renata Palisado's tower laboratory. Did the Lady know the Muck could do this? He was watching mages all over the city. Most of them probably had no idea.

Mara hadn't even known this kind of magic was possible. She knew mages spied on each other all the time, but not like this. Even Bindy, suspicious as she was with her spelled candles and secret journals, had only ever worried about another mage *hearing* her songs. She had never worried about somebody watching her in the privacy of her own home. The very possibility made Mara's skin crawl. Had the Lord of the Muck been watching yesterday when she coughed and stumbled into the Lady's laboratory tower? Had he been watching all those nights when Bindy told Mara a story to ease her to sleep while storms raged outside? Did he watch the High Mage when he met with students in the Citadel fretting before their exams? Did he look at these mirrors and laugh to himself about how easy it was to look down on the entire city from his towering fortress, how they underestimated him, how they couldn't hide a thing from him, how they would never know what he could do?

Mara turned away, her stomach twisting with anger and guilt. The mages in the mirrors didn't know they were being watched. One was an old woman scratching her nose and preparing for bed, not doing any kind of magic at all.

She had to find the Muck's laboratory. She didn't have time to search the entire library for Bindy's journals. She had already stayed too long.

Mara was heading back to the library doors when a book in a tattered red binding caught her eye. It was a big volume, four inches thick, nearly two feet on edge. It was set up on a book stand, apart from the shelves and piles that swallowed all the others. Most of the title had long ago worn away, but she recognized the words *Greenwoodland* and *Chance Islands* and, most interesting of all, *Founders*. Greenwoodland was an old name for Greenwood Island; the main road in Gravetown was called Greenwoodland Way. Mara had never heard the city called the Chance

Islands before, but sailors sometimes called it the Lucky Rocks, joking about how they had to be just as lucky as the original Sumanti explorers to find the islands in the great wide ocean. Luck and Chance were not such different things.

Mara turned to a page near the beginning and found a drawing of an underwater tower of gleaming black stone. The colors whirling around the tower were bright, but the ink was smudged in places. Fish circled the tower's apex, and seaweed and kelp grew at its base like a garden. A long green serpent curled through a window in one turret. Mara traced the serpent's length with her finger. The paper was as smooth as silk.

"It's a lovely book, isn't it?"

Mara froze.

"Very rare, as well. It might be the only one of its kind."

Mara took a deep breath, then another.

"What are you doing here, child? Turn around. Don't be rude."

She curled her shaking hands into fists, and she turned.

10

The Lord
of the Muck

Before he had become Lord of the Winter Blade, the Muck had lived in a crumbling, leaky, rat-infested row house on Quarantine Island. But you would never know it if you saw him sweeping through the markets and shops, dressed in the finest tunics and glittering jewelry, with his black hair oiled and his nose lifted above the stink of the streets. Bindy would tease him when he came into her shop, bowing and gesturing grandly, claiming that *she* could never serve such a fine mage, oh no, his exalted lordship must have the wrong shop. The Muck had never laughed at her jokes. Mara had never laughed either. She didn't like to see Bindy trying so hard to elicit a response from a man who grimaced every time he stepped through the doorway.

For two years Mara had been picturing him exactly like that, only more so. She had imagined that his clothes would become fancier, with gold brocade and elaborate embroidery. His fingernails would have grown longer, his jewelry would gleam brighter, and his sneer would have deepened until its creases overtook his entire face.

But the man who stood before her wore wool trousers, a tunic with no ornamentation, and an apron covered with ruddy-brown stains. He was thin, with sloping shoulders and a high brow. His feet were bare. His graying hair was cropped short and mussed as though he had been running his hands through it. His long brown fingers were stained with splotches of ink.

He looked like any other man. Ordinary, even. Shorter than Mara remembered. He was not sneering. His eyes were dark and alert.

"It's a translation, of course," said the Lord of the Muck, inclining his head toward the great book on the stand. "The original was lost centuries ago. The author never saw the wonders he drew so beautifully, so it is of limited use. The artistry is its chief virtue. Can you read, girl?"

Mara couldn't answer. She couldn't breathe. He was only ten feet away. He had killed Bindy. He had taken away Mara's home, her guardian, her future as a mage, everything. Now he stood between her and the door.

He took a few steps closer, without the least sign of hurry. He cocked his head to one side as he examined

Mara. There was an assessing glint in his gaze. He recognized her. Her throat felt raw.

"You're Renata's little diving girl, aren't you?"

Mara blinked. That was not what she expected him to say.

"I've seen you out on the water. You were the one who found my garbage dump."

He didn't recognize her as Bindy's old servant, only a diving girl for the Lady of the Tides. But what did he mean by garbage dump? He had to mean the bones on the seafloor—so he had sunk them after all!—but they weren't *garbage*. They were fantastic and valuable. She couldn't make sense of anything. Her thoughts kept tripping over themselves. She had to get away. She couldn't be captured.

"I imagine Renata believes a bit of housebreaking is respectable if she's the one ordering it," the Muck said. "But I'm afraid whatever it is your Lady wants, she will remain unsatisfied tonight."

Mara finally found her voice. "I'm not! I don't know who that is. I was only— I only wanted—"

The Lord of the Muck raised his hand and crooked two fingers. "Whatever lie you are about to tell me will have to wait until morning. I'm in the middle of an important experiment, and it cannot be delayed to hear your fibs and excuses."

At his gesture two men came into the library. One was tall and the other was short, and they both wore servants' livery marked by stains and tears. They moved stiffly, like arthritic old watermen, and winced away from the flickering candles as they passed. Their faces were a sickly gray, their eyes a murky green. Mara stared at them in horror, unable to draw her gaze away from their sagging skin and stringy hair.

"We have an intruder," said the Lord of the Muck.

The words broke Mara from her shock. She grabbed a small leather-bound book from a stack and flung it at the Muck; he grunted in surprise as it struck him in the stomach. Mara darted to the left, ducked around him while he was still recovering, and sprinted for the door.

She was fast, but the tall gray man was faster. She didn't even realize he was beside her until he was already grabbing her arm. Mara twisted and pulled, but she couldn't break free.

"Let me go!" she shouted, squirming and kicking. "Let me go, let me go!"

The tall man didn't speak. He made no sound at all except for a rasping, gurgling breath.

Mara batted at his hand, his arm, his face. "Let me go!"

He had such an iron grip on her arm it felt like his fingers were digging into bone, and with his other hand he clamped a hand over her mouth to quiet her. Mara bit his hand as hard as she could; his fingers were cold and damp and tasted of fish. She gagged and tried to spit, but he was covering her mouth again. She had to get away. They were going to kill her. The Muck would turn her to stone like Gerrant of Greenwood, or worse, and nobody would ever know what had happened to her. She had to escape.

"Take her away," said the Lord of the Muck. "Put her with the others. I'll decide what to do with her tomorrow."

The tall gray man didn't say a word. He swung Mara easily over his shoulder, finally removing his hand from her mouth.

"Hey!" she shouted, pounding on his back with her fists. "Hey, put me down! Put me—"

Mara stopped, her words choking off in surprise.

In the man's neck there were long slits like gills. The skin fluttered near Mara's face, opening and closing, opening and closing. She was too startled to scream.

The tall man carried her out of the library. He had no light to find his way through the tower, but he didn't seem to need one. Mara had left her murk-light behind; she couldn't see a thing. She counted two staircases down and a single turn into a long, sloping corridor—this had to be the tunnel beyond the vertebrate-stone arch on the first floor—but after that she lost track. She only knew that he carried her down and down and down, until they were so deep in the tower they had to be below the sea surface. Mara squeezed her eyes shut and tried not to think about it, all the darkness around her and rock pressing in from every side.

"Where are we going?" she asked. Her voice was small

in the overwhelming darkness. She tried to get free again, wriggling like a fish on a line because she didn't know what else to do, but he was holding her too tightly. "Please? Sir? Where are we going?"

The gray man didn't so much as grunt in response. She couldn't see his gills in the dark, but she knew they were there. It gave her an unpleasant feeling to know those flaps of skin were fluttering with every noisy breath he took.

"Can you even talk?" Mara asked. "Are you even allowed? Hey!" She beat helplessly at his back. "Can't you say anything?"

Down in the bowels of the fortress, the man finally stopped. Mara's bravado vanished under a new wave of fear. Keys jangled as he opened a door, and a candle flared on the other side. The man flinched away from the light. Mara took the opportunity to twist for a look, but she couldn't see anything except a crooked floor worn smooth where the door had scraped a groove into the stone. The air was dank and sour, like an animal pen.

A few steps more and she saw the iron bars.

Then she heard quiet coughing. Gasps of surprise. Soft whispering voices.

There were people behind the iron bars. Behind the locked door. Trapped in the dark.

It was a dungeon.

Mara began to struggle anew, beating at the man's back and kicking her legs wildly. It didn't do any good; the man barely seemed to notice. He carried her between the rows of cells, farther and farther into the darkness. The cells looked very old, the bars crusted with rust, the locks massive and bulky. Whispers rose as she passed.

"They're back already?"

"So soon after the others?"

"Ask her if anybody knows we're here!"

She couldn't tell how many people there were. A foot here, a hand there. A man with a braided beard leaned against the bars, watching with narrow eyes. She glimpsed a twist of dark hair as a woman ducked away. Another man with tattoos on his face. A pale-skinned woman with straight gray hair. She couldn't see all of them. The whole empty fortress above, hundreds of locked rooms and dark corridors, and the Muck was keeping prisoners in his dungeon.

The light from the single candle grew dimmer and dimmer. Mara could barely see when the gray man finally stopped and dumped her onto the cold, hard floor. She scrambled to her feet, but the gray man had already slammed the iron door shut. He turned a key in the lock and shuffled away, his shoes scraping noisily.

Mara shook the door as hard as she could, but she couldn't budge it.

"Hey!" she shouted.

The gray man was no more than a silhouette blocking the candlelight.

"Hey! You can't leave me here! Hey!" She knew it was no good, but she couldn't seem to stop herself. The prisoners around her murmured and muttered, so many people she couldn't even see. "You can't do this! You can't just lock us up!"

But of course he could, and he had. The gray man didn't even turn around. When he left and slammed the dungeon door, the candle sputtered, winked, finally blinked out, and everything went dark.

For a long moment, all Mara could see were the spots of light dancing before her eyes. All she could hear was the sound of her own ragged breath and her heart thumping in her ears.

Then, a quiet voice: "Mara? Is that you?"

11

Voices in the Dark

Mara shut her eyes and swallowed back a whimper. She could feel the darkness all around her. It was darker than the black stone, heavier than the island. In that moment she was five years old again, alone and lost in the crypts of the Ossuary. She was waiting for her parents to find her. They would find her. The storm would subside soon and they would swim to shore. Mum would be so worried but pretending not to be, and Dad so scared it made him gruff, and soon, any minute now, their voices would ring through the catacombs. Every howl of wind twisting through the ancient crypts became an echo of her name. A hundred times her heart stuttered with hope, and a hundred times her hopes dissolved into tears, until she had no more hope, and no more tears.

Alone in the dark, there was nothing left to do but hug her knees to her chest and sing a comforting old song to herself. Her mother's favorite song, a sailors' song about missing home, one that felt like cozy blankets on cold winter nights and embers glowing on the hearth.

"Mara? Is that you?"

The whisper seemed to come from everywhere all at once. Soft, so very soft, swallowed at once by the dungeon.

"Mara? Say something! Please?"

A spark of confusion broke through her fear. That wasn't right. Nobody had said her name in the crypts. The voice that had found her, after an interminable night, had slithered through the darkness like a sea snake winding through coral: "Little girl, where are you? What a pretty song that is. Let me help you. What a pretty little song."

Mara had been convinced the voice was coming from the ancient skulls embedded in the walls. She hadn't believed her eyes when she saw the first glow of a murk-light shining in the darkness. The person calling for her was not a crypt-dwelling ghoul or rattling skeleton, but a woman in a patched smock with ink-stained fingers and a kindly smile.

It wasn't Bindy's voice whispering to her now. This wasn't the Ossuary. The air around her smelled not of seawater and ancient stone, but of unwashed people, refuse, and fear, all together creating a thick, choking stench that filled her throat.

Mara was in the dungeon of the Winter Blade, and somebody knew her name.

"Who's there?" Mara said. The words were barely a rasp, caught in her sticky-thirsty mouth. "Who is that?"

"Mara? It's me! It's Izzy!"

"Izzy?" Mara's eyes snapped open, but there was nothing to see except darkness. "Izzy! What are you doing here?"

Izzy let out a soft laugh, one with very little humor in it. "I was about to ask you the same thing. Please tell me they didn't grab you when you came looking for me."

"No, I— What do you mean? Who grabbed you? What happened?" Mara asked.

"I don't know who they are. I didn't see their faces. I only know—"

There was an unimpressed snort in the darkness. "You don't know anything."

Mara's skin prickled all over. "Who's here?"

"There are ten or twelve of us, I think," Izzy said. "They took five others when they got me, and there were already about that many here."

"But they only brought in one this time," a man grumbled. "Maybe this one's a spy. Did they grab her too? How'd she get here?"

"Oh, *please*," Izzy said. "I know Mara. She's my friend.

She's not a spy. Whatever the Lord of the Muck wants—"

"We should give it to him," said another voice, also a man's. "You don't mess with mages. Not mages like him. Cooperate and go along. That's what we should do."

"That's the stupidest thing I've ever heard," a woman said. "I'm not going along with anything."

"I don't think he's looking for cooperation," Izzy said. "If he was going to ask us, he wouldn't be kidnapping people off the docks."

"Even a mage can be reasoned with," said the second man.

The woman chuckled darkly. "Have you ever *met* a mage?"

"You're all so stupid." That sounded like the same girl who had snorted before. "You don't understand anything."

"Why don't you explain it to us, if you're so smart?" Izzy said. "You keep telling us we're stupid but you don't *help*."

"It's not worth asking," said yet another person, a woman with a faint Lunderi accent. "She was here when they brought us in, and she hasn't explained anything."

"How did you get here?" Mara asked, before they could start arguing again. "What happened? Was it the same for all of you?"

The first to answer was a woman. Her voice was weak and cracked like weathered wood; she coughed, a rough phlegm-wet sound, and said, "They grabbed me from the docks on Summer Island. I was walking to my daughter's house. I didn't see their faces. They were wearing masks, then they put a hood over my head." She spat derisively. "What sort of cowards hide behind festival masks, like they think it'll scare us?"

Mara had been about to ask if the shuffling, silent gray men had been the abductors, but the woman's words brought her up short. "How many of them were there?"

"Four or five," the woman said. "I couldn't see once they got the hood over my head."

"Me too," said a boy, his voice trembling and soft. "Just like that. I wasn't scared of the masks. The masks are *stupid*."

They were wearing animal masks to hide their faces. That's what Fish Hook had said about One-Eyed Bennie's pirates. Bennie told so many wild stories nobody listened anymore. But maybe this time, this once, she had been telling the truth.

"I fought 'em," said a man, and his words were echoed through the dungeon. They had all fought, to no avail. "One of them had—must've been knives. My arm got sliced up."

"One of them was a skinny girl who laughed the whole time," another man said. "They put us on a ship, then dumped us into a small boat to bring us inside. I couldn't see anything, but I've been on the water my whole life. I know a ship from a rowboat."

As the prisoners spoke, Mara counted at least ten different voices, including the rasp of an old woman saying something in Roughwater. A man translated for her: the old woman had been waiting for her grandson's fishing boat when she had been taken.

The first girl who had spoken, the one who had called them all stupid, didn't tell the story of her own abduction. Mara noticed and wondered what her silence meant.

"What about you?" said the coughing woman. "You come in here asking all these questions and don't share the same about yourself? Why *are* you alone?"

Mara didn't know how much to tell them. She didn't want to give any information to the man who wanted to cooperate with the Muck, and she couldn't explain that she had sneaked inside without revealing *how*.

"I don't remember," she said finally. She didn't like to lie, but it was simpler for now. "I think they hit my head. I woke up when that horrible man was carrying me in here."

"Oh, Mara, that's awful," Izzy said. "Are you hurt? Do you feel sick?"

"No, no, it's not really that bad," Mara said quickly. "It's okay."

She wished she could talk to Izzy without anybody else listening. She wanted to tell her that the Lady of the Tides and Professor Kosta and Driftwood knew she was here and would notice when she didn't return. She wanted to tell her not to give up hope, if only because saying the words out loud might help Mara believe them as well.

"How long have you been here?" Mara asked.

A man answered, "Who can tell? One of those shuffling men brings us food once a day, so it's been about twenty days for me. My belly isn't as reliable as the rising sun, and we've got none of that down here. I was one of the first. The girl was here before me, her and the man they took away."

His words sent a fresh shiver through Mara's entire body. "The man they took away?"

"Ask her," said the man. "The girl. She knew him."

"I don't know anything," the girl said. She sounded younger now, with a hint of fear creeping into her voice. "Why don't you ask the mage when you get a chance? He's powerful and clever. He has a reason for everything. But I don't know what it is, so stop asking me!"

The dungeon echoed with the force of her words, and for a long moment nobody said anything. There was only the quiet hiccupping noise of somebody crying and trying to hide it. It might have been the girl, but why would she be crying while also praising the Muck for his cleverness? It sounded an awful lot like she knew more than she was letting on, but Mara didn't know how to draw it out of her. She had to *think*, but it was so hard to do when every time she opened her eyes she saw only darkness, a darkness so deep and so complete her mind began to invent things for her to see: reaching hands, blinking eyes, fluttering gills. There was a candle by the door. Maybe she could—but that was stupid. She didn't know any fire-lighting spells. She didn't know any useful magic at all. She rubbed away stinging tears.

"Have they taken anybody else?" she asked.

A pause.

"No," said one woman.

"Not yet," said another.

What was the Lord of the Muck doing? What did he *want*? Mara knew why he had put *her* in his dungeon, but Izzy and the others had only been going about their lives. They didn't deserve to get captured and locked up. It didn't make any sense. If he was trying to study the magic of the founders in the bones of ancient creatures, he didn't need prisoners.

But not all of the bones she and Izzy had found on the seafloor had belonged to animals.

One of them had come from a person.

"Izzy?" Mara said quietly.

"Yeah?"

"Where are you? Which way?"

"Over this way. Can you follow my voice?"

Mara tried. She crawled toward Izzy, stopping only when she bumped up against the rusted iron bars.

"Reach out toward me," Izzy said.

Mara reached blindly into the next cell. She grasped around, closing her fingers on open air, pressing into the bars until the cold metal bit into her skin.

"I'm trying," she said.

"Me too," said Izzy.

But they were too far apart. Their fingers did not meet. Reluctantly Mara dropped her hand and settled against the bars with her knees drawn up to her chest. The dungeon was so cold her teeth had begun to chatter.

"Here," Izzy said. "You're freezing. I'm throwing you my shawl."

Something soft brushed Mara's arm.

"Now you'll get cold," Mara said.

"I'm fine," Izzy said. "You keep it for now. We can switch off."

Mara wrapped the shawl tight around her shoulders, tucking her nose under the cloth. It wasn't very warm, but it was better than nothing.

"Somebody has to know we're here, right?" Izzy said.

Mara knew what she was asking. "Yeah. Somebody has to."

She tried to sound reassuring, to counter the quiet plea she heard in Izzy's voice. The Lady of the Tides *did* know where they were—where Mara was, at least. So did Driftwood and Professor Kosta.

But the Lady had warned her: if Mara was caught, there might not be any way to help her. She had to rely on her wits.

Mara didn't know what good wits were against iron locks, but she did know she couldn't count on the Lady and Professor Kosta and Driftwood to rescue them.

12

The Hall of Glass

Mara jerked awake from a restless sleep. She couldn't see anything. She was shivering, and she felt clammy and damp all over. In her stomach there was a deep hunger ache, the sort she hadn't felt in a long time. She rubbed her eyes and blinked. It didn't help. Only after a few heart-thudding moments did she remember: the dungeon.

She must have slept for hours and hours, to have grown so hungry. It had been almost midnight when she sneaked into the fortress. An hour or two before dawn when she was captured. It would be daylight now. By now, the Lady and Professor Kosta must have realized that Mara had been caught.

She didn't know what had awoken her until she heard

a loud metallic rattle, and a voice hissed, "They're coming back!"

Down the long row of cells, the door opened. The candle flared as the tall gray man came into the dungeon. The light was barely bright enough to see by, but still it stung Mara's eyes. The gray man shuffled along, keys jangling in his hand.

He hadn't brought in anybody new. He was coming to take somebody away.

Mara's first thought was: please don't let it be me.

Her second thought: it has to be me.

She had seen more of the inside of the Winter Blade than any of the prisoners. She knew at least two ways out: the sea cave and the well. She was hungry and tired, but not as hungry and tired as the people who had been here for days. She could swim for help. She would make the Lady and Driftwood and Professor Kosta understand that the prisoners needed to be rescued.

She stood up. She couldn't see much, but she was able to fumble her way to the barred metal door.

"Hey!" she shouted. Her voice bounced around the dungeon, a sudden shock of sound. "Hey, you! Back here!"

"Mara, what are you doing?" Izzy hissed.

"It's okay," Mara whispered. "I have an idea." She didn't have time to explain. She only knew she had the best chance of any of them to get away.

"Mara—"

"Hey!" Mara shouted again. "Hey, you! Do you hear me?"

The gray man swayed his head toward her. She caught a glimpse of the gills on his neck and shuddered. He blinked at her. He was listening.

"Tell your master I've got a message for him. From my master. He knows what I mean."

The gray man swayed as he looked at her. He blinked again.

"I have a message for him," she said again, enunciating each word carefully.

The gray man shuffled forward and stopped in front of Mara's cell. He picked through the keys on his ring one by one, moving with agonizing slowness.

"Leave her alone," Izzy said from her cell. She banged on the bars, making the door rattle loudly. "I said leave her alone! Take me instead!"

"Izzy, don't," Mara pleaded. "I have a plan. Trust me!"

Finally the gray man found the right key. Mara's instincts told her to shrink away from the cell door, but she didn't let herself move. Izzy's shawl was still around her shoulders, but she had no time to give it back. She knotted it around her waist like a belt so it wouldn't get in her way.

The moment the lock clanked, Mara shoved the door open and darted out.

The gray man dropped his keys in surprise. Mara was

already running. She sprinted out of the dungeon, plunging herself into the dark corridor beyond. The light from the single candle faded, and soon she was surrounded by darkness. She didn't stop running. She had to get out. She might not get another chance.

Behind her the gray man huffed and wheezed as he chased her. How did he breathe air if he had gills? Could he see in the dark? Mara didn't want to find out. She had to find the sea cave. That was her way out. She was going to get away. She was going to the Lady for help. She was going to—

Run smack into a wall.

Stars exploded in Mara's eyes. She bounced back and fell, landing hard on her butt. Fiery pain burned across her entire face, and blood trickled over her lips. She scrambled to her feet and reached out blindly, tears gathering in her eyes, groping the wall to figure out if she was at a dead end or only a corner.

She heard the gray man's shuffling footsteps, his rasping breath, and too late she realized he was right behind her. She dodged to the side, but she wasn't fast enough. He caught her shirt with one hand, her arm with the other, and before she could even yell he was slinging her over his shoulder.

"Let me go!" she shouted. "Let me go! Let me *go!*"

She wriggled and fought and beat at the man's back, but she couldn't break free.

He carried her through the dark corridors, around corners, and down stairs. Mara was hopelessly lost by the time they entered a hallway lit by flickering candles. All she knew was they were not going back to the dungeon. They were going farther than that.

And deeper, even though they were already below the sea.

In some places the walls on both sides were smooth, featureless, and shaped from solid stone; but in others they were made up of large fitted blocks, forming a tunnel as tall as two men and completely round. It gave Mara the uncomfortable feeling of being trapped in the guts of a massive stone beast.

She knew where they were.

This ancient passage had been carved by the founders a thousand years ago, or more. Tunnels like this, the ones that had once connected the city above with the founders' city below, were supposed to have been lost centuries ago, collapsed or buried. Treasure hunters and mages were always looking for ancient tunnels, hoping to find some cache of valuable or magical artifacts, but Mara had never heard of anybody finding any this extensive. The past masters of the Winter Blade had been keeping secrets even more impressive than anybody knew.

Finally the gray man stopped before a round wooden door. It was a perfect circle, like a ship's porthole, smaller and plainer than the library doors upstairs. There was a

strange noise coming from the other side. It sounded—
Mara had to be imagining things; she knew they were
deep under the island, but it sounded like a singing bird.

The gray man pulled the door open without knocking. He ducked his head to carry Mara inside—her back
scraped the top of the round frame—and dumped her
onto the floor.

She jumped to her feet immediately, but before she
could run the gray man grabbed her arm.

The room was murky with smoke and humming with
the echoes of countless spell-songs, all clashing and clanging against one another. Altogether the noise was loud and
grating enough to set Mara's teeth on edge.

This was the Lord of the Muck's laboratory. It was the
room Mara had been looking for, but she had been looking
in the wrong place. It wasn't in the tower at all. The laboratory was hidden below the sea.

It was so much bigger than Mara had imagined. Every
inch of the room was jammed with tables, shelves, and
workbenches, half of which sagged under the weight of
piles of books. The rest were crowded with jars and tanks
and cages, nearly every one filled with specimens of fish
and fowl, reptiles and mammals, so many animals both
dead and alive Mara couldn't begin to count them. Eels
writhed in buckets, colorful parrots bristled on perches,
and a school of silver anchovies swam in endless circles in
a large tank. Two fat seagulls fought over a heel of bread

on the floor. Sleek brown otters slept in cozy burrows in a large cage. In one tank an octopus glared through the glass with a wary eye. A makeshift pen built out of chairs and boxes trapped a few knee-high goats; the black one was gnawing on a book.

The dead creatures were no less numerous, both those that were whole and those in pieces: fish and eels, crabs and lobsters, tangles of jellyfish and squid preserved in green liquid. There were tanks of shark fins and shelves of walrus horns, bird feathers plucked and strung on a line, and bowls of teeth and scales and fine bones. In one huge glass tank beetles swarmed over a pile of bones, devouring the flesh in a shimmering black wave. Beside it something was bubbling in a large vat over a magic-stoked fire; Mara was glad she couldn't see beneath the foamy surface. Beside it was a butcher's block and a large cleaver.

And on the floor: a lumpy woven sack tied up with rope, ready to be dumped in the sea.

The whole room smelled of fish and smoke and animals, with a faint hint of cooked meat, and the acrid scents of chemicals and compounds Mara didn't recognize.

Against the wall there was a shelf of mirrors, some clear and some cloudy. In front of the shelf stood one mirror that was larger than the rest, the freestanding kind in a frame, like what a rich person might have in their dressing chamber. Smoke whirled and drifted in the glass, completely obscuring the view.

Beyond all that, beyond the cluttered tables, the sloshing tanks, and crowded cages, beyond the bubbling cauldrons and hazy smoke, beyond the mirrors spying across the city, it was the most magnificent room Mara had ever seen.

It was a massive round dome larger than the ballroom at Tidewater Isle. Half the dome was polished black stone, supported by smooth pillars that rose into high arches, eventually joining at a star-shaped point in the center of the ceiling. The other half was made of tall glass windows set between stone pillars. Shimmering green light shone through the glass.

Mara had seen great glass rooms like this in mosaics and tapestries, but she had not thought it possible one still existed. They were all believed to have collapsed when the founders left the city.

A school of slipfish darted past, their silver scales shining briefly before they turned as one and whirled away. There was sunlight up there somewhere, just as her stomach had been telling her. From the shade of green Mara guessed they were at least ten fathoms down. Deep enough that the weight of the water on the glass would be crushing—if the glass wasn't magic, spelled centuries ago by the founders.

A bird squawked loudly, and Mara startled. She could scarcely take it all in. There was too much noise, too much motion, too many colors.

And in the center of the room was the Lord of the Muck.

He stood at a table, his back to Mara and the gray man.

He was still wearing the stained apron over his clothes. He stood beside a broad table, holding a quill in one hand, a notebook in the other.

Without turning he said, "Bring the specimen over here."

The tall man dragged Mara over to a chair. She didn't even have time to jump to her feet before the Muck said, "It would be unwise to flee. You'll never find your way out."

Mara said nothing. He might be right, but she wasn't about to tell him that.

Something pressed against Mara's bare ankle. She looked down. It was a green lizard about as long as her arm from nose to tail, similar to those that lived among the flowers and trees at the Hanging Garden.

But this one had wings.

Mara's mouth dropped open in surprise. The wings were black and bat-like, protruding from the lizard's back just behind its front haunches, with neat rows of stitches around each base. The lizard nudged its blocky head against Mara's leg and looked at her expectantly; she felt a puff of air when it beat its wings.

Mara tore her eyes away from the winged lizard to look around the laboratory again.

In one large tank a turtle swam lazily back and forth,

but one of its flippers had been replaced by a furry paw. Perched above the tank was a monkey that had a parrot's crest of white feathers growing from the top of its head. In a mesh cage there were several little animals Mara had assumed were geckos, but when she looked closer she saw they were actually mice, except instead of fur they were covered with grass-green scales. Beside the mice cage was a skeleton strung together with bits of wire: it had the body of a goat but the head of a bird and large claws like those of a hunting cat.

The laboratory wasn't just full of animals. It was full of magical hybrids.

"My garbage dump," the Muck had said.

A low, panicked buzz grew in Mara's mind.

She hadn't found the remains of glorious ancient creatures on the seafloor. She had found the remains of the Muck's magical experiments.

Tears of disappointment and anger stung her eyes. She had been wrong. The Lady had been wrong. Her stomach turned. Mara and Izzy had brought up parts of at least a dozen creatures, maybe more, so excited about what they'd found, so happy to have uncovered a piece of history. But they had only been cleaning up the Muck's trash.

That trash had included one human femur.

There were leather cuffs dangling from chains on the sides of the table. One at each corner.

"The man they took away," the girl in the dungeon had said.

With trembling fingers, Mara scratched the lizard's head gently. The Muck wasn't looking at her. She was terrified of drawing his attention to her. She kept glancing at the leather cuffs on the table, tearing her gaze away, looking again.

If she didn't say anything—if she didn't *try*—she might not get another chance. She knew *what* he was doing, but she had no idea *why*. If she found a way to escape—No, she couldn't think like that. *When* she found a way to escape, she needed to tell the Lady everything. That meant she had to make the Muck talk to her.

"Excuse me," Mara said. The words came out as a trembling whisper. She licked her lips and tried again, louder. "Excuse me, sir?"

"One moment." The Muck was absorbed in his writing.

"If you please, sir, what are you doing?"

The Lord of the Muck lifted his gaze from his notebook and gave Mara a surprised look. "Oh, it's you. This is the wrong one." He snapped his fingers at the gray man. "I told you we couldn't use this one yet. Go back for another—a few years older, not a child."

"Sir," Mara said, her voice rising with fear. "What are you doing?"

The Lord of the Muck turned a page of his notebook

decisively. "My work is far beyond your capability to comprehend."

"That's not what my mistress says," she said.

That got his attention, exactly as she wanted. He spun around to face her. "What does Renata say?"

Mara's mind raced to come up with an answer. "She says that you're a lesser mage with no real talent."

The Muck narrowed his eyes. "Yet she sent her servant to steal from me. Do you think I am an idiot, child, or does your mistress merely think that of you? Do you see what I am accomplishing here?"

"You're trying to . . . make animals like the ones the founders used to make?"

"Ha!" The Muck's sudden laugh startled a parrot into squawking. "How quaint that would be, to use all my skills and knowledge to create charming little pets. No, I'm afraid each of these tiresome creatures represents only a single step toward my ultimate goal. Come look at this."

The Muck tapped a long finger on the open page of his journal. Mara stood to approach the table.

On the page was a set of detailed anatomical illustrations. The drawings showed the strangest creature Mara had ever seen. At first glance it looked like a founder with beautiful fins and round fish eyes, but upon closer inspection she saw it wasn't a founder at all, but neither was it human. It had two arms and two legs, but instead of hands and feet it had long, trailing fins at the ends of its limbs. It was covered from knee to toe and elbow to wrist in scales of blue and green, but the rest of its body was normal brown skin. It had a collar of spiky fins around the back of its neck like a founder, but no dorsal fins down the spine. Its round eyes were too big for its human head.

The drawing made the creature look predatory and fierce, but it was beautiful too, in a cunning, unsettling way.

Mara leaned in for a closer look. There were arrows and annotations on the drawing, and notes written in small script. *Cut. Stitch. Slice.* Tiny hash marks indicated where fins attached to the arms and legs. Accompanying the diagrams were lines of spell-songs, with instructions for how they were to be sung.

The cold feeling in Mara's gut was only growing colder. She knew what she was looking at.

"But . . . *why?*"

"Why?" the Muck repeated incredulously. "*Why?* Look around you, child. Look at this chamber. Look at this city. Look at what it used to be, and how much less it is now. The founders could carve fortresses from solid stone, call up storms on a whim, command the creatures of the sea to obey them. And what can we do? We believe it an accomplishment to light the smallest candle, to stir the weakest breath of air, to frighten the tiniest fish into a net. We are *pathetic.*" He spat the word as though it tasted bad. "You ask *why.* But surely even your small mind can comprehend the desire to elevate ourselves above the scrabbling, squabbling, inferior creatures we are?"

He wanted the power the founders had once had. He wanted their magic. He wanted to be able to shape and topple islands, call and control storms, and so much more.

He wanted to turn humans into founders.

It was impossible. It was worse than impossible. It was mad.

But he spoke with a calm sort of fervor that made Mara's skin crawl, as though he couldn't imagine anybody would disagree with him.

"Sir," Mara said, licking her lips nervously. "Can you really *do* that?"

"Of course I can do it," the Muck said, his voice sharp. "Do you doubt me? Here, with the evidence all around you? I have achieved great success in my initial experiments. I've had to use bits of the ugliest old spells, nothing anybody besides a wretched bone-botherer would care to sing, but they have their uses."

He gestured across the table to a stack of books. Mara gasped when she looked at them. They weren't just books. They were Bindy's books, her spell journals, where she had written down her bone magic. After getting caught and being tossed in the dungeon and finding Izzy among the prisoners, Mara had forgotten all about Bindy's journals. But they were right here in the Muck's laboratory. He was consulting them as he worked.

"But, sir," she said, breathless with surprise, "where did you learn magic like that?"

"Irrelevant," the Muck said, returning his attention to his own notes. "Look here—I am ready to attempt the next step of the transformation."

Mara's fear was twisting around and around in her gut, tightening into hot anger. "What do you mean? What's the next step?"

"It will become clear as soon as my servant returns."

"You want to turn your servants into founders?"

"Of course not," the Muck said scornfully.

For a second, the briefest flicker of a second, Mara felt a pang of relief. She had gotten it all wrong. Nobody could be that cruel. Not even the Lord of the Muck. Not even for the magical powers of the founders.

Then he went on, "They were merely early trials, but unfortunately the gills are largely decorative, and they can't speak a word. No great loss. They were dull conversationalists anyway. I realized it is best to perfect each step on individual subjects before I attempt a complete transformation. That's why I work in absolute secrecy. You've noted the mirrors, of course. I must be certain nobody is mimicking my work. When every step in the process is flawless, I will perform the first—and only—complete transformation on myself."

"You," Mara said faintly. He was going to operate on *himself*? With the knives and the songs both? "But—but— how? *Why*?"

"As I am the only one to have conceived of such a step, does it not follow that I am the only one worthy to wield such powers?" the Muck asked. He didn't wait for an answer. "You see, it is both a physical transformation and a magical one. Neither by itself will allow me to shed my human form and take on one far superior. Only when both changes are achieved will the complete breadth of ancient magic be available to me, and I will reveal my improved nature to the city. Ah, here he is. I'm afraid I must return to my work now."

From the corridor outside the hallway Mara could hear the gray man's scuffling steps. With those steps came the sounds of somebody fighting: slapping, cursing, frustrated cries in a familiar voice. Mara's chest ached as though she had been holding her breath. She was supposed to have gotten away by now. She was supposed to be going for help.

The gray man bent through the door, dragging Izzy behind him. She was fighting hard, clawing at his arm and face, trying to break free, all the while shouting words Mara didn't know but was pretty sure would make a dock-hand blush. She cast her gaze wildly around the room, taking in the jars of specimens, the cages and tanks of living creatures, the Muck at his laboratory table, at Mara, and she snarled, "Let go of me, you filthy worm!"

But he was too strong. He dragged her across the room to where Mara and the Muck stood beside the table. Through her twisting and turning and shouting, Izzy caught Mara's eye. She looked toward the door, toward the cages, back at Mara. She stopped spewing insults long enough to mouth a single word: *go*.

Mara couldn't move. The Muck was going to hurt Izzy. Mara couldn't leave her. She didn't know what to do.

Run. Fight. She had to do *something*. Attack. Escape. She didn't know. She didn't *know*.

Izzy said it again: *go*.

"Put her up here," said the Muck. He tapped his fingers on the worktable. "Then hurry along to meet our guests. It will be dark soon, and we have much to do tonight."

He wasn't paying attention to Mara. She took two steps toward the door. The winged lizard scampered around her feet. The Muck and the gray man didn't notice, but Izzy did. She went limp and slumped to the floor. "Oh, please! Please, sir, don't hurt me!"

The gray man looked down at her. He tugged at her arm, confused that she wasn't fighting anymore.

"Carry her if you must," the Muck said impatiently.

The gray man tugged; Izzy slid a few inches across the floor. "Oh, please! I'm so scared! What are you going to do? I'm so scared!"

Mara inched farther from the worktable. There were only about twelve feet between her and the door, and all along that distance were jars and tanks full of specimens, shelves and tables of the Muck's carefully preserved work perched precariously over his valuable books and drawings.

"Girl," the Muck said, "where are you going?"

He hadn't even finished his question before Izzy shouted, "Mara! Go! *Get out of here!*"

Mara sprang to action. She sprinted toward the door, pulling over cages and toppling specimen jars, sweeping piles of scrolls and tipping heavy books into the growing puddle. She didn't want to hurt the living animals, but there were plenty of other things to knock over. She shoved at a stool, threw a stack of books, and knocked a large vat to the floor, sending a wave of cold water and a slithering mass of preserved eels across the room.

"Catch her!" the Muck bellowed.

Mara slipped on an eel, jumped over the little winged lizard as she regained her balance, and she ran.

13

Sea Above
and Sea Below

Mara ran like she had never run before. Candles flared and faded as she raced past. Behind her the Muck was shouting at his gray man, Izzy was shouting at the Muck, a parrot was shouting impolite words at both of them, and animals were twittering and bleating in a cacophonous racket.

Mara had to find her way out of the Winter Blade. She had to go for help.

She would get lost in the dark, so she kept to the passages lit by spelled candles. Those were the hallways the Muck used the most, which meant they had to lead *somewhere*. She could hear the gray man shuffling behind her, but she didn't look back. She only ran faster, her breath coming in ragged gasps, the ends of Izzy's shawl fluttering, until finally, *finally*, she found a staircase winding upward.

Up, and up, and up. She was climbing awfully high—how far down was the laboratory? Was she at sea level yet, or above it? She passed five, six, seven locked doors. The gray man was getting closer.

Mara charged through the first open door she found. On the other side was a dark corridor. She looked frantically to the left and right. She didn't know which way to go until she saw the faintest glimmer of light to the left.

She sprinted toward it—but it wasn't a candle. It was a window. It was a whole wall of windows. She was in what had once been some sort of gallery or sunroom; the chamber faced east, overlooking the distant city, but the dirty glass was aglow with the indirect light of the setting sun. She had lost an entire day in the Winter Blade.

The first window didn't open, nor the second, but the third had a broken latch and swung outward when Mara shoved it. She leaned over the sill to look down.

Waves crashed against the black rock a hundred feet below.

She was too high. Mara wanted to shout with despair. She couldn't jump from here. She would dash herself to pieces on the base of the Winter Blade. She had ruined her one chance, the chance Izzy had fought so hard to give her. The gray man would catch her and put her back in the dungeon, and then how could she help anybody? Izzy was in the Muck's laboratory. He could have overpowered her and bound her to his table. He could at this very moment be sharpening his scalpels and consulting his notes while Izzy fought and screamed. Mara shouldn't have left her.

There was a scuffle of footsteps behind her. Mara whirled: the gray man had reached the sunroom. The gills in his neck flared when he spotted her.

She had no choice. She couldn't help Izzy if she was frozen by fear.

Mara tightened Izzy's shawl around her waist and climbed out the window. The stone was cool and slick. Mara pushed her fingers into a crack and searched with her toes for a foothold, then stretched down as far as she could for another, and another. She had climbed stone walls before, all over the steep streets of Quarantine Isle and in the Ossuary crypts. Those walls were never more than ten or twenty feet high, but if she could climb down twenty feet without falling, she could climb down a hundred feet without falling. It was just like descending five twenty-foot walls, one after another. She could do it. She *had* to.

That's what she told herself, in between thinking very hard some of those words she had just learned from Izzy.

She looked up. The tall man was lurching out of the window. He didn't lower himself as Mara was doing, with his feet below and his hands above. He climbed down like a spider: headfirst, very swift, his long limbs spread wide.

She had to go faster. Her arms and legs shook with the effort of holding on, and her toes and fingers were soon scraped bloody from jamming into the slightest cracks.

Every time she looked up the gray man was closer.

She could not let him catch her. If he caught her, Izzy was doomed. The angry girl in the dungeon, the scared boy, the old Roughwater woman who was worried about her grandson, all of them were counting on her, but most of all Izzy, who was so happy to be getting married and teased Mara like a sister and had fought the Muck to give Mara a chance to escape.

Mara glanced down. Waves crashed on the rocks far below. The motion of the sea made her dizzy. The sun was ducking beneath the clouds on the horizon. There was no way she could make it. It was too far.

Something grabbed her hair, and pain burned through her scalp. The gray man had caught up to her.

Mara smacked his hand away, but the motion made one of her feet slip, and she slid several feet down, out of the man's reach. She couldn't catch herself—she was sliding too fast, too far—she was going to fall—

Her toes caught on a ledge. Mara gasped in surprise and grabbed at the stone, fingers scrabbling until she found a crack to hold. She leaned into the rock and held tight, breathing heavily, not daring to move a single finger or toe until she was sure she wasn't going to fall. Her arms and legs were shaking, the evening air stirring all around, the waves crashing below, and the gray man was still coming. She could hear the rattle of his breath. He was only a few feet above her.

Mara leaned away from the wall the tiniest bit, so tiny not even a fish could slip between, and looked down. She had come about halfway down the fortress's formidable wall. She turned carefully, holding on to the stone blocks with one hand, then the other, her back pressed firmly against the stone. Her foothold was just wide enough for her heels to stick on the edge.

Fog was gathering, but she still could see the water. She couldn't tell if there were any dangerous rocks beneath the surface. There hadn't been where she found the tunnel, but she didn't know if it was the same all around the island.

She didn't have a choice. She felt the brush of the gray man's fingers on her hair.

She took a deep breath, and she jumped.

Mara turned into the dive and struck the sea with a slap on her hands and face. Water churned around her in blinding bubbles. For several seconds she was stunned and disoriented, then she kicked to the surface and blinked water from her eyes.

High above, the tall man was still clinging to the tower, spider-like and upside down, a gray blotch on black stone. Mara didn't wait to see what he would do. She swam away from the Winter Blade as fast as she could. Away from the gray man, away from the Lord of the Muck.

Away from Izzy.

Mara needed to bring help, and she needed to do it fast. With every breath she saw Izzy in the Muck's laboratory. She saw the delicate lines of his drawing as though they were inked on Izzy's skin. She saw the jars of preserved fins and scales, the trays of sharp instruments, the table with the cuffs. And Izzy, clever, bright, courageous Izzy, telling Mara to escape.

Like a coward, Mara had left her behind.

She swam and swam and swam until her shoulders ached and she was gasping for breath. She *was* going to bring help. She was not going to abandon Izzy.

She stopped only when night had fallen and the Winter Blade had vanished in the heavy fog. She treaded water and looked around to get her bearings. She didn't hear any sounds of pursuit. No shouts, no splashes, no oars slicing through water. She saw no lights, no boats, no islands. She couldn't even see any stars.

She was too tired and too hungry to swim for long. She had to go somewhere, find a boat or an island, even a wave-washed jut of rock where she could rest.

She wasn't lost. She couldn't be lost. She could see the city in her mind, not as it looked on Renata Palisado's map, flat and lifeless, but as she had seen it the day her father had taken her up a winding stone staircase on Greenwood Island. In the hours before dawn they had climbed the tree-choked slopes to a lookout atop a ridge. Her father sang as they walked, his voice booming through the morning with a silly Greenwooder song:

"Ask the shepherd with her staff if her sheep are well.
Ask the ranger with her ax for a tree to fell.
Ask the mason with her chisel why stone rings a bell.
Ask the digger with her spade if the dead feel swell."

When they reached the top, a break in the forest provided a view over the city. They had gazed down on all the islands and ships and ports waking with the day, coming alive with color and motion and light as the sun rose. It remained one of the most beautiful sights Mara had ever seen. She would never forget.

She knew this city. She knew these islands.

There was a light in the distance.

Mara blinked several times. Through the shifting fog, high above the water, there was a line of small sparkling lights. They were so faint they might have been stars, but Mara knew better. They were the lanterns along the bridge between Spellbreak and Cedar Isles, the one shaped like a kraken's reaching tentacles. It seemed impossibly far away, a delicate necklace in the sky, but the shape was unmistakable.

She was looking right at the heart of the city. She wasn't lost at all. She could find the nearest land from here. She headed north and west with long, easy strokes, breathing regularly, not racing. Once or twice she thought she saw a ship on the waves, not too far away, but each time it vanished like a mirage. The current pushed her along. She knew better than to fight it. The sea would always be stronger than one girl.

She had been swimming long enough to settle into a rhythm when something brushed her foot. Mara kicked in surprise, gulping seawater and coughing, but she didn't feel it again. Maybe she had imagined it, or maybe it was only a bayfish. They were big and curious but harmless. Nothing to be afraid of.

Then she felt it a second time: a nudge.

Her heart, already thumping, skipped in fear. Only a bayfish, she thought, desperate to make it true. It couldn't be a shark or a hunting whale. No predator would be so careless as to bump her before it attacked. It had to be a bayfish.

A massive shape breached the surface not ten feet away. It was so long it seemed to go on forever. Its scales shimmered black and green in the starlight.

Mara was too shocked to swim away. She didn't even remember to kick her legs until she began to sink.

There it was again, arching out of the water, so close she could touch it if she dared. Something brushed her back, her knees. Its scales were slick and smooth and warm.

A sea serpent.

It was a sea serpent.

It was impossible. She and Fish Hook had laughed about it just the other day, said Svana's son had to be imagining things. But the proof was right in front of Mara. Her heart was racing so hard it hurt. She couldn't catch her breath. It was so *huge*. The mosaics and statues had not prepared her for how big it was. If it attacked—did they attack people?— if it attacked she wouldn't be able to do anything.

The serpent circled her and nudged her feet. It wasn't an aggressive nudge, just a tap. Mara turned and turned, trying to follow the serpent's path. It didn't seem to be trying to hurt her or frighten her. That nudge seemed— almost *gentle*, she thought incredulously. They were intelligent creatures. There were stories about loyal sea serpents going on adventures with their founders, about returning year after year to where their founders had died. Those weren't the actions of vicious animals.

It wasn't attacking her. It was only letting her know it was here.

"Hello," Mara said. Her voice shook. Laughter gathered at the top of her lungs. "Hello."

That's when she saw the second one. It was smaller, not quite as fat around as the first. It drew its entire long body into the water, ending with a flick of its tail. Mara heard a splash behind her and turned. There was a third. She tried to look at all of them at once. They glided around her in lazy circles, bumping softly at her legs, never hurting her.

One lifted its big head above water. It moved to the side, its dark eyes glittering before it dove, then surfaced a few feet away. It came back to do the same thing again, moving in the same direction. When it did it a third time, Mara felt a spark of understanding.

"Are you . . ." She paused for breath; she was so tired. "Are you trying to tell me something?"

She felt a bit silly—it wasn't like they could *understand* her—but the feeling vanished when another of the serpents nudged at her back, pushing her in the same direction the first had indicated.

They *were* trying to tell her something. They were showing her where to go.

She looked across the water. Land. There was an island in the distance, just visible through the fog. The sea serpents were pointing her toward land. She had drifted off course. Without their help she would have missed her destination in the darkness.

Mara laughed again, giddy with disbelief and relief. "Thank you," she said, breathless and overwhelmed. "Thank you!"

When Mara began to swim again, the serpents swam with her. They circled her smoothly, bumping her legs when she flagged, sometimes sliding farther away but always returning, always staying near. They were watching over her.

She was too tired to swim very fast, but before long she

heard the sound of the surf dragging on a beach. When she could put her feet down, she stood on exhausted, wobbly legs and turned around.

All three sea serpents watched her with their glittering eyes.

"Bye," she whispered. "Thank you. Be careful."

Then, one by one, they dove away. Their long, slick bodies glistened before they disappeared into the waves. She watched for a long time, her heart aching with sadness, but they didn't return.

After days filled with so much strangeness and a night filled with so much fear, the serpents seemed to Mara both perfectly natural and perfectly magical. She didn't know why they were here, in the city their masters had abandoned. She didn't know how it was even possible. She didn't know why they had helped her. All she knew was that she hoped to see them again.

Bleary-eyed with exhaustion, she turned away from the sea to stagger up the beach. There were no buildings or docks along the shore. She heard a drift of music, but it came from far across the water. The island in front of her was lit only by scattered candles dotting tiers, terraces, and crooked stone pathways. It was eerie and quiet. Mara recognized it immediately.

She had found her way to the Ossuary.

14

The Graveyard Island

Mara stumbled along the black-sand beach toward the Ossuary's single dock. As awed as she was by the sea serpents, and as lonely as she felt now that they were gone, Izzy needed her help. Nothing was more important than that. The momentary calm she had felt with the serpents swimming beside her was gone. She had to get back to Tidewater Isle. She had to stop the Muck before he hurt anyone else.

She didn't think there would be any mourners or gravediggers on the island after dark, but she had to check. Her only other choice was to swim the long distance to Summer Island.

The Ossuary was made of the same black stone as the

other islands, but it was a long hump rather than a narrow spire, like a whale lying on its side. The founders had never shaped it with their magic, and it had no towers or palaces, as it had only ever been home to the dead. Here and there spots of light punctured the darkness; mourners brought candles and oil lamps to leave on the graves. The candles were said to help the dead navigate the sea during their long, dark night. Nobody ever seemed to wonder why the dead needed to navigate anywhere if they were trapped safely in their crypts, but the tradition persisted.

Mara climbed a staircase to the top of a crumbling sea wall and followed a path to the western end of the island. The fog was thickening, and a soft rain began to fall. It was going to be a chilly night. She could barely see the lights of Gravetown, just across the water on the shore of Greenwood Island.

She didn't know which of those specks of light was her old home or who was living there now. Another family of stonemasons, perhaps. A father who greeted the dawn with silly children's songs and fed stray cats with scraps from their table. A mother who loved to walk barefoot on the beaches on sunny days and kept a precise ranking of her favorite sea captains, duelists, and adventurers from history. There might be a tabletop scattered with intricate sketches, a bubbling pot of spicy fish stew, tea in earthen mugs that had been given to them by the potter who lived in the muddy valley above town. There might be a little girl who slept in the warm loft beside the fireplace. Instead of being an only child she would have brothers and sisters all around her, so many there was no chance she would ever be left alone.

Mara pushed those thoughts away. Feeling sorry for herself wasn't going to help Izzy.

A cold wind rose, twisting the fog in wraith-like whirls. The sea was growing rougher; the air smelled like a storm was approaching. It would be hard to swim to Summer Island. Mara didn't even know if she could make it.

When she reached the western edge of the island, she leaned out from the terrace for a look down at the dock. Her heart skipped in surprise.

There was a ship.

She jumped to her feet and scrambled to a lower terrace. She could beg the crew for passage to Tidewater Isle. She could be back before the Lady finished supper.

She took in a breath to call out, but the words caught in her throat.

The ship was a two-masted caravel, smaller than the ocean-going merchant ships but larger, faster, and more agile than what mourners, gravediggers, or stonemasons would use to travel to the Ossuary.

It was painted black from bow to stern.

It carried no flag.

It had no name on its prow.

Mara lowered herself to the terrace, her heart thumping with fear.

A black ship, docked on an empty island. It was a pirate ship.

She had thought she saw a ship while she was swimming, but she hadn't been sure, then the sea serpents had appeared and it went out of her mind. Maybe it had been so hard to see because it was black. But where could it have come from? None of the usual shipping lanes crossed the waters near the Winter Blade.

A pirate ship coming from that direction could have come from just one place: the Winter Blade itself.

The prisoners had been grabbed off the docks by masked pirates. Mara's stomach twisted with fear. If the pirates were working for the Lord of the Muck, what were they doing at the Ossuary? There was nobody to kidnap here, and there were better places to hide.

She saw only one figure on the ship's deck. She didn't hear any voices. She couldn't see much from this far away, but it looked like they were battening the ship for the storm. She crept away from the edge of the terrace, then stood quietly and took a step back.

A hand seized her left arm.

"What do we have here?" a voice hissed in her ear.

Mara froze. Something sharp pressed into the underside of her chin.

"Who sent you?" the voice asked.

Mara lifted her chin a little so the point of the knife—it had to be a knife—wasn't jabbing into her jaw. She was really starting to get tired of people grabbing her in the dark.

"Nobody sent me." Her voice shook, but she went on. "I'm allowed to be here."

"You're watching us." It was a woman's voice, made hoarse by the hissing, but through her whisper Mara could hear the musical lilt of the Glassmaker Isle craftsmen. It was a strangely posh accent for a pirate, but then Mara hadn't met very many pirates. Maybe they were all former glassmakers turned to freebooting.

"Why would I want to watch you? I don't even know you." Mara knew her voice was a shade too loud, but that was better than letting her fear show.

"It was a mistake for you to come here," said the woman.

"Okay," Mara said. "I'll just leave. I don't want to be here anyway."

The woman laughed softly. "I don't think so. Walk."

She steered Mara along the rows of wind-worn graves, never once letting go of her arm. Every time Mara tried to see her face, the woman jabbed the blade under her jaw and hissed a warning. They passed crypts carved with elaborate scenes of founders swimming in underwater palaces, sea battles between tall ships, great leviathans being jabbed with harpoons, before finally stopping at a curiously plain mausoleum. The only thing marring the stone door was a small, carved symbol in one corner: a tool with a pickax at one end and a key at the other. Mara didn't know this particular tomb, but she recognized that symbol as the one gravediggers used to mark their secret entrances to the catacombs. Bindy had taught her to look for it when they were robbing graves for mages' bones.

The woman felt around the mausoleum door for a hidden latch. The lock clicked, and the door groaned open.

"Inside," she said.

She nudged Mara forward. There was no light, and there was only one way to go: down.

The steps were slick and uneven, twisting sharply around corners. Mara kept one hand on the wall for balance. She couldn't see anything. She stumbled when the steps gave way to flat floor, but the woman's hand on her arm kept her from falling. A tiny flame appeared in the darkness. It was a single candle tucked into what Mara assumed was a hole in the wall—until she saw that it was actually the eye socket of a skull.

They had gone down past the neat stone crypts and fancy tombs into the bone-lined tunnels that gave the Ossuary its name. The candle winked out as they passed, and a second flared several steps later. Mara twisted for a glimpse of the woman. She saw a pointed chin, white teeth, dark eyes.

"Don't," said the woman. "Keep walking."

Before long, a glow filled the tunnel ahead. The

cloaked stranger steered Mara down a short flight of stairs, through a doorway, and into a room lit by firelight. After so much dark the brightness stung Mara's eyes. She blinked until the spots cleared.

The chamber had once been a large crypt, the sort where an entire family might have been buried. All the niches in the wall were empty of bones and coffins now; in one of them a bed had been made up with a colorful quilt folded over a shaggy straw mattress. A few woven rugs were scattered on the floor. A half circle of chairs and wooden benches huddled near a central pit, where a small fire was burning. Smoke curled into a hole in the ceiling— was a draft drawing through the cracks?—but most of it lingered, obscuring the far corners of the crypt in murky shadows. Distantly Mara could hear wind whistling and waves crashing as the weather worsened.

Somebody had been living in this crypt, and quite comfortably, for some time. There was even a kettle, a tea tin, and a few cooking pots resting on a flat stone by the fire. A single spoon sat atop a jar of sugar.

The first person Mara saw was a girl of about fourteen. She was sitting by the fire and roasting chunks of fish on skewers. The hot crackle made Mara's mouth water. She was so hungry she stared at the food for a long moment before she noticed that the girl had wings.

Mara blinked.

The girl had *wings*.

It wasn't a trick of the smoke and light. Right behind her shoulders there were two wings jutting from her back. The feathers were black on the top and white underneath, like those of an albatross, but much larger. The tips touched the floor.

"We have a trespasser," said the cloaked woman. She released Mara's arm and shoved her forward, hard.

Mara stumbled to her knees, jumped up again. Figures moved in the dark corners of the room, emerging from the drifting smoke. One, two, three—no, there were four of them. Mara held herself very still as they approached. There were no other exits from the room. The only way out was the one behind her, and that was blocked by the tall cloaked woman—who was now lowering her hood. She smirked at Mara's gasp: she had been waiting for that reaction.

Instead of skin, the woman had a hide of deep green scales covering her face and neck. She pushed back her sleeves to reveal fingers tipped with long, curved claws the color of pearls.

That was what Mara had felt beneath her chin: not a blade but one of those fierce claws.

"Show-off," muttered the winged girl.

The woman narrowed her eyes. "Excuse me?"

The winged girl jabbed at the embers with a skewer.

"I was just saying how nice and green you look in the fire-light, Captain Amanta."

The others murmured. Mara couldn't tell if it was anger or amusement.

"Watch your mouth, child," the woman said.

"Sure, Captain. Who are you?" the girl asked Mara.

Mara didn't want to tell these people anything until she knew more about them. "I was about to ask you the same thing," she said.

"Allow us to introduce ourselves," said Captain Amanta with an amused twinkle in her eyes. "We are this city's worst nightmare."

One by one the others emerged from the dark corners of the room. There was a teenage girl with large webbed feet and a long curling tail like a monkey's, and a skinny man with splayed fingers tipped with sticky pads like a frog's. Another woman, older, had big, round fish eyes and gills in her neck like the gray men. She grinned when Mara stared at her, revealing two rows of pointed teeth; Mara stepped back without meaning to, and the woman laughed. A grizzled man with a gaping hole where his left eye ought to be had a pair of curling mountain goat horns growing from his head and tough plate-like scales covering his neck and arms.

They all gathered closer, grinning. Mara knew they wanted her to burst into tears or collapse in a faint, so she tried very hard to look unimpressed. Her heart was racing so fast she was sure they could hear it; she balled her hands into fists at her sides to keep them from shaking. The strange bones, the gray men, the animals in the Muck's laboratory, and his terrible and beautiful drawings—those had all been bad enough, but she hadn't thought he could do *this*. She didn't think he could *actually* change people into other creatures.

But from the looks of the pirates gathered around her, he was getting close.

And the next person he meant to experiment on was Izzy.

"Um," Mara said. "What do you mean?"

The tailed girl was carrying a long, curved knife. She touched the point with her fingertip and grinned. "I still think it's better if we say we're worse than the worst nightmare. Worse than anything they've dreamed."

The frog-fingered man shook his head. "Nah, that's too much, you know, it might backfire? How do we know what they've dreamed? One time I had this nightmare about a giant clam with teeth and a cooking pot—"

The tailed girl snickered. "We can call ourselves the city's worst nightmare, except for the chowder nightmare."

"I like the sound of that," said the winged girl.

"Quiet," snapped the captain. "This is not the time for joking."

The girls subsided with only a little bit of grumbling. The frog-fingered man rolled his eyes.

The captain flexed her fingers; each claw glistened in the firelight. "My name is Amanta, and this is my crew."

"Do they get their own names?" Mara asked, proud that her voice didn't shake. "Or should I just make some up for them?"

"Why don't you tell us yours first? And the name of whoever sent you to spy on us."

Mara swallowed, her mind racing. "Nobody sent me. I didn't even mean to come here. I just needed a place to rest for the night."

The tailed girl laughed. "You want us to believe that you *swam* here? Do you think we're stupid?"

"I don't care if you believe it or not. It's the truth. Who are you?"

"The whole city will soon speak our names in fear and awe, so you might as well be first. I'm Ketta," said the tailed girl. She pointed to the frog-fingered man. "That's Yousef. Neske's the one with the horns. Feather"— a nod at the winged girl—"used to have another name, but she insisted we change it."

"Everybody's going to call me something birdy anyway," Feather said. When she shrugged, both her shoulders and wings moved. "Might as well pick for myself."

"And that's Mya Storm-Eye over there," Ketta finished.

Surprised, Mara looked at the old woman with the fish eyes. "I've heard of you. You're a storm-mage. You used to have that tower on Quarantine Island."

Mya Storm-Eye, if Mara remembered correctly, had drawn the ire of the High Mage when she had persuaded some students to steal the magical journals of the infamous mage Greengill from the Citadel library in exchange for teaching them forbidden spells. Bindy had taken Mya's side in that particular disagreement, claiming that if the students were stupid enough to go along, then the Citadel deserved to lose its precious books.

Mya Storm-Eye was pleased. "I like this one, Captain. Can we keep her?"

Neske, the horned man, laughed. "She didn't say she'd heard you were a *good* mage. Captain, you're asking the wrong question."

Captain Amanta glared at him. "Am I? What should I be asking?"

Neske shrugged. "Don't want to tell you how to captain or anything, but maybe you could ask why she doesn't seem all that surprised to see us, with us looking like this. Ask why she hasn't run away screaming."

They all turned to look at Mara, their eyes glinting.

"That *is* a very good question," Captain Amanta said.

Ketta's tail flicked back and forth like a whip. "She came looking for us. Why else would she be here?"

"I wasn't looking for you," Mara said. It was the truth, but she didn't think they cared much about that. "I wasn't looking for anybody."

She glanced around, weighing her options. What she

needed—more than answers, more than explanations, more than *anything*—was help getting back to Tidewater Isle. That meant she needed them to be on her side.

"But I did come from the Winter Blade. I saw the people he's holding there. The people he hasn't experimented on yet."

Even though the pirates seemed more proud of their hybrid features than ashamed, Mara was still expecting them to flinch, at least a little bit. The pirates might be free now—if hiding away in an Ossuary crypt was free—but the Muck was holding *prisoners*. Had the pirates been prisoners too? Had they escaped? She was expecting anger and scorn. She was expecting fear.

She was not expecting the captain to whirl her around, grab her by the shoulders, and shake her so hard her teeth rattled.

"You've been inside? In the dungeon?" Captain Amanta wasn't hissing or whispering now; her voice rang through the catacombs. "What did you see? Who else is there?"

"Did you see them?" Feather asked, jumping to her feet.

At the same moment Neske said, "Did you talk to them? Are they all right?"

Mara twisted out of the captain's grasp and backed away. She looked over the pirates, confusion turning her thoughts around and around. "The prisoners? You want to know if the prisoners are all right?"

"Yes, we want to know!" Feather said. "Are they hurt? Who did you talk to? What did they say?"

"But . . ." Mara was having trouble making sense of anything. If they had escaped from the dungeon, why would they keep going back? Why would they agree to help the Muck at all? "Aren't you the ones who captured them? They said they were grabbed by people with . . . masks. They thought you were wearing masks."

It was hard to be sure, with their faces and claws so terrifying, but Mara thought the pirates might look a bit sheepish.

"That was you, wasn't it?" Mara said.

"We had no choice," Feather said, when nobody else spoke. "He said—"

Captain Amanta cut her off. "Tell us who you saw. Tell us exactly."

"It was dark," Mara said slowly, stalling for time. "It's a *dungeon*. It was hard to see anything. Haven't you . . . Weren't you prisoners? Didn't he do this to you? Did you escape?"

"It's not like that," Feather said. "He didn't capture us."

"Then what is it—"

Mara stopped to think. If they hadn't been prisoners, why had the Muck experimented on them? Why weren't they still in the Winter Blade? She had so many questions, and the only way she could think to get the answers was to offer the same in return. She had information the pirates wanted, but she wasn't going to give it away freely.

"Tell me why you're—why you've got all *this*, and why you're kidnapping people for the Muck, and I'll tell you what you want to know."

Captain Amanta looked over her crew before answering. After a moment she nodded slightly. "We had a business arrangement with the mage."

"You mean . . ." Mara made herself think it through without jumping to conclusions. *Had* was not the same as *have*. "What was the arrangement?"

"The master of the Winter Blade has long had a reputation as a mage who is willing to entertain clients requiring something more than the standard magical services," Captain Amanta said.

Neske snickered. "She knows we're pirates, Captain."

Captain Amanta silenced him with a glance. "We approached him with—let's call it a problem, one that we believed could benefit from a magical solution."

"What did you want to do?" Mara asked.

"That's not important," the captain said.

"If it's not important, then you can tell me," Mara countered.

Mya Storm-Eye laughed. "I really do want to keep this one, Captain."

The captain hissed at both of them. "All you need to know is that we approached the Lord of the Muck for help in gaining access to somewhat remote parts of the city."

"What parts? Do you want to break in somewhere?" Mara asked.

But even as the words flew from her tongue, Mara knew the answer. Ketta with her webbed feet. Yousef with his sticky fingers. Feather with her wings. And most of all Mya Storm-Eye, once a respected mage, disgraced as a thief for stealing some valuable old journals from the Citadel. They were pirates. They might look strange and frightening now, they might be hiding away in the catacombs, they might be doing business with the Lord of the Muck, but they were *pirates*. And there was one thing pirates wanted above all else.

"You want to find Old Greengill's treasure," Mara said.

There was a brief, stunned silence.

"You"—Mara pointed at Feather—"you've got wings to fly up to the top of the Broken Tower and find the map. But the rest of you—" Mya Storm-Eye grinned, and Neske began to chuckle. "The legends say it's hidden in sea caves so deep nobody can reach them, so you asked the Muck to— What? Make it so you could swim like fish?"

Ketta snorted. "Our plans are so much bigger than that, little girl. You have no idea what you're talking about."

"Maybe not, but I bet he told you he would help. Then he told you what he was going to do, and you thought it was crazy." Mara knew she was right from the way they avoided her eyes. "But then he explained that it wasn't just about . . . fins and scales and tails. He told you the transformation would give you magical abilities like the founders had. Did it work? Are you magical now? Magical in a way that mages have never been able to manage?"

The pirates glanced at one another and said nothing.

Mara pressed on. "I guess not. But I'm right, aren't I? That's why you let him do this. You were never his prisoners. You offered yourselves up willingly."

"We had a business arrangement," Captain Amanta said stiffly, "but he broke our agreement. He refused to release two of our crew."

Understanding dawned. That was why they were so eager to hear about the people in the dungeon.

"Who are they?" she asked.

"My daughter, Jemi, and Feather's father."

Feather stabbed at the fire with a skewer, not seeming to notice that the chunks of fish had blackened to a crisp. There was a glimmer of tears in her eyes.

"He said he would release them if we brought him new subjects for his experiments," Captain Amanta said. "First it was one group of prisoners, then two. We've now delivered three. Still he says he'll release them next time."

"And every time you believe him, you become more of a fool," a new voice said.

It came from the corridor outside the catacomb room, echoing dully on the stone. Captain Amanta turned, but the pirates didn't look surprised or alarmed. This was somebody they had been expecting. Mara couldn't yet see the newcomer through the doorway.

"But your foolhardy path began when you went to such a man for help in the first place."

A shiver of recognition snaked down Mara's spine. Her legs wobbled, suddenly so weak she was afraid they wouldn't hold her up. It wasn't possible. It couldn't be. Her tired, muddled mind was playing tricks on her.

"He's never going to let your people go. Surely you know that by now."

The speaker appeared in the doorway. The firelight caught her familiar smile in its warm glow.

It was Bindy.

15

The Bone-Mage

Bindy had disappeared on a stormy night at the beginning of winter.

Rain and wind had lashed at the islands, and a bitter cold had crept into Mara's drafty attic bedroom. She had gone to fetch an extra blanket but stopped when she heard voices below. She hadn't known Bindy had a visitor. When she heard the Muck—he wasn't lord of anything yet—she settled on the top of the stairs to listen. She didn't like the Muck. She didn't like the way he looked over her as though he couldn't see her, she didn't like the way his eyes glittered when Bindy worked her bone magic, and she especially didn't like the way Bindy had lately begun snapping and sending her away when he came by. She was ten, not a little baby, and soon she would be Bindy's apprentice. She shouldn't be sent out of the room for mage talk anymore.

Finally Mara heard the Muck say, "We don't have time to argue, Belinda. Meet me at the docks. Don't be late."

A moment later the door slammed.

Mara ran down the steps. "What did he want?" she asked.

Bindy didn't look up; she was shoving a stack of her journals into a satchel. "You should be in bed."

"Are you going out tonight?"

"Just for a bit," Bindy said distractedly. She looked around, tapping her fingers thoughtfully on the table. "Now, where did . . . There!" She grabbed one more leather-bound journal and added it to the satchel. "I've just got to run out and help that fool with a little project of his."

"What do you need all that for?" Mara asked. "Where are you going? Can I come?"

Bindy slung the bag over her shoulder and headed for the door. "Go to bed, Mara. I'll be back by morning."

But she never came back. A fisherman found her abandoned rowboat east of Quarantine Island. Bindy and her spell books were gone. The Muck was Lord of the Winter Blade.

Mara had searched for days and days, scouring all of Quarantine Island, hoping against hope there had been some terrible misunderstanding. Bindy wouldn't abandon her shop. She wouldn't abandon Mara. Mara had tried to tell people that the new master of the Winter Blade must have done something, must have tricked Bindy and stolen her spell books and pushed her overboard, but they chased her away and scolded her for telling tales. The other mages helped themselves to Bindy's shop, never mind that they had always scorned her bone magic. Mara lived alone on the streets for months, until she met Fish Hook and he convinced the fishmonger to give her a job.

That had been two years ago.

Bindy's black hair had more gray now, and it was shorn close to her head in a curly cap. There were more wrinkles around her eyes, a more pronounced stoop to her shoulders. She wore patched trousers and a simple linen shirt. Her brown eyes warmed when she smiled.

"It's good to see you again, Mara," she said.

Mara was so stunned she couldn't move. Her pulse pounded in her ears. She had to be dreaming. So many nights she had gone to sleep wishing with all her heart that Bindy would be alive again, that she would come back to her shop on the Street of Whispering Stones and throw open the windows to air it out, and she would prowl the streets and markets of all the islands until she found Mara and took her home.

Bindy's expression softened. "Mara. I'm so sorry."

That was all Mara needed. She was awake and Bindy was here. Mara flung her arms around Bindy's waist and buried her head against her shoulder. Bindy had never been much for hugging, but she closed Mara in a tight embrace. She smelled faintly of seawater and smoke, scents so familiar Mara's heart squeezed.

"I thought you were dead," Mara said, sniffling.

"You've gotten so tall," Bindy said fondly. "How I've missed you."

A million questions crowded Mara's mind, each one more plaintive and confused than the last. "What happened? Where have you been?"

"Oh, my dear child," Bindy said. "It's a very long story. And look at you! You're all wet and shivering. Haven't my friends offered you a spot by the fire and something to eat?"

Mara had forgotten all about the pirates.

"Do you know this child?" Captain Amanta said.

"Mara is my apprentice," Bindy said. "But I'm just as surprised as you are to see her tonight."

Mara's still-stunned, flip-flopping heart swelled with pride. She had never *really* been Bindy's apprentice; she had been too young. But she liked to hear Bindy say it anyway, especially to the pirates who had been looking at her like she was a sea slug that slumped out of the water and into their secret lair.

"You didn't know she was coming here?" Captain Amanta said, her eyes narrow.

"Not at all. It's a wonderful surprise." Bindy slung her arm around Mara's shoulders, and Mara leaned into her for comfort. "I'm sure we can all make sense of it if you stop bleating long enough to listen."

Mara stifled a giggle. She had forgotten how much she liked to hear Bindy insult people who tried to intimidate her. But beneath her amusement and relief, Mara had questions for Bindy, so many that every time she thought of a new one, another piled up behind it: Where had she been? Why had she vanished for two years? What happened the night she and the Muck went out together? Why was she here at the Ossuary? How did she know these pirates? What did she know about the Muck's experiments?

And most of all: Why had she left Mara alone for so long?

"Bindy," she said, "what happened? I thought you were dead. Everybody thought you were dead. How do you know these people? Where—"

"All in good time, my dear," Bindy said. "Sit down and warm up."

Even though she wanted to keep asking more than she wanted to obey, Mara sat beside Feather. She unknotted Izzy's shawl from her waist and spread it over the bench to dry; the fine silk was bedraggled from the dungeon and her long swim. She didn't care if Izzy was mad at her for the rest of her life for ruining the shawl, as long as Izzy was alive.

There was hope now. Bindy would help.

Feather held a skewer before Mara's nose. "Hungry?

It's only mudfish, but we have plenty."

Mara accepted the food absently. As hungry as she was, she didn't want to waste time eating. She wanted to make a plan. "Bindy, what—"

"You must be very angry with me," Bindy said. She sat in a chair and folded her hands over her knees, looking so much like she had before that Mara was momentarily confused, lost between her memories and now, with Bindy here, *alive*, and talking to Mara as though it had been two days since they'd seen each other, not two years.

Mara didn't know how to answer. She took a bite of mudfish so she didn't have to say anything. She didn't know if it was anger she felt churning in her stomach. She had been angry when Bindy first died—*disappeared*—but all that anger had been directed at the Lord of the Muck and the mages who scavenged Bindy's shop and everyone who refused to listen. Only later was she angry at Bindy herself. For not telling Mara what she was doing that night. For going into danger alone. For working with a man like the Muck.

For not coming home.

For abandoning her.

"It's okay if you're angry," Bindy said, as though she was reading Mara's mind. "I understand. I'm so angry with myself, but I didn't have a choice. It was too dangerous. I wanted to keep you safe."

The mudfish was warm and filling, but Mara's next

swallow felt like a stone in her throat. She hadn't been safe when she was tossed out of Bindy's shop and she'd had to sleep on the streets through the rainy, blustery winter. She hadn't been safe scrounging for food behind inns and begging for scraps on corners. She had been cold and scared and alone until she met Fish Hook. Even in the fish market, she had awoken every morning fearing the fishmonger's strap and went to bed every night cold and hungry.

Mara said, "Where did you go? I thought he killed you."

"To explain that, I have to go back a bit farther than that night." Bindy smoothed the fabric of her trousers over her knees. When she looked up, she glanced first at Mara, then around the room at each of the pirates. "Do you know why they call him the Lord of the Muck?"

Captain Amanta said, "We don't care, bone thief."

But Mya Storm-Eye looked curious. "I've never heard him called anything else. I don't even know his proper name."

"What I mean is: Do you know why they call him the Lord of the Muck rather than the Lord of the Winter Blade?" Bindy asked. "By rights that should be his title, but he's had the same nickname since he was a student."

Captain Amanta looked skeptical. "How do you know?"

"Because we studied together at the Citadel," Bindy said.

Mara felt a chill pass through her. She had never known

Bindy had learned magic at the Citadel. Bindy had always disdained Citadel scholars, mocking the High Mage and his underlings as stuffy old warts without a shred of imagination. She had never—not once, not ever—told Mara that she had walked those obsidian halls herself.

Across the fire Bindy's eyes sparked, and in them Mara saw something like a challenge. Mara kept quiet and ate another bite of fish. If you don't know where a conversation is going, it's better to listen than to interrupt—Bindy had taught her that.

"I met Londe at the Citadel," Bindy said. "That's his real name, you know. Most people have forgotten it. He hasn't a surname, because he's an Outcaster orphan."

Mara looked at the fire. She didn't have a surname either, at least none that she recalled. She had forgotten her parents' names long ago.

"The High Mage took him on because he had obvious talent, but he made Londe work for it. While the rest of the students were reveling at masquerades, Londe was in the kitchens scrubbing pots and pans. When the others spent the summers impressing their parents' wealthy friends at parties, Londe stayed at the Citadel to mop the floors and dust the library. That's where his nickname came from. The other students called him Muck Boy. Children can be so cruel."

"Are you trying to make us feel sorry for him?" Ketta demanded. "He's a liar and a cheat."

"Not at all," said Bindy. "I wouldn't spare him any pity if it were made of salt and I owned the sea. But I did pity him, once. My parents were fisherfolk from Cedar Isle, so I knew what it was like to be poor at the Citadel. We became allies, in a way, the way people facing the same enemy do. We convinced ourselves that if we worked hard enough, we would prove the others wrong. We would show the rich daughters and sons of the ruling families that we were accomplished mages too."

Mara glanced around the circle to see the pirates listening raptly, caught up in Bindy's story as she had been so many times herself. She felt a swell of pride that Bindy could captivate a crew of pirates like children before a nursemaid.

But at the same time Mara's unease was growing, and mixed with it was a share of anger. Bindy still hadn't explained *why* she was here, nor how she knew the pirates. She had heard Mara's questions and neatly ignored them.

"We tried to do just that," Bindy went on. "We sought patrons in wealthy merchants, only to see them hire their friends instead. We devised songs to protect shipping lanes and valuable cargo, only to see the High Mage recommend his incompetent staff for the work. After a while, I lost interest in proving myself to the merchants and ruling families. And to the High Mage." Bindy spat derisively. "He wouldn't know interesting magic if the founders themselves returned to sing it in his bedchamber."

Mara had always giggled at Bindy's mockery of the city's most prominent mages, but now she saw she had missed an edge of jealousy in Bindy's words.

Bindy said, "I saved for my own shop and focused on my own craft. But Londe, he was not so easily put off. For him magic was a way to climb above others before they could trample on him."

Mara looked into the fire, ignoring the unpleasant squeeze in her chest. So many times she had thought that same thing: magic was her way out of cold attics and stinking fish markets, her way to someday being something more than just another orphan forgotten by the city. She didn't want to have anything in common with the Lord of the Muck.

"I confess I did not think he would ever go so far," Bindy said. "He came to my shop to ask my help singing secrets from the skeletons of some old mages. Nothing I hadn't done before—and he promised to pay well. I had no idea he was planning to take the Winter Blade. I didn't see the danger until it was too late."

Bindy didn't appear to be looking at anybody, her gaze resting on the flames, but Mara felt as though Bindy was watching her anyway. The knot in Mara's chest tightened. If all Bindy had been planning to do that night was use her bone magic on skeletons, why had she needed to bring all of her spell books and journals with her? Bindy was no amateur; she didn't need notes to sing songs she had sung a hundred times before.

"When I realized the bones he wanted me to sing to were the past masters of the Winter Blade, I figured out what he planned. I wanted nothing to do with it—to be perfectly honest, I thought Londe would get himself killed. Gerrant of Greenwood was a powerful mage. But it was too late." Bindy shook her head sadly. "I demanded we return to Quarantine Island, and Londe pretended to agree. But as I was bringing the boat around, he hit me in the head and shoved me overboard.

"I let him think he had drowned me, because I knew that if he suspected even for a second that I had survived, he would come after me again. So I went into hiding, and I waited, and I watched for signs of what he was up to. I knew he must have had some terrible reason to close himself up in that fortress. You," Bindy said, nodding at Captain Amanta, "were kind enough to fall into his thrall just as I was beginning to lose hope of ever uncovering the truth."

"We are not in his thrall," Captain Amanta said. "We have a mutually beneficial arrangement."

"Remind me again who has so carelessly left her daughter in his fortress?" Bindy said, lifting her eyebrows. "You are his creations. He has owned you from the day you agreed to let him turn you into abominations, all for want of a treasure that might not even exist. You walked willingly into his cage. You are foolish to think he'll ever let you out."

"We're not in a cage now," grumbled Mya Storm-Eye. "Not all of us."

Bindy snorted. "For now you're more useful to him out here, doing his bidding while nobody knows who you are. The moment that changes, you'll be back in the fortress. You'll never see daylight again."

The pirates began squabbling, and Bindy kept mocking them, and none of them spared a second of thought or breath for all the innocent people they had captured. They only cared about rescuing their own people and finding Old Greengill's treasure.

Mara touched the edge of Izzy's shawl. The silk was drying quickly so close to the fire, warm beneath her fingertips. Her urgency was turning into panic. She was the only one who wanted to help the prisoners. She was the only one thinking about Izzy. She couldn't lose sight of what she had to do. Finding Bindy alive, and here with the pirates, didn't change that. The holes that pockmarked Bindy's story didn't change that. Mara needed to get back into the Winter Blade, and she needed to bring the prisoners out before the Muck could hurt them. Prisoners in the dark. The Lord of the Muck in his laboratory.

Mirrors filled with smoke.

The Lady of the Tides in her tower.

Just like that, Mara had a plan. It fell together like shards of tile in a mosaic.

They were all talking over one another, so nobody heard Mara say, "I know how to get them out."

From her chair, Bindy was watching, eyes glinting.

Mara cleared her throat. "I know how to get them out."

One by one the pirates fell quiet.

"What did you say?" Captain Amanta demanded.

Mara did not let herself quail under the green woman's angry gaze. "I know how to rescue the prisoners. All of them, including your daughter. I have a plan."

Ketta rolled her eyes. "What do you know about anything? Be quiet, little girl."

Mara felt her fear drain away, and in its place grew a white-hot anger. She was doing this for Izzy. The bearded man, the Roughwater woman, the little boy, all of them needed help, but most of all Izzy, who was Mara's family in every way that mattered. The pirates couldn't scare her away from that.

"I will *not* be quiet. If you want to keep arguing, go right ahead, but my friend is in that dungeon, and I'm going to rescue her. I'm the only person who knows how to get into the Winter Blade without the Muck seeing."

"He'll catch you," Yousef said. "He's always watching."

"He can't see everything," Mara retorted. "And he won't be there."

Captain Amanta tilted her head thoughtfully. "He rarely leaves the island."

Mara looked over the pirates one by one, examining their strange features. Finally she settled on Feather. She smiled.

"What?" Feather said. "Why are you looking at me like that?"

"He told me he's working in absolute secrecy for now. What do you think he'll do if he finds out another mage has gotten her hands on you?" There was a brief silence. Mara's heart was thumping, but this time it was with excitement as much as fear. "And what if it's the richest mage in the city, from the oldest of the ruling families he hates so much? Don't you think that might draw him out of his fortress?"

Bindy began to laugh, a low chuckle that rolled like tumbling rocks around the crypt. "Oh, Mara, you are such a clever child."

16

Partings and Plans

Summer Island rose like an ax blade from the sea, a long, sharp spine of black rock covered with steep streets, stacked buildings, and winding staircases. The air was filled with the rich scents of smoke and spice, frying fish and roasting meat, and ripe fruits and vegetables in the markets. It was early afternoon. The rough seas and lashing rain had faded to a cold drizzle. The docks were crowded and noisy with sailors and merchants talking in a dozen languages.

"I don't like being here in daytime," Feather said. "Anybody could see us."

She was seated beside Mara in the rowboat, her wings hidden beneath a blanket. Yousef and Ketta were at the oars, and Bindy was on the opposite bench with her eyes closed and her expression peaceful. But Mara knew she was listening. Bindy was always listening.

"I wanted to leave last night," Mara pointed out. It had taken entirely too long to convince the pirates of her plan. By the time they had grudgingly agreed, the storm had grown so bad they were stuck on the Ossuary until it passed.

Mara hunched down and shivered. She was wrapped in Izzy's shawl, which didn't smell like Izzy anymore. It smelled like seawater and smoke, and it barely offset the chill. She looked away from Bindy, away from Feather, and gazed across the water.

There was no sign of the sea serpents. She might have thought them a dream, except that she could still feel the gentle bump of the big square head against her legs. She could still see those watchful, intelligent eyes. She didn't know what it meant that the serpents had returned to the city. She didn't want to believe it was the Muck who had brought them back, that he might be getting close to wielding the founders' magic after all, and the poor, lonely sea serpents mistook his efforts for a sign of their long-lost masters. It was too cruel to contemplate, that such beautiful creatures could return to their ancient home, to find only the Muck and his caged hybrids.

All through the night the thought of Izzy on the Muck's laboratory table had spun around and around in Mara's mind. With every passing hour the horrors she imagined had grown more terrible. More than once she had been certain, absolutely *certain*, that it was too late. Izzy was already transformed or dead, and it didn't matter if Mara stayed in the Ossuary tombs for the rest of her life, because she had failed her friend and nothing would be okay ever again.

The storm was still blowing when the day dawned cold and gray, but by midday the seas were low enough not to capsize an open rowboat. Captain Amanta had taken the black ship and most of her crew to a hidden cove on the eastern side of Greenwood Island. Ketta and Yousef agreed to row Mara and Feather to Summer Island, and Bindy to Quarantine Island, but they refused to go as far as Tidewater Isle. When Mara protested, Yousef had laughed and said, "Pirates and ladies don't mix, little girl. We're staying well clear of your fancy mistress."

The pirates slotted the rowboat into a free spot at the docks. Mara helped Feather climb out, but when she went to follow, Bindy stopped her with a hand on her arm. "You know what you have to do."

Mara nodded. It was *her* plan, after all. "I know."

"I know too," Feather put in. "In case anybody cares."

Bindy didn't even glance at her. "I wish we had more time to prepare. There's so much I could tell you about Londe's magic."

"You can tell me after," Mara said impatiently. They had already wasted too much time.

Bindy smiled and tapped Mara's nose. "I will. I'll explain everything."

Mara watched as Ketta and Yousef rowed away from the dock, Bindy relaxed and smiling in the prow of their boat. They were headed to Quarantine Island, where, Bindy claimed, she still had friends who would be willing to speak against the Muck when the time came.

Mara wondered where those friends had been two years ago when Bindy had vanished and Mara had been cast out into the streets, but she hadn't dared ask. Asking would only lead to another discussion, and another discussion would only waste more time, and they had no time to waste, no matter how certain she was that Bindy wasn't telling them everything.

She turned away from the water to find Feather watching her.

Feather tilted her head thoughtfully. "You know, when we first met her, she told us she was all alone. She said there was nobody in the world she trusted. She wouldn't even let us meet the foreign kid she had rowing her around. She definitely didn't mention an apprentice."

"So? She's been in hiding," Mara said. "She faked her own death so the Muck wouldn't come after her."

"That's what she said, sure," Feather said. "But she seems okay trusting you now, and sending you off to do this while she stays away."

Mara bristled and turned away. "Look for a blue-and-yellow boat. They'll be loading up right about now."

Mara stomped down the docks, searching for the fishmongers' boys and girls, and most of all for Fish Hook. He would help them without question. She didn't have time to deal with whatever Feather was trying to say. Bindy had hidden to stay safe from the Muck. To keep Mara out of danger too. She wouldn't lie about something like that.

But, a little voice whispered in Mara's mind, hasn't she been lying to you for two years? Wasn't faking her own death about the biggest lie she could have told?

Mara scowled as she swerved around a group of laughing Blackcliff sailors. She was *happy* Bindy was alive. Maybe she didn't understand everything that had happened, but she knew the Lord of the Muck was dangerous and must be stopped. Hadn't she tried to convince everybody of that from the start? Bindy had been right to hide from him. Hadn't she?

Mara caught a glimpse of blue and yellow, and her heart squeezed with relief. She shoved her way down the crowded dock and grabbed the nearest girl. "Where's Fish Hook?"

The girl scowled as she heaved a spotted flounder into a cart. "Good question. When he finally shows up, the master's gonna have his hide."

Mara's ears began to buzz with fear. "What do you mean? Where is he?"

"How should I know?" the girl said. "He took off yesterday before dinner, saying he was out to see a friend, and
he never came back. Left all his work for the rest of us to
cover."

"No," Mara said.

The girl's scowl deepened. "Are you calling me a liar?"

Mara barely heard her. The Summer Island docks
faded to a blur of noise and color. A great black wave of
fear washed over her.

She had asked Fish Hook to check on Izzy. He would
have followed Izzy's footsteps from the docks to the candlemaker's shop, right along the dark streets where the pirates
had already taken people without being seen. Just last night
they had delivered new prisoners to the Muck. He had told
his gray man they were waiting for guests. In the confusion
of being caught by Captain Amanta and learning Bindy was
alive, Mara hadn't given a thought to those new prisoners.
All of her worry had been for Izzy.

Fish Hook had agreed to help so readily, as he always
did. Mara hadn't once considered that she was sending
him into danger.

Now he was a prisoner of the Muck, and it was Mara's
fault.

Mara spun away from the girl. She marched over to
Feather and shoved her with both hands. Feather stumbled backward, nearly losing her balance.

"Did you take him?" Mara shouted, shoving Feather

again. "Did you take him last night? Did you take my best friend?"

"Stop that!" Feather said, stepping hurriedly out of the way as Mara advanced on her again. "Are you crazy? What's wrong with you?"

"Last night! I saw your ship! I know you went there! He's my *best friend*!"

"Will you be quiet?" Feather hissed. She looked around frantically. "People are staring!"

"I don't care!" Mara shouted, but Feather was right. People were watching with entirely too much interest. Her heart was drumming in her ears and her blood was racing and her stomach was all twisted up in knots, but she took a breath, swallowed painfully, and lowered her voice to a hoarse whisper. "You took more people last night, didn't you? I saw your ship. I saw it when I was swimming away. That's when you brought them in!"

"*I* didn't," Feather retorted, her voice just as low, just as angry. "They don't take me anywhere anymore. I'm too clumsy like this to be a sailor. I'm useless. This is the first time I've been out of that wretched crypt in ages."

"They're still your crew, and they took my friend. Do you even care?"

"What choice do we have? He has—" Feather's voice cracked, and her shoulders slumped. "He has my dad. And the captain's daughter. He told us he would let them go when he'd had enough. It was never supposed to be like this. We were supposed to be hunting for treasure by now. What would you have done?"

Mara glared at her and didn't answer. She didn't know what she would have done in Feather's place. She was tired and hungry and scared. The past few days had made her feel like a boat tossed about on wild, unpredictable waves. The excitement of finding the bones, the fear of losing Izzy, the terror of the Winter Blade, the joy of learning Bindy was alive, and now this—it was all too much, too many conflicting worries and feelings crammed into her mind. She was having trouble keeping track of everything she was supposed to be thinking about.

"What?" Feather said. "Crab got your tongue?"

"I'm thinking," Mara snapped. "How did you meet Bindy? Where did you find her?"

"We didn't find her," Fish Hook said. She looked like she wanted to know why Mara was asking, but she explained. "She found us. About a month ago, right after the mage told us he wasn't going to let Dad and Jemi go unless we did what he said. We had this hideout on Greenwood, and one day when we went out to the ship she was waiting. Captain probably would have killed her, but Mya knew her and convinced us to listen. Bindy said she could help us."

"Doing what?" Mara asked. "What exactly is she helping you do?"

Feather looked at her for a long moment. "She told us

there were mage bones in the catacombs that would show us a secret way into the Winter Blade, then we could rescue our people and the Muck wouldn't have any leverage over us."

Something was prickling at the back of Mara's mind, a bothersome thought just out of reach, like a sticky burr hidden in a wool sweater. "That's what she said the Muck wanted from her two years ago. Secrets from the old bones."

"She didn't tell us that part before," Feather said. "We figured out that she knew him, but lots of mages know each other. Even Mya said she'd met him, back before he was master of the Winter Blade."

Mara didn't care who Mya Storm-Eye knew or didn't know. "Did Bindy learn anything from the bones?"

"She hasn't said. She won't even let us be around when she's singing to them. She says it's because her songs are secret, but Mya says it's because bone-mages are all charlatans. Bindy kept telling us to be patient."

"She's not telling you that now."

"No, she isn't," Feather said. "The thing that's changed now is you. She doesn't need to find a way into the Winter Blade, because you already know one."

That was where Mara needed to be headed right now. She didn't have time to spend trying to figure out what Bindy was thinking. Izzy and Fish Hook needed her help. Nothing changed that. Nothing would stop Mara from rescuing them.

As she and Feather began to race along the docks again, looking for somebody to take them to Tidewater Isle, Mara realized what it was that had been sticking in her mind like a burr. It was something Bindy used to say, every time she caught Mara making up tangled excuses for why she had forgotten her chores, or taken the long route home before dinner, or spent the day swimming instead of sweeping. She never got angry enough to shout, and she rarely offered any punishment other than more chores. She would only smile, and tap Mara on the nose, and say, "Next time, little fish, make up a simpler story and stick to it. It'll be easier to remember, and nobody will catch you in a lie."

A bone-mage searching for secrets in the Ossuary. Nothing was simpler than that. Bindy could tell that story a hundred times and nobody would doubt it.

But that didn't make it true.

17

The Worm
on the Hook

By the time Mara found an oysterman willing to take them to Tidewater Isle, it was well into the afternoon. The day was growing gloomy as another storm rolled in. The oysterman and his crew muttered darkly about how quickly summer had ended and how fierce the winter was sure to be.

Tidewater Isle was lit up with lamplight, giving the rain-slicked towers a shiny gleam. Upon seeing it, Feather whistled under her breath. "I can't believe you live here."

"It's not my house," Mara protested. "I'm a servant."

Feather shook her head. "But *look* at this place."

The islands of the city were so familiar, from those crowded with shops and markets to those dominated by the palaces of the ruling families, Mara rarely paused to do just that. Look, and marvel at the magic it must have taken to carve those terraces and towers and caves.

That was the kind of magic the Lord of the Muck wanted for himself. The kind of magic that could shape a fortress from jagged stone, level a tower to rubble, or raise storms big enough to drown entire islands. It was thrilling in stories, such dangerous magic wielded at the whims of capricious founders, spells flung about as easily as harpoons in their endless feuds and battles and quests. But this wasn't history, and it wasn't a story. It was terrifying to imagine a single man with that much power.

Feather nudged Mara and gave her a questioning look. Mara realized she had started humming her mother's old song, the way she had always done when she was scared. She stopped immediately. It wasn't just a song anymore. She couldn't forget that.

As soon as they were docked in the sea cave, Mara took Feather by the arm and led her through the palace at a run. Feather's blanket rippled behind them like a cape.

When they reached the door at the base of the tower, Mara marched over to the two women standing guard. "I need to talk to the Lady and Professor Kosta."

Feather sucked in a startled breath. Mara knew what she was thinking. Mara was only a servant, in no position to make demands, and the Lady didn't have to listen. She didn't have to believe Mara's story. She didn't have to help. She didn't have to do anything at all. She was the

Lady of the Tides, master of Tidewater Isle, and she could send Mara and Feather away as easily as snapping her fingers. Mara's plan counted on the Lady not doing that. She needed the Lady to understand the danger.

When the guards hesitated, Mara added, trying to sound serious and stern rather than pleading, "It's about the task she sent me to do. She'll want to see me right away."

Without a word, the women opened the door to let Mara and Feather through. When they were only a few steps up the staircase, the door slammed shut behind them. They climbed the tower stairs through the thickening smoke, the Lady's spell-song echoing all around them. Feather coughed and covered her mouth, but Mara didn't even pause. When they reached the top, she pounded on the door until it opened.

The Lady looked down at her. "Where have you been?"

"Don't be like that, Renata," Professor Kosta said, emerging from the smoke behind the Lady. "Mara, don't listen to her. We've been very worried about you. Come in, come in. What's happened? Who is this?"

"This is Feather," said Mara breathlessly, the words tumbling over her tongue. "She's—she's been— I escaped, but there are more, he has more people, there's a dungeon, he has my friends, and we have to help them, we have to, we have to—"

"Breathe, Mara," the professor said. "Tell us what happened. Where have you been?"

Mara took a deep breath and started over. "The Lord of the Muck is holding people prisoner in his dungeon. He has Izzy and a bunch of others. He's using them for his experiments."

There was a brief, weighty silence.

The Lady lifted a single eyebrow. "Experiments?"

As quickly as she could, Mara told the Lady and Professor Kosta what had happened after she'd found a way into the Winter Blade. She told them about getting caught in the library, about the dungeon and what the people there had said, and about being taken to the underwater laboratory filled with hybrid creatures.

"Whatever is he doing that for?" the Lady asked. Her expression was thoughtful as she looked over the bones laid out on her long worktables. The ginger cat slept between two long, curving ribs, peaceful as could be. All the rocks and coils of rope that had been used to sink the bones were piled on the floor beneath one table. "If these bones are his work—and I *was* beginning to suspect they weren't as old as we first thought—it is very impressive magic, but what is the purpose of it?"

Mara started to answer, then stopped herself. It still sounded mad, no matter how she phrased it. But the Lady was waiting for her to reply, and Professor Kosta was looking at her with obvious concern, and Feather was watching Mara anxiously.

"He told me," Mara began. She hesitated, cleared her throat. "He told me that he's working out . . . he told me that he wants . . ."

"What is it?" the Lady said, a snap of impatience.

"He wants to turn himself into a founder," Mara said all in a rush. "He's practicing bits and pieces on other people, but when he gets them right he's going to—the whole thing, the whole transformation, he's going to do it to *himself*, because he wants to be able to do the founders' magic and he thinks he's the only person who deserves it."

There was a stunned silence. Mara's face warmed.

"It's true." Feather's voice was very small, but she spoke without wavering. "That's what he told us too. He thinks he can do it."

"I suppose that explains . . . Well, naturally he would need human subjects, but the rest of it . . . That's very . . ." The Lady shook her head. "I confess, Mara, I have never heard of such of a thing."

"I'm not lying," Mara said, and all at once there were tears stinging her eyes. She was so tired and so scared and her friends were in so much danger, and this was her only hope. If the Lady didn't believe her and agree to help, she didn't know what to do. She didn't have any other options, aside from diving into the storm-roughened sea and swimming for the Winter Blade by herself.

"We know you're not lying," Professor Kosta said gently. "But why would he want to do such a thing?"

"Power," said the Lady, with a delicate shudder. "Riches. Status. Oh, Etina, you haven't been in this city long enough to understand, but there is nothing—*nothing*—as valuable as magic. And ancient magic, the sort we all believe has been lost to history? Goodness." The Lady was quiet for a moment, her eyes fixed on some distant point beyond the magical smokescreen. "Goodness," she said again. "The consequences of a single man gaining such power would be . . . vast."

"I admit I don't fully understand," Professor Kosta said. "What is it he's trying to achieve? Why go to so much trouble?"

"What *can't* he achieve, if he wields that sort of magic?" the Lady countered. "The founders carved the island fortresses from solid stone with nothing but a song—so who's to say a petty little man in possession of their power couldn't level them again? He could trap the entire city in a cage of storms. Punish those who don't worship him with floods and fires. Set a fever sickness to strike down an entire family for generations. Send creatures of the sea after the ships of merchants who don't curry his favor. The question, Etina, is not what he *hopes* to achieve, but whether there would be any way for us to stop him if he succeeds."

Professor Kosta nodded solemnly. "Then we had best see that he doesn't. What happened after you escaped, Mara?"

She told them about meeting the pirates at the Ossuary, about Captain Amanta's daughter and Feather's dad, but she left Bindy out of her story. It would only complicate the story, and Mara didn't want complications. She wanted action, and fast. She tugged at the ends of Izzy's shawl, still damp with rain, and shifted her weight from foot to foot. Too much time had passed already.

She didn't mention the sea serpents either. She didn't know what to make of them, and she didn't know if anybody would believe her. They were, for now, her own secret.

Mara finished her tale with a desperate "We have to rescue them. I have a plan. I know how to help. We *have* to help them."

"Of course we do. You must be so frightened for your family." Professor Kosta nodded at Feather, who ducked her head and did not answer.

"Do you have fins?" the Lady asked. She fixed her gaze on Feather, who shrunk away in alarm. "It's only that you're holding that blanket so tightly about your shoulders, and there's clearly some manner of oddity underneath. I am trying to guess what you and your . . ." The Lady paused, searching for the right word. "Your *crew* would have requested, but I confess I am having trouble coming up with many plausible possibilities."

Feather straightened her shoulders. "I don't have fins," she said. There was a pause where she seemed to be considering adding *my lady*, but instead only jutted her chin.

"Then what is it?" asked the Lady. "I should very much like to see."

"Please don't be afraid," Professor Kosta said, rather more kindly. "We only want to know what he's done to you."

Feather started to unknot the blanket at her neck, but Mara stopped her. "Wait."

She couldn't risk the Lady and Professor Kosta getting distracted by Feather's wings before they agreed to her plan. She needed them to understand that rescuing Izzy and Fish Hook was more important than the Muck, more important than his magic, more important than anything he thought he could do.

"There's something else I saw in the Winter Blade," Mara said. "In the library and the laboratory."

The Lady was still looking at Feather. "What was that?"

"Mirrors," Mara said. "Tons and tons of mirrors. More than I could count."

The Lady's gaze sharpened as she turned to Mara. "Ah. Yes."

"He's watching *everybody*," Mara said.

The Lady's lips twitched. "I'd always suspected as much. I told you this noxious smoke was a necessary precaution, Etina."

"And you were quite right. What are you thinking,

Mara?" Professor Kosta asked.

"He's not just spying on everybody," Mara went on, not letting herself rush, not letting herself skip anything important. "He's making sure none of the other mages see what he's doing. He's afraid people will find out before he's perfected it."

The Lady began to nod, still watching Mara with a knowing, speculative gaze. Mara felt a spark of relief. Bindy had been wrong; the Lady of the Tides *was* clever. She knew where Mara was leading.

"That's my plan," Mara said. "We're going to clear away the smoke so he can see inside and . . ."

Mara tugged the blanket from Feather's shoulders.

"We're going to set a trap."

Feather flexed her wings. The professor gasped in surprise, and the Lady's eyebrows flew up to her hairline.

"And I'm the bait," Feather said. "Aren't these better than fins?"

18

Into the Fortress Again

*A single boat slipped away from Tidewater Isle at twi-*light. The rain was steady, the sea unsettled. Smoke twisted from the windows of Renata Palisado's tower laboratory; she was clearing away the obscuring spell that kept other mages from spying on her. Before Mara had left, the Lady had taken up a fan and said to Feather, "You might as well help, as you've got the proper appendages for it." Feather had grumbled but obligingly began flapping her wings. By the time Mara left, the Lady was peppering Feather with questions about the Muck's procedure.

Mara huddled down in her cloak. Driftwood was at the oars, but otherwise she was alone. This next part of the plan was entirely up to her. She hoped the old boat at the Winter

Blade's dock was still seaworthy; they would need more space for all the prisoners. She should have brought blankets, maybe food and fresh water too. The prisoners hadn't been eating regularly. They would be weak and hungry. Fish Hook was always hungry. He never got enough to eat, was always grumbling about how stingy the fishmonger was. She should have brought something for him.

It was too late for that now. All she could do was get back inside the Winter Blade.

Once, Mara thought she heard the slick sound of something moving through the water. Her heart skipped, and Driftwood turned to peer into the darkness without missing an oar stroke. Mara couldn't bring herself to say anything. She couldn't see the sea serpents, if they were even there. More and more they felt like part of a fading dream, and the more desperately she hoped to see them again, to recapture that fleeting feeling of peace and comfort she had felt swimming alongside them, the more they slipped away.

When they were near the eastern side of the Winter Blade, Driftwood stopped rowing.

"We'll wait here," he said.

Mara nodded, trying hard not to shiver. Driftwood lifted a spyglass to watch the island. He had never been a man to waste words, but Mara wished he would say something now. She could have used the distraction. The longer they waited, the more certain she became that her plan wouldn't work. The Muck might not be looking at his spy mirrors tonight. Maybe he wasn't watching the Lady of the Tides. Maybe he was too engrossed in whatever horrible things he was doing to Fish Hook and Izzy to watch anybody. The whole plan hinged on his noticing, but what if he didn't? Mara didn't know what she could do if they couldn't draw him out. She would have to sneak into the fortress anyway.

"Ah," said Driftwood.

Mara sat up straighter. "Do you see him?"

Driftwood wiped rain from the spyglass lens. "There's a boat. A small one."

Mara squinted but couldn't see anything through the rain. She thought she spotted a flash of light at the base of the fortress, quickly shuttered, but it could have been a trick of the eye.

"I can't believe he fell for it," she whispered.

Driftwood grunted softly. "Never underestimate how prideful a clever man can be."

"Is he alone?"

There was a pause before Driftwood answered. "There's another man with him."

One of the gray men was at the oars. That meant the other had been left behind.

As swiftly as he could, Driftwood rowed up to the base of the tower. The statues were even more unsettling now that Mara knew Gerrant of Greenwood's fate. The horned woman above the hidden tunnel might have been a person once, so long ago nobody remembered her name. She might have been given horns using the very same magic the Muck wanted to master.

Mara lit one of her murk-lights; she had three spares in an oilskin sack. She wasn't going to risk being lost in the tower without light.

"I'll be watching for your signal," said Driftwood. "And for the black ship."

The pirates were supposed to be nearby, ready to help, but Mara had no idea if they would keep to their part of the plan. She only nodded. She didn't trust herself to speak. She hoped Driftwood couldn't see how frightened she was.

She dove into the black water. She found the tunnel and swam its length. When she emerged in the well, she climbed out quickly, shivering in the cold.

The door to the well room was still unlocked. Still hidden by magic. Mara breathed a sigh of relief. The Muck hadn't found out how she'd gotten into his fortress.

The tower was just as silent as it had been before. Mara crept along the hallway, counting the doors until she found the sea cave. She ran down the steps, holding her light high. The rowboat was gone, as she'd expected, but the old pleasure boat was still there.

Mara lit a second murk-light and slipped into the water. She swam toward the mouth of the sea cave, but slowly, cautiously. If she swam too far, she might not be able to get back through whatever spell hid the cave. But if she didn't swim far enough she wouldn't be able to show Driftwood the location of the entrance.

She stopped when she could feel the spell thrumming through the air and stone around her, a faint pressure in her ears and a tickle on her skin. She didn't know any songs for revealing obscuring spells, and certainly not a spell so ancient as this. She didn't even know if it was a single spell. There could be spells from the founders and all the island's human masters piled on top of one another, protection after protection, tangled together for centuries.

She thought about what she knew: this spell wasn't just about hiding the sea cave. It was about hiding it so well that it looked like unbroken stone from the outside, so indistinguishable from the rest of the fortress that even people who had lived in the city their entire lives couldn't remember where the mouth was supposed to be.

Mara didn't know much about obscuring spells, but she had a song for stone magic. It was worth a try. She sang out a few notes of her mother's song: "Over the sea and under the sky, my island home it waits for me."

Nothing happened, so she tried to mimic the melodious song she'd heard echoing from the hidden tunnel the first time she'd found it: "Over the waves and under the storms, my heart is bound but my dreams are free."

Still nothing. Mara frowned, trying to think in spite of the urgency she felt in every heartbeat. She had heard a powerful obscuring spell just a few hours ago, when she and Feather had charged through the Lady's smoke-screen, but that was for hiding a room from spying eyes. She wanted to do the opposite. If you wanted to switch a song around, she thought, you had to switch the words around too.

She mulled it over, then began to sing:

"Over the sea and under the stone, my island home it
welcomes me.
Across the waves and into the cave, the way is clouded
but my eyes can see.
As I sail near and my home awaits, my island opens
to the sea."

The air before her *flickered.* Mara was so surprised she stopped singing, and the flickering vanished.

She sang again, the same melody at the same pitch, but with words of her own devising—*"The tall black spire calls to me"*—and the flicker returned. It was as though the darkness itself had turned to water, rippling like a puddle disturbed by raindrops. The ripples grew stronger and stronger, and a low hum surrounded Mara, trembling through the water and stone and air. The water became choppy, splashing over her head and pushing her side to side, and the reverberations grew louder and louder, trembling through the stone walls like thunder in a storm until finally—

A shudder passed over the entire cave.

The obscuring spell vanished like a popped bubble.

For a moment Mara was so stunned she only stared. She had only wanted to *find* the spell. She hadn't meant to take it down entirely! She hadn't even known she could do that.

With the spell gone, the mouth of the sea cave was open to the night. She threw the spare murk-light as far as she could: that was the signal Driftwood was waiting for.

The cave hummed with the echo of her song as she swam back to the dock. It made her teeth ache, that low vibration in the stones, and something about it felt *off*. But there wasn't anything she could do about that. It wasn't even a proper spell-song, just something she had made up in the moment, and it had done what she needed it to do. She had friends to rescue. She hoisted herself onto the dock and raced up the stairs.

In the corridor the gray man was waiting.

He stood directly across from the door, his long arms dangling from his slumped shoulders, the gills on his neck fluttering. When he saw her, his milky eyes widened. With a wet, rasping groan, he lurched.

Mara jumped back. Her foot curled over the top step, and she began to tip, flailing her arms for balance. The gray man caught her shirt with his spidery hand and dragged her through the doorway.

Mara kicked and thrashed, trying to get her feet under her again and wrest free, but his grip was too strong. He caught her around the waist and lifted her. Mara clawed at his hands and arms; her fingernails dug into his skin and salt water dribbled from the wounds. She reached for his face, for the gaping gills on his neck, but nothing hurt him. He didn't even flinch.

The gray man plodded down the corridor, Mara struggling futilely in his grasp. The murk-light dangling from her wrist swung back and forth, casting dancing shadows all along the walls.

Then she remembered when she *had* seen him flinch.

She stopped fighting abruptly. The gray man was so surprised his grip around her middle loosened—not enough for her to break away, but enough for her to twist one arm free and swing the murk-light wildly over her shoulder.

The light struck the man's neck with a solid thunk. The glass was strong; it didn't break. The gray man dropped Mara to the ground to bat it away. She whipped the light at him again and again, hitting his shoulder, his neck, his face, and finally his brow. One glass pane cracked in a spiderweb of fractures.

The captured flame surged with its first taste of fresh air, and fire escaped through the cracks in delicate golden wisps. Mara untangled the rope from her wrist and hooked it around the gray man's grasping arm. His watery eyes grew wide, and he let out a frightened groan. Mara snatched the ring of keys from his belt and scrambled away.

The gray man tried to shake the murk-light from his arm, but he only managed to knock it against the stone wall. The glass shattered and flames exploded from the broken globe with a bright pop. He screamed.

Mara was already running. She looked back only once to see him batting angrily at his flaming sleeve. His cries were a terrible thing, agonized and wild, but she didn't stop.

She paused only when she reached the long hallway that sloped into the heart of the island. The dungeon was down there, through the vertebrate-stone arch, and that's where she had to go. She dug into her oilskin sack for another murk-light. The gray man was bellowing behind her, his shouts carrying through the fortress, but he wasn't following.

Mara took a deep breath, gripped the keys tight, and returned to the depths of the island.

19

Rescue

Finding her way to the dungeon was harder than Mara expected. There were more intersections than she could count, and all the hallways looked the same: floor, walls, and ceiling of black stone, distant drips of water the only sound, and nothing but darkness beyond the reach of her murk-light.

Thinking that she might get a useful reaction like she had in the cave, she tried a bit of her mother's song with the new words again: *"Over the sea and under the stone, my island home it welcomes me."*

The answer was a low rumble in the walls, so deep she felt it more than heard it. It came from all around— left and right, above and below, no direction stronger than any other—which was exactly the *opposite* of what she wanted.

Mara stopped singing, and the rumble faded. She needed something else. But all she remembered about being carried to the dungeon was the dragging shuffle-scrape of the gray man's feet in the darkness.

Footsteps. Stone.

"Magic can't solve every problem." Mum used to say that, and she had never been sad or disappointed when she did. She had always said it with a smile, like she was facing a challenge she was happy to take on. "Even if mages sometimes forget that."

Mara looked down.

The gray man didn't lift his feet when he walked. He shuffled along, his heavy shoes rasping over the stone. He must have walked from the sea cave to the dungeon a dozen times or more, every time he brought a prisoner inside.

And he had left a path: a trail of fresh scuff marks.

Sprinting as fast as she could, Mara followed the scuff marks all the way to the dungeon. She skidded to a stop in front of the door and began searching through the gray man's ring of keys. The lock was big and old, so she tried the biggest and oldest key on the ring. The rusty metal shrieked, and something inside the lock clanked.

At the same moment, Mara felt a kick of dizziness, as though the floor had lurched beneath her. A low sound groaned through the fortress, like rocks grinding on rocks, but it faded quickly.

Behind the door somebody shouted, "What was that?"

"Is he coming back?"

"What's happening?"

They had felt it too. But what *was* it? Had the Lord of the Muck placed some kind of protection on his fortress since last night? If he had, it hadn't stopped Mara from getting in, hadn't stopped her from breaking the obscuring spell on the sea cave, hadn't stopped her from escaping the gray man. It hadn't done anything at all that she could see, and she didn't have time to worry about it.

Mara reached for the key again. It turned slowly, stubbornly, until finally the tumblers clacked into place. Chips of rusted metal pattered to the floor. The door was so heavy Mara had to pull with all of her weight. The hinges screeched in protest.

From the other side came a frightened cry: "They're coming back!"

She slipped inside. The candle by the door flickered to life.

"Mara!"

"Izzy!"

She ran down the aisle between the cages, her murklight swinging wildly. Voices called out as she passed, but she didn't stop until she was in front of Izzy's cage.

Izzy was sitting on the floor, leaning into the corner of her cell so that half of her was lit, the other half shadowed. "What are you doing here? We thought you got away!"

"I came back for you. I have the keys." Mara's hands shook as she searched for the right one. "I'm going to get you out of here. All of you."

Izzy was shaking her head. "It's too dangerous! He could come back any moment."

"He's not here. We saw him leave. Driftwood is waiting outside."

She tried another key—there! The lock opened with a click; Mara pulled the door open. Izzy winced and hissed in pain as she rose to her feet.

"Are you hurt?" Mara demanded, looking Izzy over frantically. Izzy's right arm was strapped across her middle by a ragged sling. The cloth was dirty and stained, but Mara couldn't see what injuries it was hiding. "What did he do to you?"

"I just need a second," Izzy said, panting. "I'm fine." She swayed before leaning heavily against Mara.

"You're hurt," Mara said.

She didn't like the way Izzy was staggering, as though she couldn't find her balance. She didn't like the strange angles and points pressing from underneath the dirty bandages. She felt sick to her stomach. She'd left Izzy for a whole day and night. That was more than enough time for the Muck to have begun his work.

"Not as bad as I might have been," Izzy said. "You running out of that laboratory like a madwoman messed up his plans. After he got it all cleaned up, he only had time to do one side. Come on, come on. Let's get the rest of these open."

Izzy couldn't balance on her own, so together they went from cage to cage, turning every lock and opening every door. There were fourteen prisoners in all. A scowling, dreadlocked girl about Izzy's age stared when Mara asked if she was Jemi, Captain Amanta's daughter.

"You've met my mother?" Jemi asked warily.

"I've met your whole crew," Mara said. She held the cell door open to let Jemi out. She was the last; the next cell was empty. "Where's the man who was with you? Is he here?"

There was a gleam of tears in Jemi's eyes. "They took him away. He never came back."

Feather's dad. Because she had found that femur, Mara had known one of the prisoners must have died, but she hadn't known who it was. Feather was back at Tidewater Isle, eagerly helping the Lady trap the Muck, believing her father would be safe soon. The sick feeling in Mara's stomach only grew worse.

"We have to go," Mara said, "but where's—"

For a second, Mara couldn't breathe.

Fish Hook was nowhere to be seen.

She ran through the dungeon, searching every cage, shining her light into every shadow. There was a new roar of fear rumbling through her ears.

"Izzy!" Mara called out, her voice wavering. She ran back to the prisoners clustered by the door. "Was my friend here? Was Fish Hook here?"

"Those men brought him in last night. He was right over—" Izzy looked around in confusion. "He was right there."

"They took him earlier," said an old man. He hunched up and coughed, his body quaking. "While you were sleeping. That creeping man came in and dragged him away."

"Oh," Izzy said. "Oh, no, Mara. He said he got caught when he was looking for me."

And he had only been looking for Izzy because Mara had asked him to. Mara sucked in a short breath and pressed her lips together. There was no time to panic. The Muck had taken him away. That meant Fish Hook was already in the laboratory. She could go to the laboratory. The Muck wasn't here. She could still save Fish Hook. He was going to be *fine*.

She dropped the oilskin sack from her shoulder. With trembling hands she dug out the spare murk-light. She started to hand it to Izzy, changed her mind, and handed it to a sturdy-looking gray-haired woman who didn't need to be propped up.

"Driftwood is waiting outside the sea cave," she said. "There's a boat at the dock. I don't know how seaworthy it is, but it can get you away from the island. You have to go quickly. One of the gray men is still down there and he's—"

"Mara." In the glow of the murk-lights Izzy's eyes were big and round. "We don't know how to find the dock."

"But I have to—"

Izzy was right. She couldn't send them into the fortress without help. Izzy was hurt, and the others were thin and shaken, and nobody knew the way. She couldn't abandon them.

"Okay. Okay." Mara was thinking rapidly. "I'll show you the way, then I'll come back for Fish Hook."

Frightened whispers and wheezing breaths filled the tunnels as they fled, and the prisoners' stumbling footsteps were as loud as drumbeats. Mara scarcely breathed until they passed through the vertebrate-lined arch. There was no sign of the gray man where Mara had last seen him, no sign of their fight except the glass shards of her broken murk-light. The door to the sea cave was still open. Mara waved the prisoners through, then bounded down the steps after them.

Just as she reached the bottom step it happened again: a jolt shuddered through the entire island, as though the stone floor had dropped beneath them. The unmistakable sound of stone grinding on stone filled the cave, reverberating briefly before fading.

"What is that?" somebody asked, his voice rising with panic.

"The island is collapsing!" another shouted.

"The mage is angry!" The prisoners clung to each other, looking around the cave with wild eyes.

"Don't be stupid!" Izzy shouted, her voice rising over the others. "Get in the boat!"

The prisoners climbed into the boat. A young man took up one of the oars; the tall gray-haired woman took the other. The boat was barely big enough, but it would have to do until they were outside.

"I have to go back for Fish Hook," Mara said to Izzy. "Get out of here. Find Driftwood."

"We can—"

The floor rocked again, and for the briefest moment Mara spotted something shimmering in the shadows by the dock. She stared at it, her heart pounding. A remnant of the obscuring spell? She didn't know. She didn't have time to worry about it.

"Mara?" Izzy said.

Mara could see now that some of the stains on Izzy's bandages were blood, and when the light flashed a certain way it caught a shimmering green just below her collar. The other prisoners had noticed too; the young boy was shying away from Izzy's right side as though he was afraid of touching her.

"Go," Mara said. "Get in the boat. Driftwood is waiting. We'll catch up."

Mara didn't wait to see the last of the passengers loaded. She left the sea cave and raced back to the dungeon. From there, she followed the mage-lit candles along the route to the laboratory; every light that flared as she approached told her she was going the right way. She was panting for breath by the time she reached what had to be the final turn. She had been paying attention when the gray man carried her this way; she *knew* she was in the right place. She rounded the corner—

And the floor *lurched* beneath her, tossing her sideways into the wall.

She flung her arms out to catch herself. The blocks ground against one another again, the noise so loud she expected one of them to squeeze itself free right in front of her.

She counted to ten silently, then took another step.

Nothing moved. Nothing trembled.

Another step. Down the corridor a candle sparked and flamed.

Then: a distant thump.

The walls trembled. Sand pattered from the ceiling.

It had been so easy to get back into the Winter Blade. So easy to get the keys and find Izzy and the others. Too easy, when everybody in the city knew the fortress had ways of protecting itself. She couldn't ignore it now.

There was something in the fortress that knew she was here.

Again: *thump.*

She couldn't let it stop her. She took another step.

Thump.

Mara squared her shoulders, gripped the murk-light in one hand and keys in the other, and ran down the corridor toward the laboratory.

Thump. Thump. Thump.

She rounded a curve in the hallway and another lurch slammed her into the wall, knocking her feet out from under her. She scraped her knees raw on the stone.

Thump.

The door was just ahead.

Thump.

Mara pushed herself up.

There was somebody waiting at the door. But it wasn't the gray man, and it wasn't the Lord of the Muck.

Bindy's eyes glinted in the glow from Mara's murk-light.

"Mara," she said, smiling. "Thank you for showing me the way."

20

The Truth
and the Lies

"*I've been trying to get into this fortress for two years.*" Bindy tapped the laboratory door, then listened as though she expected it to answer. "There were always rumors of a secret way inside, one hidden so long by magic nobody could remember it. I thought you'd be gone by now."

Mara clutched at her side, gasping for breath. "I can't— my friend— What are you doing here? You said you were going to Quarantine Island!"

Even as she asked the question, she understood. The shimmer of magic in the sea cave: that had been an obscuring spell to hide Bindy's boat. Bindy must have been on the water just like Driftwood, waiting for Mara's light to come bobbing out. She had found her way to the laboratory while Mara was releasing the prisoners. That was why she had parted ways with the pirates earlier. She had her own plans for the evening.

"How did Renata find it?" Bindy asked.

"She didn't find it," Mara retorted, stung. The Lady may have shared her family secret, but it was Mara who had found the passage and swam not once but twice through that terrifying throat of stone. "All she did was tell me where to look. I found it myself. With *magic*."

Bindy was still examining the door; she showed no sign of being impressed by Mara's accomplishment. "It certainly took her long enough to figure it out. If she'd waffled another day or two I was going to send her an engraved invitation. This is his laboratory, isn't it?"

Mara's thoughts were all jumbled up, confusion and worry and fear twisting around like eels. Bindy was saying that *she* was the reason the Lady had sent Mara to the Winter Blade. But the Lady had sent Mara into the Winter Blade because she and Professor Kosta believed the Lord of the Muck was responsible for dumping the bones in the sea. They had been wrong about what the bones were, but not wrong about who had discarded them. It was the bones that had started it all.

Mara had found the bones because a Roughwater boy on the docks told her where to look.

He had approached her with his tale during her afternoon off, when she was visiting Fish Hook. She had never

seen him before, nor since. He hadn't said which fisherman he worked for. She hadn't asked. Mara thought of
how sullen he had been, how scowling. He could have
been working for Bindy all along, but maybe not because
he liked to. Maybe he wanted something too. The old
Roughwater woman in the Muck's dungeon had been worried about her grandson.

Mara knew that just because two people were from
the same foreign land didn't mean they were related. But
she also knew better than to trust coincidences. It wasn't
so hard to imagine: an old woman stolen away, a boy who
wanted to find her, and Bindy with a plan. She had known
where the Muck was dumping his cast-off experiments—
she had been watching him for two years—and she had
sent the Roughwater boy to point Mara in the right direction. She had known Mara would bring the bones to the
Lady, and the Lady would look to the Winter Blade for the
source.

"What *are* you doing here?" Mara asked. "If you wanted
to come along, you could have just asked."

Bindy did not answer. "I wonder what Londe has
learned about locking songs since we used to sneak into
the kitchens at the Citadel for a midnight snack." She
pressed her ear against the laboratory door, listening. "Has
he got a menagerie in there? Is that a parrot?"

Mara was still holding the keys. "My friend is in there.
We have to help him."

"Of course we do," Bindy said absently. She poked at the hinges of the door. In the candlelight, her features looked sharper, the shadows of her fingers long and spindly. "I must say, this fortress isn't as impressive as I'd always imagined. Rather cold and grim, isn't it? I wonder what happened to—"

A loud thump interrupted her, and the walls shook. Mara spun around and raised her murk-light. That thump had been louder and closer than the others.

"What is that?" she asked, her voice wavering.

Bindy was looking down the corridor with narrowed eyes, her lips pursed. That was the look she wore when she didn't know the answer but also didn't want to admit it.

"Do you remember how this fortress was first built?" Bindy asked.

"The founders," Mara said absently. She didn't know why it mattered. She couldn't tear her gaze away from the long hallway. Her murk-light and the flickering candles barely penetrated the darkness. "They made it with their stone magic."

"It's the very oldest kind of magic," Bindy said. "Stone remembers magic better than anything else. It never truly forgets the songs it hears. Which is a good thing for us, because if magic faded from stone the same as it faded from water or wind, this entire city would have crumbled into the sea centuries ago."

That was what Mara had been taught all her life, in

every story and every song, beginning with her mother's murmured bedtime tales: the only stone magic in the city was that which the founders had cast themselves. It was as good as extinct, no more than a magical artifact from centuries ago.

But Gerrant of Greenwood might disagree.

"There is so much magic in these old stones, and the people who built this fortress were vicious," Bindy said. "The island does not take kindly to intruders."

"Everybody knows *that*," Mara said impatiently. She wondered if Bindy had always tried to explain the obvious in a tone that made it seem profound. Maybe Mara had been too young to recognize it for what it was. "But this didn't happen when I was here before. I was here for hours and—"

And she *had* heard something that first night. Something strange and unexplained. Not the distant song and loud clanging door, but after that, when she had sung her mother's song while searching for the laboratory. Right before she had found Gerrant of Greenwood.

"And?" Bindy said.

Mara licked her lips. "So it's just us being here that's making it—do that? Whatever it is?"

"There are surely nasty curses at work in this fortress that have been here for hundreds of years," Bindy said. "Who's to say what wakes them from their long slumber?"

That wasn't an answer, Mara thought. It wasn't an answer because Bindy didn't know the answer. Had she always mistook Bindy's cageyness for wisdom?

"Maybe it was a spell," Mara said. She drew her gaze away from the dark tunnel to look at Bindy. The longer the fortress was quiet, the more nervous she became. "Maybe it was a song the stones remember."

Bindy didn't laugh or dismiss the idea as childish. She wasn't looking down the corridor anymore. She was looking straight at Mara, her expression both knowing and guarded.

"It's possible," she said, as though granting Mara a favor by considering it. "It may be that a pretty little song sung in just the right way was enough to wake the spells in the stone."

Mara's whole head was filled with a low, insistent buzzing. "What a pretty little song." Words she would never forget, for they had been the first sign of warmth and kindness after her parents died. She had been huddling in the crypts of the Ossuary, surrounded by darkness and cold and walls made of ancient bones, singing to herself in the way little children do when they wish their mothers were there to comfort them. *My heart is bound but my dreams are free.* Bindy had appeared in the darkness, first her lantern's light in dancing yellow, then her shadow, then her voice: "What a pretty little song."

It had been a spell all along. Mara hadn't known, all the years she had been humming that old sailors' song to herself, but Bindy had. She had heard a spell one night in the catacombs, and she had searched until she found the source.

Thump.

Mara stared down the hallway again. Something moved in the darkness, just beyond the reach of the murk-light.

Thump.

Something large, and slow, and coming closer.

Thump.

A stone fortress. A stone spell. A stone man.

And in the water: bags full of stones. The Lord of the Muck had weighted down his cast-off experiments with stones from the Winter Blade. It was the *stones* that had answered when Mara sang her mother's song. Not the bones. What she had heard was magic answering from pieces of the fortress itself. She didn't know why her mother's song called to the Winter Blade, but she knew she was right.

"We had better hurry," Bindy said. "Give me the key."

Mara's grip was so tight her palm was sweaty, her arm trembling.

"Mara. Give me the key."

Fish Hook was in the laboratory. Bindy could open the door with a spell. Think, Mara told herself frantically. *Think.* The shadow in the hallway was moving closer, slowly but inexorably. She had to ask. She might not get another chance.

"Did you know?" she said.

Mara's voice was small, and small it might have remained if Bindy had turned to look at her. But Bindy studied the laboratory door as though it was the most fascinating thing she had ever seen.

"Did you know my mother's song was a spell?" Mara said, louder now, a thunder-low gathering of anger giving her courage. "Did you know when you heard me singing in the crypts? Is that why you helped me? It was only because of the song?" Her voice cracked on the last word.

"You're being ridiculous," Bindy said. "Give me the key."

"I want to know. Tell me the truth."

"We don't have time for this," Bindy said.

"Did you ever take me back to Gravetown?" Mara asked. "Did you ever ask if I had any other family? Did you even try?"

"You had no family left. Nobody wanted you. Give me the key." Bindy's voice lashed like a whip. She held out her hand and snapped her fingers.

But Mara did not jump to obey, as she would have two years ago. She remembered how Bindy had taken her straight from the Ossuary to the shop on the Street of Whispering Stones. She remembered Bindy telling her that her parents were gone and this was her home now. She remembered promising with the solemnity of a grief-stricken five-year-old not to tell anybody where she had come from. Bindy had told her she had nowhere else to go, and Mara had believed her.

"You must have been so disappointed," Mara said quietly, "when you found out I only knew the one song."

Deny it, she thought, staring hard at Bindy. Deny it. Tell me you were never disappointed. Tell me you never wanted the song. Tell me you only ever wanted a little girl to raise and teach and care for and love.

"Oh," said Bindy, her voice as soft as Mara's, the two of them almost whispering. "You have no idea what a disappointment you were. I tried for years to pry more out of your little mind, all for nothing. It was a worthless song anyway."

Tears sprung into Mara's eyes. She scrubbed them away, angry and embarrassed and hurting all over. Instead of handing over the keys, she searched through the clump for the right one. Fish Hook needed help, and Bindy was Mara's only hope of getting into the laboratory. Even with all the unexpected, surprising, magical things Mara had done in the past few days, the simple task of unlocking a spelled door was beyond her.

She put the key in the lock and turned it. The door didn't budge, so she stepped back to give Bindy space. When Bindy brushed against her, Mara flinched. Only a day ago she'd flung her arms around Bindy, so relieved to find her alive, so sure Bindy would help. But it had all been a lie. Bindy had been using Mara all along.

After a few seconds of studying the door, Bindy began to sing. Mara recognized one of the unlocking spells Bindy used to break into crypts at the Ossuary. Her song and the Muck's locking spell intertwined, like instruments slowly falling into tune, one rising to a higher pitch and a faster melody, the other slowing to meet it.

Thump.

The shape in the corridor was moving again.

Thump.

There was a snap, like a string breaking, and the locking spell was broken. Bindy opened the door. Mara pushed by her to run. She sprinted across the laboratory to the Muck's worktable, where Fish Hook was lying with his hands and feet bound in the leather cuffs.

"Fish Hook!"

"Mara?" Fish Hook craned his head toward her. His voice was a weak, rasping croak.

Mara skidded to a stop beside the table. There were bloodstained bandages on Fish Hook's neck, a swath wrapped around his head, and she couldn't see what was underneath. She reached for the scraps of cloth, then withdrew her hand quickly when Fish Hook hissed.

"Did he hurt you? What did he do?"

"Don't know," Fish Hook said. The words sounded as

though they caused him terrible pain. He coughed; it was a horrible, racking sound. He strained against the bindings, but weakly.

"Stop squirming and let me rescue you." Mara swatted Fish Hook's shoulder softly, well away from the bandages on his neck. He could still talk. It wasn't like the gray man. It couldn't be like that.

But there were dashed ink lines around his eyes that disappeared beneath the bandage across his forehead and black-thread stitches closing cuts on the sides of his face. Just under the edge of the bandage, where the motion of his head had pushed it up, Mara spied a gleam of iridescent greenish blue. She swallowed painfully.

"Almost free," she said. She opened the last cuff and helped him sit up. She wanted to throw her arms around him, but he looked so shaky she was afraid she would knock him over.

"Londe may not be here now, but I'm sure he'll be back soon." Bindy was making a slow circuit around the laboratory, peering curiously at the Muck's experiments. The little winged lizard followed her with chirping, hopping steps.

Fish Hook started to say something, flinched in pain, and pointed instead.

"That's Bindy," Mara said.

"But she's—"

Mara interrupted before he could hurt himself. "Supposed to be dead, yes."

Bindy laughed. "I've always found it so very tiresome to be what everybody says you're supposed to be."

"She wants the fortress," Mara said to Fish Hook. "That's why she pretended to be dead. She's wanted the Winter Blade all along."

From the corridor outside came a thunderous *THUMP.* The room shook. A cage full of parakeets squawked in panic.

"We have to go," Mara said. "Izzy and the others are already out. I'll explain everything later. Can you walk?"

Fish Hook slid down from the table and gave Mara a shaky nod.

"Then we're leaving," Mara said.

"Not until you hear what I have to say," Bindy said. "You'll like it, I promise."

Mara dragged Fish Hook toward the door. "I'm not listening. You lied to me about being dead and you lied about wanting to help people. You lied to me about everything! I'm not listening to you anymore."

Bindy only smiled. "Mara, don't you see? All of this is ours now. I'll make you a proper apprentice, now that you're ready for it."

That brought Mara up short. "I'll be your apprentice?"

"Isn't that what you've always wanted?" Bindy said.

For as long as Mara could remember, she had wanted to learn magic. When she was little and her parents were still alive, she would make up playful songs, pretending they were spells. She had never heeded her mother's warnings that magic was not the solution to all problems. She would demand to hear stories about great mages over and over again; her mother, laughing, always complied. Even when her parents were gone, when Bindy was gone, when she was living on the streets, when she was toiling in the fish market, through every challenge and change she'd faced, she had never given up the dream of learning magic. When she had dove into the inky black water at the base of the Winter Blade only a few days ago, she had been driven in part by the Lady's promise.

It had always been magic. That had never changed. She didn't think it ever would.

But *she* had changed. She wasn't five years old anymore, so desperate for a home she would believe anything Bindy said without question.

"Why?" she asked.

Bindy looked at her. "Why?"

"Why do you want me as an apprentice?"

"Don't you want to learn magic?" Bindy asked, baffled, as though Mara was speaking nonsense. "Hasn't that been what you've wanted all your life?"

"I know what I want," Mara said. "But you could have made me your apprentice at any time. You could have come back for me. And you didn't."

It was another chance—not for Mara, but for Bindy to explain herself. Mara stared at Bindy so hard her eyes felt hot. She was on a precipice, a strong ocean wind pushing her toward the edge. All she needed was a sign that Bindy was sincere, and Mara could say yes.

There was another ominous *THUMP* from the hallway. She only needed Bindy to answer.

"We haven't time for this, Mara," Bindy said. "Stop playing games. Are you with me or not? If you know any useful songs, now would be the time to use them."

Mara had not thought her hopes and her heart could crumple any more than they already had. Bindy didn't want an apprentice. She didn't want Mara. It had only ever been the song.

In the end, Mara did not find it such a difficult decision after all.

"I am *never* going to work with you," Mara said to Bindy, then she grabbed Fish Hook's hand. "We have to go!"

She ran, Fish Hook right behind her, but she knew even before they reached the door that it was too late. A shadow filled the doorway, just beyond the reach of the candlelight. It stood there for a long moment, agonizingly still.

Then slowly, slowly, as though reaching deep for great effort, it moved forward.

THUMP.

The stone man stood in the doorway like a sentry. His broad-shouldered bulk blocked the entrance completely.

There was no way out.

The candlelight caught the yellow gemstone eyes, twin bright sparks blazing in his dull gray face. Fish Hook gasped in shock, and Bindy's jaw dropped.

"Gerrant," said Bindy, her voice oddly strangled. "You— are you—all this time?"

Mara had never heard Bindy sound like that. She had never seen her gaping at something with such wide eyes, so utterly at a loss for words. It was so unfamiliar it took Mara a moment to understand what was happening.

Bindy was scared.

"Mara," Bindy said softly. Her voice shook; she sounded like somebody else entirely. "What have you done?"

Fish Hook made a soft, surprised noise. Mara looked to see where he was pointing. When Bindy realized where they were staring, she turned as well.

In the large upright mirror, thick smoke was swirling and billowing. The smoke parted and thinned, and Mara's breath caught.

The mirror spied into Renata Palisado's tower laboratory, but the room looked as though a storm had passed through. There were bones scattered over the tabletop and on the floor; a few of the smaller ones had been crushed. A bench had been overturned, vials shattered and jars toppled, books and scrolls strewn about wildly. There was no sign of Feather or the Lady. The horned skull, the first Mara had found, lay in a puddle of rainwater on the floor.

Fish Hook made a sound in his throat and squeezed Mara's hand.

The glass shimmered like water. Something moved at the side of the mirror, almost out of sight. The edge of a sleeve, the bend of a knee. A hand appeared. The fingers were long and stained with ink.

"Curious," said Bindy, her voice soft.

The hand tapped the mirror from the other aside. The glass rippled like a puddle disturbed by a raindrop. The hand became an arm, the arm a shoulder, and the Lord of the Muck came into view.

He reached into the mirror from the other side. There was a sound like a splash, but slower, droplets falling one after another to strike the stone floor. The Muck's arm broke through the surface, and the mirror shattered. The glass changed to water as it fell, melting and liquefying just before splashing to the floor.

He stepped through the rippling glass with one foot, then the other, hunching his shoulders through the frame. Glass broke all around him and turned to water in a sudden, brief cascade.

The Muck shook droplets from his sleeves. "Hello, Belinda. It's good to see you again."

21

The Battle of
Water and Bone

A pool of water spread across the floor at the Muck's feet.

"That's a neat trick," Bindy said, the tightness in her voice belying the casual words. "Bit messy, though."

"Thank you," said the Muck. "I've not had a chance to test it before. I wasn't quite sure it would work. It used to be quite common, if the history books are to be believed. Can you imagine how tiresome that must have been, mages splashing through each other's chambers like seals any time they fancied a visit?"

Water sloshed around his shoes as he stepped forward. With another step the water began to harden, and by the time he had taken a third, the puddle was solidifying into glass again.

"I don't recall inviting you into my home," he said. "How did you—"

The Muck's mouth dropped open in shock when he spotted the stone man.

"How—what—*what is he doing here?*"

Bindy raised a single eyebrow, but there was obvious unease behind the casual expression. "You don't know? Was it not your spell that trapped him?"

The Muck's mouth worked, lips opening and closing. "I didn't—the fortress—the founders—how can he move? He's never moved!"

"Ah. Not your work after all," Bindy said tightly. "I suppose you haven't had time to learn all the tricks your new home has hidden away. Too busy betraying a friend. Stealing her songs. Leaving her for dead."

The Muck drew his gaze away from the stone man to glare at Bindy. "Don't be petty. I seized an opportunity. You would have done the same if only you'd thought of it first."

"Ah. Well." Bindy's lips curved into a slight smile. "You're not wrong about that."

Mara's skin prickled all over. They were only talking, talking and watching each other warily, like seagulls eyeing the same dead fish. But the air crackled between them like storm clouds before the first strike of lightning.

"It was reckless to come here," the Muck said. "When I have succeeded, and I am transformed, the city will be mine to command as I please. Do you truly believe you can stand against me?"

Bindy opened her mouth. Mara expected another sharp comment, an insult or a jest.

Instead, Bindy began to sing.

The Muck spun around to face her. "Belinda. Don't be rash."

Bindy's voice rose, her song growing stronger. Mara heard familiar words from an old funeral song—*"Sail, sail away my love, across the darkest sea"*—mixed in with words from the founders' language. It set to a repetitive chant she didn't know, but she thought it might be a rowing chant. It wasn't pretty, it wasn't elegant, but it was powerful, and when Bindy changed the words—*"Sail, sail to me, return across the darkest sea"*—the air began to quiver. Mara felt every note in her teeth, in her bones.

She heard a splash behind her. She turned to look.

On a high shelf against the laboratory wall, a large glass specimen jar began to rock back and forth. The fat black eels inside, dead and dissected only moments before, were slithering now, turning and wriggling. On another shelf, fish eyes rolled around and around in a jar, looking in every direction at once. From a table by the window a vase toppled and shattered; a spidery mass of birds' feet scrabbled over the wreckage.

Bindy's voice rose sharply: "*Sail, sail to me, my children, leave this mournful sea.*"

The eels thrashed against the glass, tipping the jar from the shelf. It shattered on the floor. The Muck took a startled step backward. His eyes were wide, his mouth open in surprise.

Another jar crashed on the stones, and still Bindy was singing: "*Sail, sail to me, my children, return your light to me.*"

Mara had never seen such magic before. She had watched Bindy sing to skeletons of mages to learn their secrets, to bones from creatures to borrow their instincts, to sharks' teeth and whales' bones and human skulls. But she had never seen this.

Bindy was waking the dead.

All throughout the laboratory, in the specimen jars and glass tanks, across the shelves and worktables, dead things were sloshing and splashing in answer to her voice. The commotion rattled the living creatures: the little winged lizard scampered around the room frantically, chirping and fluttering its wings. In its tank the lonely octopus stirred, white suckers pressing against the glass, arms lifting the lid as it searched for escape. Birds squawked angrily in their cages, loosing clouds of downy feathers.

"What do we do?" Fish Hook whispered.

"I don't know!" Mara admitted helplessly.

They couldn't get past the stone man, and there was no other way out of the laboratory. She considered wild, dangerous, *stupid* ideas—breaking the windows, swimming for the surface. They would never make it. The water rushing into the chamber would crush them. Mara looked around and around, searching for anything that could help, any ideas at all.

The Lord of the Muck hadn't moved when Bindy's song began animating the dead specimens. Now, as he watched, his expression twisted from surprised to calculating. His hands hung idly at his sides. His lips moved. He tilted his head to one side. He took a breath, and he muttered something. To Mara it sounded like *"aahgraal mmumgraal,"* grumbling syllables from the language of the founders, words she couldn't even begin to understand. The spell wasn't very loud, but the notes shuddered through the air, and Bindy stumbled.

It was so slight Mara nearly missed it. Bindy didn't fall or trip, only swayed a bit before catching her balance. The Muck's voice rose to sing the powerful spell-song—those same syllables again and again, with slight variations each time. A new sound joined the sloshing and rattling of the dead things: the gentle scrape of glass on stone.

Bindy looked down.

The shards of glass on the floor softened into droplets, the droplets gathered into larger globs, the globs into puddles. The Muck kept singing, his voice rising and falling with an easy, rolling melody. In the tanks and jars that had not yet toppled, liquids of every color began to churn rhythmically in time with his song. It was water magic. The Muck was singing to the water all around them, bringing it under his control, just as Bindy was doing with the dead creatures.

Bindy narrowed her eyes. She began to sing again, louder than before: *"Sail, sail back to me, and leave the darkest sea."*

The wriggling knot of preserved eels crept across the floor toward the Muck, leaving a trail of pungent green liquid. A bucket of crabs tipped over and skittered noisily after them.

"Sail, sail to me, my children, and leave the dead seas empty!"

The Muck paid no attention to Bindy's song. He just kept singing his own spell, that rolling muddle of syllables and piecing high sounds, the language of the founders, angrier and more commanding than Mara had ever heard it. The Muck had not transformed himself yet, but he sounded as though he believed it inevitable. The certainty in his spell-song chilled Mara to her core.

In a fish tank to his left, the water sloshed from one side to the other, back and forth, until the Muck sang out two ringing words—and these Mara understood perfectly.

"Seize her!"

The water froze momentarily at one side, then it twisted and stretched and reached out of the tank, forming into a long-fingered hand of shining, greenish liquid. The hand grabbed the shelf and tipped its own tank over; it smashed to the floor.

The Muck's song changed, shifted back to the language of the founders, and took on a storm-swift energy. All across the laboratory water rose into a rolling wave. Knee-high and roaring, the wave swept over the eels, over the crabs, over the flopping, slipping, struggling creatures, before it crashed into Mara and Fish Hook, knocking them over, and slammed into Bindy's legs. She didn't lose her footing, but her song faltered. Before she could even take a breath, the wave gathered again on the other side of the room.

Fish Hook helped Mara to her feet. They needed an escape. A plan. *Anything.* The only way out was the door, and that was still blocked by the stone man. Bindy's bone magic hadn't moved him. The Muck's water magic had no effect.

The scrambling crabs reached the Muck and nipped at his ankles. He swept them away, but even as he stepped out of reach a slither of eels surrounded him. He kicked at them clumsily, trying to shake several crabs free from his trouser cuffs. His mouth twisted in a disgusted scowl.

Bindy's song fluttered briefly with laughter, and she danced through the puddles, snapping out a bit of spell-song. The wired-together bones of a sunfish stirred above the Muck's worktable, scraping across the shelf, bone dragging on wood. The big skull, pushed along by its inching spine, nudged a stack of books over the edge of the table. Mara recognized them: Bindy's journals, the ones the Muck had stolen, her cherished handwritten record of all of her bone magic.

Bone magic. Water magic.

A man of stone.

"Oh," Mara whispered.

Fish Hook looked at her, his mouth forming the silent question: What?

Mara began to whisper the words to herself. It wasn't going to work. She wasn't even a real mage. You have to be bossy, Bindy had always said, and Mara felt anything but bossy. She felt trapped, with two powerful mages battling around her, Fish Hook hurt and scared at her side, water moving with a mind of its own, dead things dancing to Bindy's spell, and just one idea for how to get out.

It was only a song, an old sailors' song, but it was all she had.

She began to sing: *"Over the sea and under the sky, my island home it waits for me."*

The noise in the laboratory was deafening and chaotic: crashing bones and sloshing water, wet dead creatures and angry living ones, and voices rising in ever more urgent songs. Neither Bindy nor the Muck spared Mara the slightest glance. They were singing so loudly they didn't even hear her. But it didn't matter. Her song was having no effect. The stone man remained a statue. All she was doing was throwing empty words into the cacophony. Her voice would never be stronger than the voices of two trained mages. She hadn't even meant to call to the stone before, so how would she ever be able to convince it to do what she wanted—

But that *wasn't* what she needed to do, was it?

Mara stopped singing. You have to be bossy, Bindy always said. To make dead creatures scurry as though they were alive again. To make puddles of spilled water gather into hands and whirlpools and waves. To make elements and creatures and objects *obey*.

Mara didn't want the stone to obey her. She wanted it to remember.

Somewhere deep inside, the stone knew it wasn't supposed to be stone. It wasn't a statue blocking their escape; it was Gerrant of Greenwood, a powerful mage, caught and trapped by magic so ancient nobody knew how it worked.

Stone remembers: that's what Bindy had said. Gerrant was a part of the fortress now—and the fortress had responded to Mara's song. Even broken pieces of it, chipped away and drowned in the sea, they had heard her song, and they had answered.

Maybe somewhere behind those yellow gemstone eyes, Gerrant of Greenwood remembered the green hills and deep valleys he'd left behind. Maybe he remembered looking out over the city from above, marveling at how small the boats looked sailing between the islands, how the vast ocean gleaming with sunrise took his breath away. Maybe he remembered learning magic from hedge witches in remote green meadows. Following the muddy road out of the mountains. Standing on the black-sand beach for the first time.

Her voice small at first, but gathering courage, Mara began to sing. The first song that came to mind was the silly rhyming song her father had sung that morning they climbed the south-facing slope of Greenwood to look over the city.

"Ask the shepherd with her staff if her sheep are well.
Ask the ranger with her ax for a tree to fell.
Ask the mason with her chisel why stone rings a bell.
Ask the digger with her spade if the dead feel swell."

But as she sang, other Greenwood Island songs came back to her. Woodsmen's spells and children's rhymes, farmers' ballads and pub songs, she sang everything she could remember.

*"The lad and his dog came to Green Inn, oh hey, oh
  hey!
The girl and her dog came to Green Inn, oh hey!"*

She wasn't a Gravetown girl anymore, but she wasn't
singing for herself. She was singing for the memories trapped in the ancient stone, for the man who had
become part of the fortress, for the boy he had been and
the mage he'd grown to be. She remembered her mother
on a rainy morning, singing as rain drummed on the roof,
singing and saying, "Who are you to say the difference
between music and magic if it's not your heart a song is
meant to stir?"

*"The mage and his bird came down from the hills, oh
  hey, oh hey!
The mage and her bird came down from the hills, oh
  hey!"*

And Mara remembered feeling light, so light she
might fly, when her mother twirled her around the little
house at the foot of the green hills. Her voice grew stronger as she remembered more and more. Songs flowed
more easily from her tongue. Her voice rang through the
room, carrying over a sudden hush in the raging magical
battle.

> *"To the inn on the river in the green, green dell, oh*
> *hey!"*

Bindy and the Muck had fallen quiet.

"To the green, green dell," Mara said, her voice dropping to a whisper.

In the doorway, the stone man turned to look at her.

22

A Song for a Stone

A hush fell over the laboratory. The stone man's yellow eyes glittered. For the first time Mara thought she saw something other than sadness in them.

Then: "What are you doing?" shouted the Lord of the Muck. All the animals and birds began screeching and squawking again. "By the founders, child, *what have you done?*"

Mara felt a burst of pride. The Muck was afraid of *her* song, *her* magic. This powerful mage who had caused so much fear and pain for others, and he was looking from Mara to the stone man, back to Mara, with an expression of pure panic on his face.

"Stop that! You don't know what you're doing! You have

no idea—" The Muck yelped in surprise as the sunfish skeleton scuttled right up to his feet. He kicked at it frantically and sent it clattering across the floor.

All the while, Mara kept singing. The Greenwood songs had gotten the stone man's attention, but they weren't breaking the founders' spell. The spell-song needed to be stronger. *She* needed to be stronger. There was so much noise around her it was hard to concentrate, with the birds squawking and animals chittering and water sloshing, and over it all Bindy's singing, never stopping, never breaking, keeping the dead things dancing—

Bindy's songs. The ones she was singing right now. *That's* what Mara needed.

Bindy had turned a funeral song around to call the dead back to life. Mara had to do the same, only she had to call a living person out of stone.

She changed her song again. She took the words from the Greenwood Island songs, from Gerrant's home, but she wove them into the inside-out funeral song Bindy was using to wake the bones. Where Bindy had called the bones with *"Sail, sail back to me, back across the darkest sea,"* Mara sang, *"Wake, wake, from cold dark stone to valleys of green."* Where Bindy made the dead things dance with *"Sail, sail to me, my children, and leave the dead seas empty!"* Mara urged the stone to *"Walk, walk the trails of green, along the rivers and through the trees!"*

The longer she sang, the more certain she became. She

could feel when the song was going wrong with a flatness that sounded like cloth in her ears—"free" when she ought to have said "green," a high note where a low one should fall. But when she got it right there was a giddy flutter high in her chest, and she kept singing.

The stone man turned his head. He clenched his fingers into fists and released them. First one arm bent at the elbow, then the other. The magic was working. He was breaking free of the curse!

She was so caught up in her song she didn't notice the dead things thrashing toward her until Fish Hook rasped, "Mara, look out!"

A tangle of spiny lobsters and slumping jellyfish had already surrounded her. She yelped in pain as they stung and nipped at her feet, hard enough to draw blood. She slipped on a jellyfish, lost her balance, and toppled into a wooden table, knocking over a jar of fish eyes with the jolt. Bindy was barking commands at them—harsh, snappish bits of song, stirring them to a greater and greater frenzy. Somewhere above the cacophony stone ground against stone, and with it came a sharp cracking sound.

Fish Hook lunged at the largest of the lobsters. "Keep singing!"

Mara sang even louder, doing her best to drown out Bindy's voice.

The sunfish skeleton clattered toward her, with the great toothy jaw of a shark snapping right behind it. Bindy was good, to be sure, but Fish Hook had worked in the fish market for most of his life. He plucked and kicked the dead things away from Mara as quickly as he could, flinging them across the room and laughing out loud when one of them struck Bindy in the face.

Bindy's expression turned thunderous. She stopped singing abruptly.

When she uttered another spell, it was completely different. Lower, slower, darker. Mara didn't understand any of the words; it was a language she didn't know at all. She tried to ignore it, tried to focus on her own spell-song, but she felt a steady drumming of fear in her heart and a breathless tightening in her chest. Bindy was singing louder and louder—

No, that wasn't it at all. The laboratory was going quiet.

One by one the reanimated dead things fell still. They slumped where they'd scrambled, collapsed into piles of wired-together bones, dropped out of the air in tufts of feathers. The living animals began to fall silent too. Fish Hook turned to Mara, his mouth open in question, but when his lips moved no sound came out.

Mara tried to ask, "What's wrong?"

Tried, but failed, because she couldn't speak. She felt herself forming the words, taking in the air and moving her lips and her tongue, but no matter what she did, she couldn't make a sound.

"There," said Bindy. "That's better."

Mara tried to shout at her, tried to scream, but she couldn't make a sound. It felt as though there was a hand on her throat, lightly squeezing out all sound. Bindy had taken away her voice, taken away her spell-song, taken away every sound in the laboratory except her own words.

"Oh, Mara," Bindy said. "You don't know what you're doing. Magic is not a toy for children to play with."

"I quite agree."

Mara blinked in confusion and spun around.

The reply came not from the Muck, who was struck as silent as Mara, but from Gerrant of Greenwood.

He flexed his fingers slowly, rolled his head from side to side, and worked his jaw. His motions were at first jerky and cautious, like a man waking from a dream. But as he moved, his skin softened, became pliable and brown again as the grayness faded. It started with the crown of his head, washed over his face, over his collar, and down his sleeves. The buttons on his shirt turned from gray to a shimmering pearl, the buckle of his belt from gray to silver, his trousers from gray to deep green. All of the gray drained from him like rainwater running over a statue.

His boots were last. As he lifted first one foot, then the other, they became battered brown leather again, and the laces an unexpected crimson.

"I would suggest," he said, his Greenwooder brogue like rocks rolling down a hillside, "that you direct your attention to the ceiling."

Bindy blinked twice, stunned. "What—"

"*Look.*" The Muck had broken free of her silencing spell. He was pointing upward.

Bindy looked up. Mara looked up. Fish Hook too.

Long, spidery cracks were spreading across the glass windows, and there were fractures in the stone buttresses. A trickle of seawater seeped through one crack and began to drip steadily. Chips of black stone snapped free and fell to the floor.

"What *have* you done, you stupid girl?" Bindy said.

"I—did I—" Mara stared in openmouthed shock. Had *she* done that? With her song?

Fish Hook slapped at her arm frantically, then did so again when Mara didn't respond. She tore her gaze away from the ceiling to see what he wanted. He pointed at Gerrant, who was staring at the floor in front of his feet.

Just a few inches away from the toe of one boot was a small stone figurine in the shape of a frog. It was poised on hunched legs, as though preparing to leap. Right behind it was another figurine, a fish flopped onto its side with its tail fin curved up toward the ceiling. Beside the fish, a hermit crab had been caught mid-scuttle with half its legs raised. Other animals were leaping over them, bounding through puddles of water, fleeing the laboratory through the door as though the room were on fire.

Mara stared at the little statues in confusion, but then Fish Hook was slapping her arm again, and tearing a strained word from his injured throat: "Look! *Look!*"

Mara looked again, and she understood.

They weren't figurines. They were animals turned to stone.

The curse that had fallen from Gerrant of Greenwood had not vanished. It had only slipped away from him, freed by Mara's song to slide across the floor, creeping like a gray shadow, changing everything it touched into stone. Animals both dead and alive, bones stirred by Bindy's song, the legs of a stool and a table, they were all transforming before Mara's eyes. The curse swept up the pedestal of one round table, bleaching the rich red wood to a dirty bland gray, then crawled across the books on the top, changing vellum and leather to stone. It caught a seagull by its clawed feet and froze the entire bird even as it tried to launch itself in a panic; the stone bird overbalanced and crashed to the floor, where it shattered over the newly stone skeleton of a snake. A stampede of beetles tumbled into one another and rolled over and over like marbles as the ones leading the charge turned to stone.

The only creatures that remained safe were those splashing through water, for the stone magic and the water magic seemed to repel each other.

Gerrant of Greenwood was backing away from the laboratory, his alarmed expression perfectly framed by the round doorway. Bindy was saying something—a song or a shout, Mara couldn't tell. There was a deafening noise like thunder; the cracks in the ceiling were spreading and water spurted through fissures in the glass windows.

There was a bellow from across the room. The Muck was singing again. There was no finesse in this song; it was all force, and all directed at the breaking ceiling.

Mara grabbed Fish Hook's hand. *"Run!"*

They sprinted for the door. The gray curse had overtaken too much of the floor, and the puddles and rivulets repelling its touch were too small for human feet, so they scrambled onto a long table and raced to the other end. There Mara jumped to a chair that was just beginning to turn to stone in its legs. But she hesitated. She didn't know if she could make it to the doorway. It was too far.

"Come on, child!" Gerrant shouted, holding out his arms. "I'll catch you!"

Mara glanced back at Fish Hook, waiting on the end of the long table.

"Go!" Fish Hook urged her. The pained rasp of his voice cut through the cracking, crashing chaos of the laboratory. "You can!"

Mara took a breath, bent her legs, and flung herself toward the door.

Gerrant caught her and pulled her through the doorway. He set her on her feet, and Mara scurried out of the way. Fish Hook leapt a second later. When he landed, with

Gerrant's help, he tumbled to the floor and let out a yelp of pain. He curled over onto his side, clutching his knee to his chest.

"What is it?" Mara asked, dropping to her knees beside him. "Did you sprain your ankle?"

"The chair," Fish Hook said through gritted teeth.

"What? What happened?"

Fish Hook extended his left leg.

His foot had turned to stone.

For a second Mara could only stare.

"No," she said. She felt numb and cold all over. "No, no, no—"

"We can't delay. The dome is collapsing." Gerrant took Mara by the elbow to lift her to her feet, then offered a hand to Fish Hook. "Look, child, it's not spreading, now that contact is broken."

He was right. The stone curse had encompassed Fish Hook's ankle, but it didn't seem to be reaching higher on his leg.

"Can you walk?" Gerrant asked.

"I think so," Fish Hook said, but on his first step he stumbled.

Gerrant picked him up easily—he was a big man, and Fish Hook was so skinny—and he said, "We must hurry."

Mara spared one last look through the round doorway. The animals were fleeing the laboratory, following a maze of puddles and spills to freedom. The winged lizard beat its wings powerfully to hop through the doorway, tumbling head over tail when it landed.

Bindy and the Muck were still flinging spell-songs at each other as stone and glass and water fell all around. They were oblivious to the gray curse spreading through the laboratory.

"Bindy!" Mara shouted. "The stone!"

She didn't wait to see if Bindy heard her. She ran.

The fortress shuddered as they fled. Stones blocks worked themselves loose from straining walls, and a rain of mortar sand pelted Mara's face. She ducked her head and sprinted. The winged lizard followed her, fluttering a few inches in the air with every bound. Soon they were overtaken by a stampede of frightened animals. The tiny goats bleated as they bounded along, snakes slithered with astonishing speed, long-legged rabbits raced ahead, and birds and bats beat their wings through the air.

Mara had just reached the vertebrate-stone archway when the singing in the laboratory cut off sharply.

She skidded to a stop.

There was a shout—a yelp of pain—quickly silenced.

For one long, uneasy moment, all Mara could hear was her own panting breath and the soft patter of falling sand. Gerrant had run ahead with Fish Hook to the sea cave. In the fading glow of the murk-light Mara saw a couple of rats scurrying toward freedom. They seemed to be the last of the animals.

Then, down the long corridor, Bindy began to sing.

Her voice was strong and clear and alone. The Muck had fallen silent. The restless stones were silent. There was only Bindy's song. It was powerful and eerie, echoing through the cavern and rising to beautiful, clear high notes before falling again. Mara didn't recognize any part of it. There were no familiar funeral songs to be found in that spell, no mourning dirges, no rowing chants. Everything about it was alien and strange and lovely.

Then the song stopped abruptly. There was no yelp of surprise, no shout for help. A single clear note rang in the air—then it was swallowed by the low, distant grind of stone against stone, and the fortress was silent.

23

The Waking Island

As she sprinted toward the sea cave, Mara *worried that* she had been wrong about the shimmer of spell she'd seen before. She could swim, but could Gerrant? Could Fish Hook, with his stone foot? And what about all the animals?

But finally one thing was going right. When she burst through the doorway, there was a rowboat waiting at the dock. At the oars was a broad-shouldered, red-haired Roughwater boy with pale skin and a smattering of freckles. Beside him was the white-haired woman from the dungeon. The other boat and the rest of the escaped prisoners were gone.

"Hey," Fish Hook rasped as Gerrant set him down.

"Yes, he's the one who told me about the bones, I know," Mara said. "Bindy put him up to it. She promised to help his grandmother."

"Gran made me wait for you," said the boy. The old woman gestured for Mara and the others to hurry into the boat. "She said you helped them, so we had to help you. She wouldn't let us leave with the others."

"Thank you," Mara said to the old woman.

She helped Fish Hook into the boat and jumped in after him, scooted over to make room for Gerrant. The little lizard hopped in with them, followed more clumsily by the tiny goats and a few terrified rabbits. The birds and bats were already swooping out of the cave as fast as their wings could carry them—and right on their tails came a terrible thunder rumbling through the entire fortress.

"How fast can you row?" Mara asked.

"Fast enough," the Roughwater boy said grimly.

The roar chased them through the sea cave and out of the fortress. It was a deafening crash of cracking stone and rushing water, like a storm, a river, a waterfall scouring away a mountain, so loud it hurt Mara's ears and filled her entire body with fear. That sound could only mean one thing.

The dome had collapsed. Water was rushing to fill the passages and dungeons below. There was no stopping the force of the sea.

The Roughwater boy rowed faster and faster, even as

the waves grew choppier and threatened to capsize the crowded boat. Mara clung tightly to the side with one hand and to Fish Hook with the other. The little goats bleated incessantly, and the winged lizard was nipping frantically at Fish Hook's arms.

A whirlpool formed at the base of the island, a yawning dark swirl of water. Fish Hook was shouting for the boy to row faster, and Gerrant was singing a spell with his strong voice, and the old woman's eyes were squeezed shut, and Mara couldn't breathe, she couldn't *breathe*, because the laboratory would be underwater by now, utterly drowned, with no way out, no possible escape, and she had left Bindy behind.

She had left Bindy behind.

Mara was losing her all over again, only instead of fear fading away to grief that would never ebb, this time it was hope crumbling under the weight of a betrayal that could never be righted, and that was so much worse.

Gradually, slowly, the waves calmed and the noise lessened. The whirlpool softened to a gentle sweep, but it did not entirely vanish. The sea was still pushing into the depths of the Winter Blade. Gerrant ended his spell-song, and Mara belatedly realized that he had been helping the Roughwater boy propel the boat away from the whirlpool. Without his magic they might have been sucked into the vortex. She should be impressed by magic that power-ful—she wanted to be impressed by it—but all she felt was cold and hollow inside.

The light rain had gathered into a heavy fog, and the night was damp and dark and cold. Already the Winter Blade was vanishing into the mist.

"Mara?" Fish Hook said.

She hurriedly wiped tears from her eyes. Fish Hook was sitting next to her, with the winged lizard clutched to his chest and his stone foot jutting awkwardly forward. She took in a determined breath and shoved the bleating little goats aside.

She gently touched Fish Hook's leg, and he flinched.

"It hurts?" Mara said, snatching her hand away.

"No," he said, but he didn't sound sure. "It feels . . . weird."

The transition from flesh to stone wasn't abrupt, but gradual, pliable skin giving way seamlessly to solid stone. Looking at it made Mara feel ill, her stomach twisted up with horror and guilt. She couldn't even begin to imagine how Fish Hook must feel. She had been so confident, so proud of herself, drawing on her mother's old spell-song to use it against two experienced and dangerous mages. But it had all gone out of her control, so far beyond what she had intended.

She reached out again, but stopped herself just before touching it.

"Are you sure it doesn't hurt?" she said quietly.

That time Fish Hook didn't answer. He was clinging to

the little winged lizard, shushing it softly when it chirped and wriggled.

"If I may ask," Gerrant of Greenwood began. He hesitated and cleared his throat. "How long has it been? How long was I—"

He didn't finish the question. He wasn't looking at Mara or Fish Hook or the Roughwater woman and her grandson. He was staring across the water to the lights of the city glowing weakly through the fog.

"Two years," Mara said.

A brief pause, then Gerrant said, "It passed like a dream. A terrible waking dream. Sometimes I convinced myself the darkness was a starless sky, but the sun never rose."

Mara bit her lower lip. She didn't know how to ask what she wanted to. "I don't understand how the curse trapped you when the tower was yours."

"I'm afraid I lost the tower before the curse overtook me," Gerrant said. "The Muck sneaked in and overpowered me in quite a mundane way—a blow to the head. I was unprepared for a challenge. Nobody had been interested in so long. When I awoke, he had already claimed the tower as his own. The protective spell set by the ancient builders overwhelmed me before I could fight back. That was always their greatest power, you know, their command of great elemental magic, such as turning flesh and blood to stone."

Gerrant tilted his head to the side, and at once Mara

heard it too: a low, low rumble emanating from the Winter Blade. The island was barely visible through the fog. But she could still feel it, that tremble in her chest. The stone grumbled and groaned for the span of only a few breaths, then fell silent again.

"The stone curse rolled over me like mist creeping over a lake, and all the while he watched with the most curious expression. He was not surprised. He knew the fortress would protect its master. Even so, he was awed to see such power at work—awed, I think, and eager." Gerrant's voice was little more than a whisper. "The Blade is a capricious old place. It obeys a new master as easily as a hungry dog will beg for scraps—as you demonstrated so well."

"What?" Mara said. "Me?"

"You sang the spell that woke me, did you not?"

"Yes, but . . ."

But Fish Hook's foot was turned to stone, and the spell that had slipped away from Gerrant had trapped a little frog and a frightened seagull and who knew how many other animals, and two powerful mages too. Mara could not shake that last clear note of Bindy's song from her mind. All she had wanted to do was escape with Fish Hook. She had never meant to hurt anybody.

But she had felt so powerful when she was singing her songs. Songs she didn't fully understand, calling upon magic she had no idea how to control. She couldn't stop thinking about what it had felt like to realize the Muck was afraid of her magic, to turn the same fear she'd felt back at him. She had not considered the consequences. She rubbed the center of her chest, trying to ease the echo of the rumbling stone. The sea was eerily calm, as though the weight of the fog had pressed all the waves flat.

"There's somebody here," the Roughwater boy said. He pointed away from the Winter Blade.

A soft circle of light was moving through the heavy fog: a murk-light held high by a passenger aboard the flatboat.

"Mara?" Izzy sounded like she was trying to shout without actually shouting. "Is that you?"

"We're here!" Mara answered.

A moment later Driftwood was there too; he had taken a few of the passengers into his boat.

Mara saw no sign of the black caravel, although Captain Amanta had promised they would be here. "Is it just you? Did the pirates come?"

"They did, and they've already gone. They took their girl and left," Driftwood said.

"Who is that?" Izzy asked, looking at Gerrant. "Did we leave someone behind?"

"I am Gerrant of Greenwood. I am Lord of the Winter Blade." A pause, and he added, "That is, I was. I don't know quite what I am now."

A murmur arose from the prisoners when they heard his name, and Mara spoke up quickly. "We should leave now. We'll go to Tidewater."

She didn't like being adrift on the water so near the Winter Blade. She didn't like how quiet the night was, and how dark. She just wanted to return to Tidewater Isle, to get the prisoners back to their homes and families, and try to forget the feel of the stone song thrumming in her chest.

The boats moved farther away from the fortress, and the spire of light that was Tidewater Isle grew closer. Soon Mara could make out the features of the palace: the tall windows ablaze with lamplight, the ornate balconies with torches flickering at every corner, its beautiful face so familiar it seemed impossible that it should still be here, exactly as she had left it hours ago. It felt like everything should have changed. Izzy and Fish Hook were safe now, but they had been hurt, and Mara still didn't know how badly. Bindy was gone. The Muck was gone. The Winter Blade was quiet.

"Look!" The shout came from a woman in Izzy's boat.

Mara whipped her head around. The woman wasn't looking back at the Winter Blade, nor at Tidewater Isle. She was pointing at the water.

At first Mara didn't see anything. She heard somebody ask, "What are we looking at?"

"I saw something," the woman said uncertainly. "I thought— There!"

The inky water between the boats rippled.

Mara's heart skipped.

"I don't see anything," a man said.

Another asked, "Why have we stopped?"

"There's something in the water," the woman said. "*Look*."

Even as she spoke, the scaled shape of a sea serpent rose from the water in a slick, glistening arch. It slid quickly into a dive, its scales reflecting the murk-lights with a greenish-black shimmer before it vanished.

One of the prisoners moaned. "He's sent his creatures after us."

"We'll never get away!" cried another.

Mara was staring so hard at the water her eyes began to burn. She barely heard the others shouting, all of them fearful and panicking as they searched the water for the serpent.

"Mara?" Fish Hook nudged her shoulder.

"It's okay," Mara said. Her heart was beating so fast she wasn't sure she could tell if it was fear or excitement. She repeated herself, loud enough to carry. "It's okay! It's not him!"

"You don't know that!" a woman said. "You don't know—"

She broke off with a sudden shriek.

A few feet from the side of Mara's boat, a sea serpent lifted its large scaled head above the water. Its green eyes glittered. She couldn't breathe. It was looking right at her. Right at *her*, and she knew without a doubt it was one of the serpents who had swum with her last night. The ones who had helped her find her way to land. The ones who had kept her company when she was most alone.

"Hello again," Mara said quietly.

The serpent dove away, and the brief, stunned silence was broken. She became aware of several noises all at once: Driftwood and Izzy speaking to each other from separate boats; a woman shouting that they were all going to die; whimpers of fear and gasps of alarm; Fish Hook saying her name in a strange, tense voice; and the soft exclamation, under his breath, from Gerrant of Greenwood, "*Oh.*"

"It's okay!" Mara shouted, trying to make her voice carry. "They won't hurt us!"

"*They?*" somebody yelped.

The water around them began to bubble and roil. Seawater slid from curved flanks of green and black scales, and tails flicked like whips. Serpents lifted their heads before diving to the left and right, front and back, and Mara realized, with growing trepidation, there were a great deal more than three of them this time. There seemed to be dozens, all swimming and tangling together, so many it was hard to tell where one ended and another began.

The boats rocked and swayed, jostled by the massive creatures. Mara clung to the side of the rowboat. The great churning mass of them filled her with fear in a way her three companions last night hadn't. There were so many. She had never imagined there could be so many—not anymore, not anywhere, and especially not right here in the city.

As she stared at the serpents, an eerie orange glow shimmered over the choppy water.

The Winter Blade wasn't dark anymore. Bright light shone from a row of windows high on the tower, and that light spread like sparks across the face of the fortress until the entire island was aglow. The light stung Mara's eyes, but she couldn't look away. Windows and doors that had been blocked for years, balconies and ramparts that had been hidden by magic, all of them were being cracked open and set aflame from within. The Winter Blade was transforming from a spire of shadow and darkness into a blazing tower of light.

With the blinding brilliance came a soaring spell-song, quiet at first, as though coming from a great distance, but it grew louder and louder as more and more light was revealed. It wasn't possible. The Muck was gone. Bindy was gone. Turned to stone, or drowned, there was no mage in the tower, nobody left to sing a spell.

Nobody left except the tower itself, and the echoes of magic trapped in its stones for hundreds of years. Another sound joined the song, something deeper and more terrible. It was the sound of breaking stone, cracking and grinding, so loud it was as though the heart of the island was shattering. Mara felt it both as a sound and as a spell, a noise in her ears and an ache in her chest, and her dread gathered.

Just when she was sure she couldn't bear it anymore, the

terrible explosion erupted from the Winter Blade.

Waves pulsed from the island, spreading in every direction, lifting the boats and dropping them again and again. Mara clutched at Fish Hook and he clung to her, and Driftwood was shouting, the freed prisoners crying out in fear, and Mara was certain they were going to capsize, and she didn't know if they were strong enough to swim, if *anybody* was strong enough to swim in waves like that. There was nothing for those at the oars to do but row with the force of the water, row as quickly and frantically as they could.

Then, as quickly as they had begun, the waves stopped.

The Winter Blade was silent and dark again.

But the sea was still glowing—this time from *below*.

There were orbs of yellow light ascending from the depths of the sea. The nervous cries of the prisoners fell to a hush. Nobody spoke. The lights grew brighter and brighter, like murk-lights rising, but the orbs were bigger than any murk-light. The silhouettes of the sea serpents twisted around the lights, casting the whole night into flickers of brightness and shadow. Warm light reflected from the fog, the choppy water glinted, and still the lights grew brighter.

"Mara," Fish Hook said. "*Mara*. The serpents, they're never . . ."

The first of the lights broke out of the water. It was a massive curve of glass in the shape of an oyster half shell, so thin and delicate it shimmered like a soap bubble.

Reclining in the shell was a woman. She had huge green eyes set in a face of gray and green scales, and her teeth were sharp and gleaming white. Her long arms ended in even longer fins, and a colorful frill of spines framed her face and shoulders. Her long, elegant tail flicked and curled as she looked around.

"The serpents are never alone," Mara whispered.

One by one, all around them, gleaming glass shells rose to the surface.

The founders had returned.

24

Mara the Stone-Mage

All around the boats, more and more founders were emerging from the sea. Two, three, four, so many Mara quickly lost count. Every one of their glass half shells was lit a warm golden color, filling the foggy night with a soft glow like firelight. Soon they dotted the sea like stars.

But it was the one nearest to Mara who captivated her attention. None of the paintings, statues, mosaics, or tapestries did the founders justice. They were so much more terrifying than Mara had ever imagined.

The founder's frill of spines looked blue when she turned one way, green when she turned another. Iridescent shades of blue and green shone so brightly from her scales that her entire body shimmered. She rested one of her long, bony hands on the side of the glass shell, the fins at her fingertips trailing in the water; the fins flashed to golden when she was in motion. Her eyes, so large for her thin face, so bright and uncanny and green, seemed to be lit from within.

Gerrant of Greenwood started to say something, then stopped. Fish Hook was gaping, and the winged lizard clinging to his shirt had fearfully tucked its head into the crook of his elbow. The escaped prisoners were silent. Nobody dared say a word.

High above the boats, people gathered on the balconies of Tidewater Isle. Shouts of surprise and alarm rang over the water. Mara thought she glimpsed Renata Palisado watching from a high balcony, but she didn't want to look away from the founder for more than a second. Shouts echoed within Tidewater's sea cave. Soon the whole city would know. The founders had returned.

When the founder spoke, Mara was so surprised she let out a terrified gasp.

The founder's voice was strange and musical, like a flute trying to capture the sounds of the storm at sea. Her words made the hair on the back of Mara's neck rise, raised goose bumps over her skin, an altogether strange experience—but not entirely unfamiliar. It felt, in a way, like magic. Like chasing the sensation of a spell drifting on underwater currents. Like stepping directly into the path of a powerful mage's song and standing still to withstand its power.

And Mara could not understand a single word. The founder sounded angry, exasperated, impatient, all of those things, none of them good, but Mara couldn't make any sense of it. The woman looked around in frustration, her voice rising as the humans shrank away in terror.

"We don't know their language anymore," Gerrant said, his voice breathless with awe. Mara spared a second to feel a bit sorry for how shocking this must be for him: to spend two years trapped as a statue, wake up in the middle of a mage battle, and escape to *this*. "It's been lost for centuries, and we could never speak it properly anyway. It's meant to be spoken underwater."

"I don't think that's their language," Driftwood said. He cleared his throat, cleared it again, then he spoke a few words, more hesitant than Mara had ever heard him.

"Ah," said Gerrant softly. "Yes. That might work."

After a moment Mara understood: Driftwood was speaking Sumanti. The language the first human settlers to the islands had spoken, in the days before the founders left the city.

The founder reacted immediately. She turned to stare at Driftwood, her collar spines flaring, her green eyes growing even more massive. She spat out another bunch of words. Driftwood listened intently, even as the people in Izzy's boat began to whisper and murmur.

"Can you understand her?"

"Is she threatening us?"

"What do they want?"

"Quiet." Driftwood's voice was low but firm. He said something else, and the founder answered. Driftwood nodded. "She's using Old Sumanti. I can't understand everything she's saying, but I recognize some of it."

Fish Hook tapped Mara's arm and pointed. There was light shining from the base of Tidewater Isle: a boat emerging from the sea cave, lit by lanterns on tall poles. It was the Lady's personal boat, with six rowers at the oars.

"What is she saying?" Izzy asked.

Driftwood said something else to the founder, who gestured impatiently, fin-fingered hands sweeping majestically to encompass the water, the city, the islands. Other founders spoke up, their musical voices coming together for a brief chorus, but Driftwood remained focused on the one nearest. She emphasized her words with a sharp nod that made the spines of her head flare like blades.

"She wants to know . . ." Driftwood began slowly, frowning. "I don't understand. I think she wants to speak to the emissary?"

"The emissary?" Izzy said, incredulous. "There hasn't been an emissary for hundreds of years!"

"What use do we have for an emissary without anybody down below?" somebody else said.

"Maybe she means the ruling families? Somebody important?"

"Or the High Mage?"

"Professor Kosta is coming with the Lady," Mara said quickly, before the founder could grow frustrated with so many people talking at once. The Lady's boat was drawing nearer, and the professor was standing at its prow. "She can help. She knows Old Sumanti."

Driftwood spoke to the founder and pointed. When the Lady's boat was near enough that he didn't have to shout, he called to Professor Kosta in Sumanti. The Lady listened as well, nodding as Driftwood finished. She spoke quietly to Professor Kosta for a moment.

"I see," said Professor Kosta. "I will do my best to translate."

"Tell them we welcome them to our city," the Lady said. Then she amended quickly, "No, tell them we welcome them *back* to *their* city. Tell them—"

"You don't speak for us!" one of the men in Izzy's boat shouted.

"She better not tell them *she's* the emissary," another muttered.

"Somebody's got to say *something*," a woman countered.

"Nobody can say anything if you don't shut up!" Izzy said.

Professor Kosta relayed the Lady's greeting. As soon as she began to speak, the founder fixed her eyes on her, and the spines along her back fanned and frilled as she listened. When Professor Kosta finished, the founder answered immediately, unleashing a rapid torrent of words.

The response from the boats was immediate.

"What is she saying?"

"What do they want?"

"Why have they come back?"

Professor Kosta lifted a hand and waited for quiet. "She says they've come back because they want to know who woke the island with a song."

The Lady frowned, her brows drawing together. "What does she mean?"

"What do you think she means?" a woman said. "The whole fortress lit up like a torch!"

The light, Mara knew, had been the least of it. The fortress had also groaned and ground and shook to its very foundations.

Professor Kosta asked, and the founder considered a moment before she began to speak. The professor translated: "She says they've been telling stories about their ancient city and the air people—that's her word for us—for generations. Long ago they came to believe the stories were more fiction than fact."

"We were as mythical to them as they were to us?" the Lady said. "How is that possible?"

"She says that they've spoken of their lost city for a long time, but most people believed it existed only in myth." Professor Kosta paused to listen as the founder went on. "But when they heard an ancient song from far away, they decided to search once again. They first heard it several days ago, but again off and on since then, and most strongly tonight. They've been traveling hard for several days, as fast as their magic could carry them, to come farther than any of them has dared travel in a very long time. They sent their serpents, who are much faster, ahead as scouts."

Mara could scarcely believe what she was hearing. "Maybe they remember us as we remember them," Mara's mother used to say, on winter nights so many years ago, when the people of Gravetown gathered to share stories and warmth. It had been a fanciful idea, a Gravetown superstition, but she had been right.

And it was an underwater spell-song that had drawn them back. First sung a few days ago, then more strongly tonight. Strong enough to stir the ancient spells within the Winter Blade from their centuries-long dormancy to a frightening awakening. Mara's heart was in her throat. Her hands were shaking.

The founder was speaking again. Professor Kosta listened a bit, then said, "She says they didn't know what to expect. They were discussing what to do when they heard the magic from the—she says the first island, which I suppose is the Winter Blade. That rather impressive outpouring of magical power made the decision for them." She waited a moment while the founder spoke again. "She really is very insistent in speaking to the mage who sung the spell-song that woke the island."

"Does she mean the Muck?" Izzy said.

"Or the bone-mage?" the Roughwater boy put in.

A debate broke out among the boats, but Mara barely heard it. She felt herself shrinking smaller and smaller into the boat. Fish Hook was looking at her, one eyebrow raised, lips curved in something almost like a smile. She turned away uncomfortably, only to find Gerrant of Greenwood was watching her too.

"Child," Gerrant said, so softly nobody outside the boat could hear, "you need not fear your own magic."

Fish Hook nudged her side. "You know he's right."

Mara hesitated, frozen by indecision and fear. She knew she was being a coward, but the truth was, she *did* fear her own magic. Her song had broken the Winter Blade. It had trapped Bindy and the Muck. It had loosed an ancient curse that hurt Fish Hook. She didn't even know if she could do any of it again. She couldn't be who the founders were looking for. They were expecting an experienced mage, somebody worth traveling across the ocean for the first time in centuries. Not a fish girl singing her mother's favorite song.

But there wasn't anybody else. There was only Mara. She lifted her hand.

"Um, I, um." She was shaking so much it was hard to speak. "I think it might have been me?"

The founder whirled to face her at once. She gripped the side of her shell and stretched across toward Mara. She was so much *bigger* than Mara had ever imagined. Her head was nearly twice the size of Mara's, her arms nearly twice as long even before counting the fin-tipped fingers.

It was astonishingly, impossibly absurd that the Muck could have ever believed he could transform himself into *this*. All of his experiments, his hybrid creatures, his trials with the pirates, all of it seemed so very clumsy and desperate in comparison. Whatever the Muck might have achieved, whatever terrible magic he might have wielded, however many animals and people he hurt in the process, the one thing he never would have done was match the terrible beauty of the founders.

Mara felt like a tiny fish cowering before a shark—but the founders weren't mindless animals. They were terrifying and strange, but they were also people. People who had believed so much in their beloved ancient stories they had followed a song across the sea.

"It was me," Mara said, her voice stronger now. She straightened her shoulders and forced herself to meet the founder's brilliant green eyes. They were the same color as seaweed growing in the shallows on a sunny day. "I sang the stone song."

"Mara?" the Lady said. "Wherever did you learn—"

"Why would you do that?" a man wailed, then everybody was shouting all at once.

"Were you trying to bring the island down?"

"Were you trying to seize it for yourself?"

"She's working with the mage, you know she is!"

ONYX & IVORY

MINDEE ARNETT

BALZER + BRAY

An Imprint of HarperCollins *Publishers*

ISBN 978-0-06-265266-9

Typography by Torborg Davern
Map illustration by Maxime Plasse
18 19 20 21 22   PC/LSCH   10 9 8 7 6 5 4 3 2

❖

First Edition

For Lori M. Lee, friend and champion

GAR

MOUNTAINS

Rin

Wandering
Wood

Jade Forest

Norgard

Thorne
Hall

Penlaurel River

ENDRA

Tyvald

Shieldtown

RHOSWEN

Penlocke

Belloss

Florri

Algot

The Mistfold

Luxana

Gindris

Solara

SEVA

2017

ONYX & IVORY

PART ONE

The Traitor's Daughter

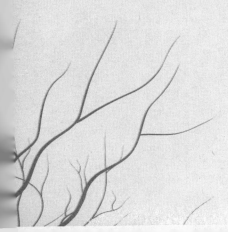

⌇

OUT HERE, DARKNESS MEANT DEATH.

Kate Brighton urged her weary horse ever faster as night crept over the land of Rime. The gelding labored with the pace already, his pants like whipcracks in the air, and his shoulders and neck lathered with foamy white stripes. But they couldn't stop, and they couldn't slow down. They had to make it inside the city before the gates closed.

How much farther? Kate thought for the hundredth time, Farhold still nowhere in sight. The road wound between hills too tall to see beyond, the shadows deep and dark. The swaths of everweeps spilling down the slopes toward them were already drawing their petals closed, while the moon with its pale silvery ring peeked over the crest of the hills to the east like a watchful eye in the bruised face of the sky.

"Come on, Pip," Kate whispered. She stood in the stirrups as she rode, her legs burning from the effort to keep her weight off the horse's back. After so many hours in the saddle, her muscles felt like wood gone to rot.

Pip's sleek ears twitched at the sound of her voice, but his pace remained the same. He had no more speed to give. It was more than fatigue. Even without her magic, Kate could sense the horse's pain in the way his neck dipped whenever his left foreleg struck the ground. When she reached out with her abilities, though, Kate felt the pain as if it were her own, a hot throb running up from the base of the hoof. What must've started as a tiny fracture had only spread and worsened on their long journey.

Fear clutched at Kate's heart. *If the bone shatters* . . . She cut the thought off before it could grow roots and spread.

The guilt was harder to keep at bay, though. If only they'd stayed a bit longer in the Relay tower, where she and Pip had spent the night on their return journey from Marared, a city more than fifty miles to the east. Another Relay rider would've come along to help them. The royal courier service of Rime kept strict protocols about searching for riders who failed to return with the mail they carried. Most riders who went missing were assumed killed by the nightdrakes that roamed the surface of Rime after sunset. The creatures ruled the night in this land, devouring any human or horse they could find. The only safety was behind the fortified walls of the cities and Relay towers or a magist wardstone barrier.

But she hadn't sensed the injury. Pip had left the tower sound, if a little sluggish from the previous day's ride. Then halfway to Farhold—snap. The foot went from fine to on fire. At once Kate had dismounted and wrapped the leg with the cloth bandage she kept in her saddlebag. She wanted to stay put, fearing further damage, but they had to press on. She'd slowed their pace in an effort to keep it from worsening, but that too had been a mistake—one they were paying for now with this hellish race against the encroaching darkness. If she just had the power to halt the sun in its descent . . . but only Caro could do that, and she doubted the sky god was listening.

"We're almost there," Kate said, struggling to convey the complex idea to the horse. Although her gift allowed her to touch the minds of animals, and to even influence their behavior, making them understand wasn't easy. Horses didn't think in words and ideas but in images and feelings, a language much harder to speak in.

Still, for a few seconds she sensed something like relief from Pip, his steps a little lighter, his head a little higher. Then the road began to climb upward, and the horse fell out of the gallop into a trot. Kate resisted pushing him back into a run; Pip needed to catch his breath, and daylight still lingered, if only by a single brushstroke of pink on the sky ahead. *Farhold can't be much farther,* she hoped. They'd been in the hills that formed the city's eastern border for more than an hour now. But this was only her second time taking this route, and she couldn't be certain. The Marared route, with its lengthy distance and taxing pace, was reserved for veterans, and Kate had only just made three years as a Relay rider for Farhold.

Nevertheless, her instinct proved true. When they finally crested the hill, she spotted Farhold's towering stone wall less than a mile ahead. In the deepening darkness, the wardstones set in the embrasures at the top of the wall glowed bright as starlight. The magic inside each stone served a single purpose: to repel the nightdrake packs. No one knew where or how the drakes passed from under the earth to the surface, but they always appeared at dark and terrorized until dawn.

Kate ran her gaze over the cornfields on either side of the road, which started at the base of the hill and stretched all the way to the city. The green stalks, high as Pip's knees, swayed in the breeze, making gentle *whish-whish* sounds. At least, Kate prayed it was the breeze. In the weak light, the stalks offered enough cover for the nightdrake scouts to venture out without fear of being burned by the sun. The smaller, more timid drakes of the pack, scouts always appeared first to spy for prey. With teeth like knives and claws like razors, a single scout could bring down a horse with little effort. The drakes came in every size. Some small as pigs, others large as horses. All of them deadly.

The path ahead appeared clear for now, and she allowed Pip to slow to a walk as they descended the hill, the pressure in his hoof too great for anything faster. Each step sent needling pain through both horse and rider. Kate wanted to withdraw from it, the agony making her dizzy, but she didn't dare. Sharing the pain with Pip was the only way he would endure this final stretch. The horse had great heart, but even the strongest spirit couldn't push a broken body forever.

With her nerves on edge, Kate kept her eyes on the fields, flinching at each twitch of the stalks. She retrieved the bow tied to the back of her saddle and held it crossways over her lap. The quiver on her back contained twelve arrows, half of them fashioned with ordinary steel tips and the other half bearing tips enchanted with mage magic, same as the wardstones. Piercing a nightdrake's hide was no easy task—only arrows imbued with mage magic could do it from a distance. Pistols could as well, but they fired a single shot, which made them next to worthless against a pack. The remaining drakes would be on the shooter before she had time to reload.

Kate closed her legs around Pip's sides, asking for more speed. He snorted and tossed his head in protest, the bit jangling in his mouth. She couldn't blame him; the pain was more tolerable at this pace. For a second, she considered letting him stay at the walk, but then two sounds reached her ears. The first was the clang of Farhold's evening bell, calling for the gates to close. The second was the distinctive screech of a nightdrake from somewhere behind them. Both had the same effect. Digging her heels into Pip's side, Kate sent him a vision of an attacking drake. The horse had no trouble understanding the concept this time, and he charged into the gallop.

Turning in the saddle, Kate spotted a pair of bright, glistening eyes peering out from the stalks just behind them. The scout gave chase, flanking them on the left but staying hidden beneath the cover of the corn. *For now.* With her heart thrumming, Kate grabbed an arrow, nocked it, and loosed it, all in the span of a second. She missed, but it didn't matter. Scouts spooked easily, and it backed off.

But there would be others. There always were.

Turning back around, Kate heard the wind shriek in her ears even louder than the bell. Ahead she saw the teams of oxen hitched to the insides of the gates, pulling them closed.

"Wait!" she shouted. "Wait!" Once the gates closed, they wouldn't reopen until dawn—not for one lowly Relay rider. There was another way into the city, through the hidden mage door, but only mage magic could find and open it. Hers was wilder magic, outlawed and secret and good only for influencing animals.

If the men driving the oxen heard her, they didn't respond. She urged Pip even faster, but the horse was failing by the second as the pain in his foreleg spread. She heard the rustle of corn behind her, louder than before. In the distance, the rest of the pack began to screech, closing in. Kate spied the Farhold guards waiting atop the wall with arrows nocked to repel the beasts should they approach the gate before it closed.

Come on, Pip. Gritting her teeth, Kate closed her eyes and went deeper into the horse's mind until she found the very center of him, his essence. All animals possessed it—a glowing brightness like a burning candle that she could see and feel only through the eye of her mind and the magic that gave it sight. She found the brightness and wrapped her magic around it, shielding the horse from the pain. She took that pain into herself instead, gasping at the sensation. The ploy worked, and the horse shot ahead, his strides lengthening.

Moments later they charged through the narrow space between the gates and into the safety of Farhold. The gates thudded closed, sealing them in. Kate resisted the impulse to let go of the horse's mind, fearing what the shock would do to him. She eased back on the reins and brought him to a halt. Then she slid from the saddle and slowly withdrew her magic. Immediately the horse began to tremble, struggling to stay upright with only three legs able to bear weight now.

Ignoring the curious looks from the Farhold guards, Kate led the horse forward, one slow, hobbling step at a time. The Relay house wasn't far from the eastern gate, but it was like miles to poor Pip. Now that she'd withdrawn from his mind, he bore the pain in full, but she couldn't risk maintaining the connection. There were magists in Farhold, same as in every city in Rime, and all of them carried enchanted stones designed to detect wilder magic. If they ever discovered what she could do, she would face imprisonment and execution, a fate she feared for more reasons than the obvious. Not that she would even be able to use her magic much longer today, with true night descending. Wilder magic worked only during the day. Like the everweeps on the hills outside, the power closed up inside her and would remain dormant until dawn.

Still, Kate did what she could to help the horse. Halting him, she removed both saddle and mailbag, slinging them over her shoulder despite the weight and her own weariness. She tried to find comfort in knowing that at least they'd made it into the city, but she couldn't stop the tears stinging her eyes. She had done this. Broken this horse to save her own life.

By the time they arrived at the Relay house, the ringed moon had risen high overhead, drenching the cobbled street below in silver light. Irri, the goddess whose nightly charge it was to spin that shining orb, was hard at work. Kate wished for darkness, if only to hide her guilt. The iron gates into the stable stood closed and barred from the inside. She started to shout for entry when the door into the main house opened and a young man stepped out.

"You're late, Traitor Kate," Cort Allgood said in a mocking, jovial tone.

Kate ignored him. He used the name far too often for it to bother her like it once had.

A grin twisted Cort's lips. "We thought you died. Even started making bets on it. You cost me more than a few valens."

Clenching her teeth, Kate adjusted the mail pouch across her shoulder. Of all the people to be here now, why did it have to be him? *The gods must hate me.*

"Open the gate. Pip is lame."

Cort examined the horse, cocking his head so that his blond curls bounced foppishly. Instead of his usual Relay rider uniform he wore a green tunic over breeches and tall black boots. The sight of his dapper appearance made Kate regret her own state of disarray. She smoothed down the front of her soiled tunic and brushed back raven-black hair from her face, where it had escaped the neat braid she'd plaited this morning.

"That horse isn't lame," Cort said, finishing his examination. "He's good as dead."

Kate's hands balled into fists around the reins. *"Open the gate."*

"How'd he get like that anyway?" Cort cocked his head in the other direction, his curls doing another ridiculous bounce. "You ride him off a cliff? Could've sworn they trained us not to do that."

Turning to the gate, Kate opened her mouth to shout for someone else but stopped as Cort made a quick retreat. A moment later he appeared on the other side of the gate and swung it open.

"Come on, Pip. Just a little farther." Kate tugged the horse forward.

"Poor thing." Cort slapped the gelding on the rump, making him flinch. "But that's what happens when you're forced to carry a traitor." Cort touched a mocking finger to his chin. "How does the Relay Rider's Vow go again, Traitor Kate? The part about protecting the horse at all costs?"

She kept walking, head up and lips sealed, but her blood heated with every word he spoke. She had reason to hate Cort Allgood. He was the one who had first discovered who she really was: Kate Brighton of Norgard. Daughter of Hale Brighton, the man who tried to kill the high king of Rime.

The traitor's daughter.

After her father was executed for his crimes, she'd come to Farhold hoping to escape her past, to start over with a new life and a new name. For the first ten months she'd managed it, but then Cort had seen an illustration of her in the *Royal Gazette*, a new monthly newspaper published by the royal court and sent to all the city-states that formed the kingdom of Rime. The story that accompanied the illustration marked the one-year anniversary of Hale Brighton's attack on the king. Within days of its publication the anonymous Relay rider Kate Miller became Kate Brighton once more. She was lucky not to have been dismissed from the position.

"Then again, Traitor Kate," Cort said, catching up with her, "if you had kept the vow, you would've ruined your reputation." He paused, frowning. "You know, I've always wondered why it is your father did it. None of the stories ever say. Do you know why he did it?"

Kate ignored his question as well as the same one that echoed deep inside her. No, she didn't know. She never would. *The dead tell no truths,* as the priests were fond of saying.

Spying a stable boy ahead, Kate waved him down. "Fetch Master Lewis."

The boy looked set to argue, then changed his mind when he saw Pip stumble sideways, struggling to maintain his awkward three-legged balance. While the boy made a dash for the foreman's quarters, Kate continued on, guiding Pip toward the eastern stable.

Cort started to follow her, another cutting remark on his lips, but someone shouted his name from across the way. He shouted back a response, then turned and addressed Kate.

"Well, I'm off, Traitor Kate. Good luck saving that doomed horse."

"Shut up," Kate said, her hold on her temper finally slipping. "He's not doomed."

Cort barked a triumphant laugh. "I'd say let's make a wager on it, but there's no sport in a fixed game." He winked, then turned and jaunted off without another word.

I hope you choke on your own spit, Cort Allgood, she thought after him.

By the time Kate managed to get Pip inside the stable, the foreman had arrived. Small and lean as a tree branch, Deacon Lewis looked fit enough to still outride any of the riders in his charge, despite his years. Short-cropped black hair, tinged with silver, framed his angular face, his brown skin leathered with age. He was intimidating on a normal day, but in this moment, Kate could barely bring herself to look at him for fear of his judgment. Over and over again, she ran her hands down the front of her tunic, trying to make it lie flat, trying to give herself the shield a good appearance could bring.

At first, he stood examining the horse from a few feet away, acknowledging Kate with a glance. Then he came forward and ran his hand down Pip's injured leg. The gelding hopped sideways, protesting the touch.

Sighing, Deacon let go of the leg and straightened up. "I'll summon a healer," he said, and his doubtful tone felt like a punch to Kate's gut.

"I might be able to mend the bone," the magist healer said sometime later. "But I doubt he'll ever be sound for hard work again." He straightened from his hunched position and smoothed his green robes, the mark of his order. The magestone he'd used to diagnose the horse's injury remained fastened around Pip's pastern on a piece of leather. It glowed bright red, pulsing like a heartbeat.

Kate stared at the green robe, frustrated that she couldn't read his expression behind the mask he wore and despising his matter-of-fact tone. All magists wore masks, the cut and coverage of them signifying rank. This one's covered his whole face, marking him a master, the very best of his order—and the most expensive.

"How much?" Deacon said, his face as expressionless as the magist's. Nevertheless, the way he kept rubbing his fingers along the four scars on his left forearm betrayed his concern. The scars ran so deep, they made the muscles beneath look permanently twisted in a cramp. There weren't many riders who survived a nightdrake attack, but Deacon had come through two in his long years with the Relay.

"Seventy valens," the magist said.

A wrench went through Kate's stomach. That was nearly as much as it would cost to replace the horse, and she knew what Deacon's answer would be.

Forgetting her position, Kate touched Deacon's arm. "Please, Master Lewis, let me pay for it. If you hold back my wages this month and the next, maybe—"

Deacon brushed her off and raised a hand for silence. He turned to the green robe. "Thank you for your services. We'll pass on further treatment."

The green nodded, then stooped to untie the piece of leather around Pip's injured foot. The glow in the magestone faded the moment it was removed.

Once the green robe had gone, Kate wheeled on Deacon, unable to stay silent a moment longer. "Please reconsider. Please. I'll do anything. I'll give up a month's salary. I'll do extra rides for free, muck out the stables for the next year. Anything. Please, Master Lewis."

Deacon turned to Kate, meeting her gaze for the first time, it seemed. "I'm sorry, Kate, but I can't let you."

"But, sir . . ." Tears burned in her eyes, making her cheeks flush. If she didn't stop speaking she wouldn't be able to hold them back. "He's a good horse, and it's my fault. I didn't mean—"

"Hush now. There's no place for such foolishness here." Deacon folded his arms, fingers worrying at his scars again. "I know he's your favorite, but Pip's a working horse and only as good as his legs. If he were a mare, it would be a different story, but a lame gelding is worth more dead than alive."

"But, sir, given time he could be sound again. He's still young. If you just let me buy him, then maybe—"

"I said no, and that's final." Deacon glared down at her now, his dark eyes sharp enough to cut. "How would you feed him? Where would you keep him? He can't stay here, and don't tell me you're paid so handsomely that you can afford to be wasteful with your coin, because I know better. No, I won't let you sacrifice for nothing."

Kate flinched at every point he made, each harsh truth laid bare. He was right. She couldn't afford the coin, and a part of her even understood the practicality of his reasoning. Saving a lame horse was more than pointless—it was wasted space, a great selfishness in a city already overfull with humans and animals both. There wasn't room for anything that didn't serve a purpose. Even the elderly and infirm were encouraged by the priests and priestesses to give their lives in sacrifice to the gods. But the rest of her had touched Pip's very essence, had caressed his soul with her magic. That part couldn't bear the idea of his death. A piece of her would die with him.

But she couldn't tell Deacon any of that, not in a way that he would understand and accept. Although Deacon always treated her fairly, even after he learned who she really was, he wouldn't tolerate her wilder magic if he ever found out. Wilders were outlaws, subject to the Inquisition.

Sagging in defeat, Kate swallowed. "Yes, sir." She reached for Pip's lead. He was her charge, and it was her responsibility to take him to the slaughterhouse. She'd never had to take a horse there before, and her fingers shook as she untied the rope.

Deacon took the lead from her, his expression softening. "Go home, Kate. I'll see it done."

Kate looked up at him, torn between what she knew she ought to do and what she wanted to do. But in the end, she couldn't refuse his kind offer, the escape too welcome, too easy a path to choose any other.

She turned to Pip and ran a hand over his sleek neck, wishing she could touch his mind one more time, to give him the peace he deserved. He leaned into her touch, burying his muzzle in her belly. She stroked his nose for a moment, whispered good-bye into one velvety ear, then turned and walked away.

Shame and regret dogged each step she took on the way to her rented room, a few miles from the Relay house. Cort's taunts echoed in her mind, taking on weight. It was true—as a Relay rider, she had vowed to always bring Pip back safely, to hold his life equal to her own. But she had broken that vow tonight, an act of betrayal as sure as any other.

Have I become my father? Did oath breaking run in her blood? She was so much like him. Even her magic was inherited from him. Hale Brighton had been master of horse to the high king, a position he'd earned with the help of his secret, forbidden gift. He'd been the king's friend and liegeman, and yet he had tried to kill him. Kate didn't know why, but there was no denying her father's guilt. *Just as there's no denying mine.* Traitor's daughter. Traitor Kate.

Once again, she had lived up to her name.

THE MORNING CAME TOO EARLY, as it always did, night slipping away like a thief afraid of discovery. Fingers of sunlight pressed against Kate's eyelids, and she rolled over out of their reach. It was more comfortable on this side, cooler, though the bed remained hard, nothing like the beds she used to sleep in. Memories disguised as dreams—of feathered mattresses wrapped in silken sheets and long luxurious mornings spent dozing only to be awakened by the smell of sugar-glazed sweet rolls—started to lull her back to sleep.

Then a more recent memory slid through her mind—of Pip, and the disaster of the night before. Kate groaned, coming fully awake. She forced her eyes open, breaking apart the crust of dried tears that had sealed her lashes together. The urge to renew that crying rose up in her, only to be shoved aside by a sudden jolt of alarm. The sun beyond the narrow window shone too brightly and too high in the sky, more than an hour past dawn. *But the dawn bell didn't ring!* She was sure of it. She never slept through the loud gong that signaled the opening of the gates.

Panicked, Kate scrambled out of bed just as the door swung open and her roommate stepped in, carrying with her the faint, sweet stench of barberry wine.

"You're still in bed?" Signe's pale eyebrows climbed her forehead, almost disappearing into her golden-blond hair. "What happened?" Yawning, she gestured to Kate's unmade bed. She wore a sleeveless jerkin and breeches, both disheveled from whatever activity had kept Signe away all night from their shared room.

"I don't know." Kate stooped and picked up the clothes she'd discarded on the floor the night before, their presence there, instead of carefully folded and put away, a telling sign of her distressed state of mind. Scowling at the soiled state of her Relay rider's tunic— *whoever thought light blue and horses was a good pairing should be drawn and quartered*—she slid it on over her shift. "What time is it?"

"Nearly eight." Signe stepped in and dropped onto the bed nearest the door. There wasn't much room for standing and the two narrow beds were the only places for sitting. "If you hurry, you should make it to roll call." Signe was a Relay rider too, and both of them knew the consequences of a late arrival. Fortunately for Signe, it was her day off.

"Gods, let it be so." Kate pulled on the rest of her uniform of black breeches and overskirt, wishing she had time to rebraid her hair and wash the dirt from her face.

"Did you hear?" Signe asked, a gleam in her voice. "There's a royal in the city."

"What?" Kate's hand stilled in the act of fastening her belt over the tunic.

Signe nodded, raising one leg to pull out the knife tucked inside her boot. She leaned back on the bed and idly began to toss the knife in one hand. "I don't know who, but it must be someone important."

"Obviously," Kate said, breathless. A royal was in the city. A Tormane. *But who?* She shook the thought from her head. Whoever it might be was not her concern anymore. She'd left that life behind. "That explains it, though. The dawn bell doesn't ring when there's a royal in the city."

"It doesn't?" Signe cocked her head, birdlike. Even with her gaze fixed on Kate, she didn't stop juggling the knife, catching it absentmindedly. Although they'd been friends for more than two years now, Kate had no idea where Signe had learned such a skill. She was from the Esh Islands and never talked about her life there or what had brought her to Rime, but Kate often suspected she'd either been a circus performer or a thief. "If I'd known that," she continued, "I would've come home sooner to wake you. Why doesn't it ring?"

Kate made a face. "Because royals don't like to have their sleep disturbed so early." That wasn't precisely true, but she didn't have time to explain the political nuances involved. Although there were kings in Esh, there weren't sealed city gates. All the islands were free of the nightdrakes that plagued Rime after sunset.

Why did you ever leave? Kate wanted to ask, the memory of Pip ambushing her again. If the horse had been reared in Esh, he would still be alive.

She shoved the regret down deep inside her and headed for the door. "I've got to go."

"Wait," Signe said. "I brought you a gift."

Kate turned back automatically, unable to resist her friend's infectious enthusiasm. She gaped as she saw the object in Signe's hand, a silver chain with a series of small colored stones fastened between the links. The magestones glowed faintly, the enchantment on them strong and new. "A moonbelt?"

Signe grinned. "I swore I would find you one." She thrust out her hand. "Take it. And learn to enjoy life. Like I do."

Against her better instincts, Kate accepted the moonbelt. The very hint of its purpose made her insides squirm like she'd swallowed a jar full of worms. It was indecent for an unmarried woman to possess one, let alone wear it.

"Uh, thanks, Sig, but I enjoy life enough already." Kate tried to hand it back.

Signe brandished a finger at her like a whip. "Working all the time is not enjoyment."

"It is if you're me." There was nothing Kate liked more than riding, and—last night aside—she loved working for the Relay. "Besides," she added, "you know I've no need for it."

A suggestive smile stretched across Signe's face. "Yes, so now you must choose a nice boy for a plaything and create the need."

Ignoring the blush creeping up her neck, Kate shoved the moonbelt into the single outside pocket on her overskirt, making sure it was hidden from view. She would put it on—or not—at the Relay house.

"I've got to go."

Signe shooed her toward the door. "Yes, yes, may the luck of Aslar be with you."

With a determined bent, Kate hoisted her overskirt and trotted down the narrow hallway to the even narrower staircase. If she was late to morning roll call, she would get bumped from her route by one of the other riders to either a less lucrative one or a more difficult one. The latter was the last thing she wanted, especially after the tragedy with Pip.

Grease hung thick as smoke in the air as Kate descended, the walls and railing slick with it. She would be slick with it too by the time she made it outside. A greasy face and hair were an inevitable consequence of renting a room in the Crook and Cup. So was the stench of boiling meat and ripe onion (a smell she despised) that lingered on her clothes nearly as strong as the ever-present scent of horse (a smell she loved). She and Signe would've preferred staying at the Relay house, but there wasn't a bunk for women riders, only the men, who vastly outnumbered them.

Turning right into the kitchen, Kate darted between a cook and a serving girl on her way to the alley door. The cook shouted that she wasn't supposed to be in here, but Kate batted her eyes at him and smiled before heading outside. She turned left down the alley, her boots splashing mud over the hem of her overskirt with each step, and soon reached Bakers Row.

"Oh hells," she muttered at the congestion in the street. Always a little crowded, this morning Bakers Row looked like a fisherman's net after a good catch, full of flailing, chattering people piled one next to the other. There were women in brightly colored gowns embroidered with lace and with long gaped sleeves, and men sporting velvet or silk tunics and boots polished to a high sheen. Jewelry hung from belts and around necks, some glowing with mage magic designed to enhance beauty or hide disfiguration, others merely glinting in the sun. Kate clucked her tongue in dismay. Such finery had no business in a marketplace as common as Bakers Row.

One man, a merchant by the looks of him, wore a sash made

from the carcass of a small nightdrake. The reptilian head hung over the man's shoulder with its fanged mouth fastened to the scaly tail, and its body wrapped crossways over his back and chest. Shiny black stones had been placed in the eye sockets, making it look alive. Kate suppressed a laugh at the absurdity of such a person wearing such a trophy. No one would believe this portly, gray-bearded man had actually killed the drake.

She pushed her way into the crowd, elbowing sides and stepping on toes without care. *The royal is to blame for this,* she realized. Why else would everyone bother with such finery if not with the hope of impressing whichever of the Tormanes was here? *Not that they're likely to be seen right now.* In her experience, the nobility preferred to breakfast late in the quiet comfort of whatever palace or stately home was grand enough to host them.

With her agitation building, Kate couldn't keep the glare from her face. Some of the people stepped out of the way at the sight of her blue tunic with the silver galloping horse on the left breast, but most did not. A Relay rider uniform commanded respect only from atop a horse and with a full mail pouch in tow—the contents of those pouches too important to impede, containing everything from personal missives to newsletters to royal decrees.

Booths and vendor carts lined both sides of the streets, some beneath canopies, some leaning with off-angled sides, but all displaying savory wares like sweet buns, pumpkin-glazed crumpets, or flatbreads slathered with butter and honey. The smell of yeast and sugar filled Kate's nose, making her stomach quiver. She'd been too distraught last night to eat, and hunger sabotaged her now when there was no time to assuage it.